DARK OF THE SUN

Maynard Sims

First Edition
978-1-937771-57-7

Dark of the Sun © 2013 by Maynard Sims
All Rights Reserved.

DarkFuse
P.O. Box 338
North Webster, IN 46555
www.darkfuse.com

Become a fan on Facebook:
www.facebook.com/darkfuse

Follow us on Twitter:
www.twitter.com/darkfuse

Copy Editor: Steve Souza & Robert Mele

*Dedicated to family and friends,
the solid bedrock of a happy life.*

1

Ahead of them the sea in the secret bay was clear blue, the afternoon sun glinting from it as if a torch was shining onto a mirror. Gentle waves tickled the white sand at the shore, the beach stretching lazily in both directions, empty and inviting.

The three boys were best friends, and now that school was out, the rest of the day was theirs. They planned to spend it doing absolutely nothing, and being diligent about it.

Most of the previous couple of hours had been spent laughing about what their teacher, Miss Robertson, had said to them.

They were in a crafts lesson, making a model aeroplane out of balsa wood. Harry was doing most of the assembly, gluing and sticking the pieces together, Jack was giving him advice, while Alan watched both and talked about what the finished plane would look like and where they could fly it.

'Bahamas industrial structure in miniature,' Miss Robertson laughed.

'What do you mean, Miss?'

'The Worker.' She pointed at Harry Beck. 'Doing all the work. The Supervisor.' She pointed at Jack. 'Involved in the job, Mr Dylan, but not doing much to help.'

'And what about me?' Alan asked.

'You, Mr Lancaster, you are the manager, the owner, the entrepreneur. Giving the instructions, not getting your hands dirty, and probably reaping most of the profits, if there were any. Time to break for lunch, boys.'

All three boys were headed for eleven years of age, starting to notice how their personalities were taking on patterns that repeated themselves.

'Worker.' Jack pushed Harry from behind, making him stumble on the steep path down to the beach.

Alan, as he regularly and instinctively did when Harry was even mildly threatened, pushed Jack. 'Supervisor.'

'Owner, owner.' Harry and Jack ran ahead calling out and laughing.

The sand was warm and they hopped and skipped across to the cluster of rocks that was their den, their beach house. Alan laid his towel out on the best spot, slightly shaded, but facing the sea. Jack and Harry let their towels fall close by.

'Swim?' Alan said.

Harry jumped up. Jack shrugged.

'Last one in is a tarpree.' Alan shouted, his shirt already on his towel.

They all had their swimming shorts on under their school trousers and they were so busy laughing and splashing each other that no one noticed who was last into the sea, because no one cared.

The pecking order of the boys was becoming well established. None of them acknowledged it, and maybe didn't even notice it consciously, but they all obeyed it as the natural order of things. Life was good in the Bahamian summer of 1982.

'I can hold my breath underwater for ten minutes,'

Jack announced.

'Course you can't,' Alan said. 'You'd die.' And he swam away from the other two as if the pronouncement was final.

'I can,' Jack insisted. 'Watch me.'

'I wouldn't if I was you,' Harry said.

Jack had started to submerge himself, but he trod water instead. 'Why not?'

'Whether you stay underwater for ten minutes or ten seconds, who cares?'

'It's a challenge.'

'So?'

Losing interest in diving underwater Jack laid on his back and swam parallel to shore. 'You never want to do anything, Beck.'

Harry looked up at the sun. 'I just want to enjoy doing what I like.'

Alan had swum back so all three were close together in the water. 'And what do you like, Harry?'

'Lots of things and nothing.'

Before anyone could say anything else a roar of engines damaged the quietness of the day.

During the late 1970s and the early 1980s the US Coast Guard increased its resources to attack the growing threat of drug smugglers. They tested and evaluated the surface effects ship *Dorado* for a period between 1981 and 1982 to check its effectiveness as a patrol craft for the shallow waters around the coast of Florida.

When the tests proved successful, the Coast Guard acquired three SESs for active use: *Sea Hawk*, *Shearwater*, and *Petrel* beginning in the summer of 1982. Although the Coast Guard had experimented with non-traditional vessels such as hydrofoils as late as the 1970s, no such craft had seen extensive service until the SESs.

They were rigid sidewall hovercraft constructed of a lightweight aluminium alloy. Their lift engines powered fans that created a pressurized air cushion under the cutter, lifting the craft, reducing drag and draft. The solid sidewalls pierced the water, creating a catamaran hull, and the air cushion was sealed by flexible rubberized skirts at the bow and stern. This allowed the boats to operate at high speeds in waters both shallow and deep, making them ideal for the waters off the coast of Florida and well out into the Caribbean. Their wide beam and the catamaran hull also made them extremely stable craft, even in high seas.

What had disturbed the boys was one of the first patrols in the waters around the Islands of the Bahamas.

'Wow, what must it be like to ride in one of those?' Jack said.

'I'd love to skipper something like that one day,' Harry said.

Alan dived to the bottom of the sea and surfaced a few seconds later with a handful of small shells. One by one he slowly let them fall from his hands, watching fascinated as each made a small ripple in the calm surface of the sea.

'Would you like a boat like that, Alan?' Harry said.

'I'll own one someday.'

'When's that?' Jack said 'When your father gives you all his money?'

'No,' Alan let the last shell slip back to the sea. 'When I own the Islands. When I'm rich.'

'Owner, owner.' They began to splash water over Alan until he leapt as far out of the sea as he could and tried to jump on both of them at once.

They fell backwards into the warm water, the teasing forgotten, futures unplanned, dreams still asleep, just boys with the whole world ahead of them and a lazy afternoon to spend at the beach and in the sea.

Friends forever.

When forever was just another sunny day in paradise.

2

I sat on the end of the bed smoking a cigarette, staring out through the window of the bungalow. From where I sat I had a pretty good view across the Grand Bahamian landscape, all the way down to the small, private harbour where my boat, *The Lady of Pain* was moored, bobbing gently on the incoming tide.

The girl on the bed stirred and rolled over, the sheet slipping from her naked body, exposing her sun-kissed breasts. She murmured something dreamily and gave a throaty laugh, but didn't wake. She had her arm raised above her head, curled on the pillow like a golden snake, her fingers tangling in her blonde curling hair.

Her name was Jane and she was on vacation; holidaying in the Bahamas with three of her girlfriends. I was not sure how she'd ended up in bed with me; I'd been too drunk last night to remember anything that clearly. But now morning was here and the bungalow smelt of stale cigarette smoke and sex, so it was reasonable to assume that I'd had a good time.

There was a short, sharp knock on the back door. I stubbed the cigarette out in a shell-shaped brass ashtray and went to answer it. Stevie was standing there dressed in a purple halter neck and denim shorts. She said nothing but pushed past me into the bungalow. Her bare feet padded across the wooden floor and she'd reached the bedroom before I could stop her.

'See you're still banging the tourists, Harry,' she said in a voice loud enough to rouse the recently and not so recently deceased from their slumbers. Jane didn't stir. 'I thought you'd mended your ways.' She was grinning mischievously as I reached past her and closed the bedroom door.

'So what are you suddenly, my keeper? And keep your voice down. Someone's sleeping in there.'

She shook her head, a gesture of giving up on a lost cause. 'You're beyond help, Harry. A pretty face, a whiff of perfume, and you're no better than an alley cat. No, on second thoughts, most alley cats have more self-control than you.'

'Have you just come here to insult me?' I said.

She looked at me hard, taking in the stubble on my chin, the dark half-moons under my eyes. I looked like shit, and I felt worse than I looked. She chuckled and flopped down on the couch. 'Feeling fragile are we?'

'Obviously *we* aren't, but *I* most definitely am.'

She picked up a magazine and started leafing through it. She looked up. 'Mine's white, no sugar. For you I recommend black, and as strong as you can take it.'

I glared at her half-heartedly and went through to the kitchen to make the coffee.

Stevie Bailey, like me, was a native white Bahamian. She had just turned nineteen; tall and willowy with light brown hair, cropped boyishly short. Her skin was tanned and flawless, unless you counted the smattering of freckles across the bridge of her slightly uptilted nose as a flaw, and she was really quite pretty, though if you told her that she would probably flatten you with one of the fiercest and most feared left hooks in Freeport. She'd been crewing for me since she was fifteen and her father Tom Bailey died, leaving her with a list of gambling debts and not much else.

Stevie had inherited very little from her father except a love of the sea, a ferocious temper, and a skill with things mechanical that defied belief. She knew her way around *The Lady of Pain's* Penta engines better than I did myself, and in all the time she'd been crewing for me we hadn't lost more than a day due to mechanical failure.

Running flat out the engines gave *The Lady* a top speed of thirty knots, quite respectable for a boat of that class. She was a Striker 38', built with a steel hull back in '74, original in every way except for the engines. When I first acquired her she was powered by twin Daf 165hp diesels, but I pulled them out and replaced them with the Penta 235hp diesel turbos, making her a much more powerful craft. Stevie kept her in immaculate condition; a job she loved. A job she was very good at.

She threw down the magazine, grabbed an apple from the bowl on the side table and bit into it. Juice dribbled down her chin and she wiped it away with the back of her arm, leaving tiny droplets of apple juice glistening in the down-fine hairs.

'So what are you doing here?' I said, placing a cup of coffee down on the table beside her. 'It's Sunday, or don't we have a day of rest in this outfit anymore?'

'One boat, a handful of commissions and he thinks we're an outfit,' she said. 'Alan's looking for you.'

'Oh? Where did you bump into him?'

'He showed up at the harbour. I was down there on *The Lady*.'

'Why didn't he try here first?'

'I didn't ask him. He was on his boat. What a beast that is. I'd love to get my hands on her engines. Anyway, I told him you'd probably be here, but he didn't seem to take it in. He was acting as if he had something on his mind. You know, distracted. I went back to what I was doing and when I turned round again he was heading out to sea.'

I lit another cigarette. 'Did he say why he wanted to see me?'

'You smoke too much,' she said disapprovingly.

'Christ! Since when have you cared what I do?'

'Just keeping an eye on my future, that's all. Good employers are hard to come by.'

'At least I score some points on the positive side of the scale. Well?'

She bit into the apple again and shook her head. 'Just said he wanted to see you, that's all.' She changed the subject. 'What's on for tomorrow?'

'Pleasure trip. A family from the hotel want a tour around the island.'

Stevie mimed an extravagant yawn.

'I see you're impressed.'

'Squawking kids, henpecked husbands and whinging wives. Hardly the stuff of great adventures.'

'True, but it means we can eat for another couple of days. Drink your coffee. I'm going to take a shower, and then I'll go up to Alan's house. He might be back there by now. Will you still be here when I come out?'

'No. I'm going back down to *The Lady*. A bearing on one of the shafts is beginning to wear. I want to check it out before it seizes. Are you coming down later?'

'Maybe. I've a few things that need attending to here first.'

She smirked at me. It wasn't one of her more attractive expressions. 'Young enough to be your daughter that one.' She nodded her cropped head at the bedroom door.

'That's not what I meant. I was thinking more of giving the place a clean. I wouldn't want the word getting around that I'm a slob.'

'Why not? The truth never hurt anyone,' she said with

a grin and jumped up from the couch before I could throw something at her. In two mouthfuls the coffee was gone and she was out the door. After she'd gone I checked on Jane, who was still sleeping, then went and took a shower.

When I came out the bedroom was empty and Jane had gone. *C'est la vie.*

3

The boy was sitting in the rear seat of a Dodge Grand Caravan. The car was white and clean. It was a standard vehicle, large, comfortable enough, but not even top of the range. To him it was a spaceship.

He'd never seen anything like it. Perhaps on TV when they got a signal back in the two room shack he had shared with his parents and his three brothers. Maybe on the American shows he watched when his parents were out. Never in real life. They didn't have a car, his parents, or anyone he knew.

Travelling in his personal starship he had been thinking about his family. Since the earthquake, Haiti had been in chaos, had been fairly crazy before the disaster, and now it was lawless and wild in too many places.

He had been living in a makeshift camp, in a tent donated by some organisation in Europe, which was somewhere he had never heard of, had no idea where it was or what it looked like. The tent leaked when the rain got too heavy.

His parents had been killed when the first huge tremors hit the island. His mother had been swept away down the hillside when the slum city of similar wood and cardboard buildings had collapsed in on themselves and then formed a landslide that moved with the mud and the rocks like a slow moving tide. His father he hadn't seen die; he had been told the street his father had been walking along opened up like a mouth and the people were swallowed into the huge cracks and craters. He didn't know what had happened to his brothers.

He was at school when the noises began. He'd seen a tree fall in the forest once, but that was nothing like the sight of buildings splitting apart and collapsing in heaps of dust and bricks. All the children began shouting, some were crying, others screaming. Everyone was scared. The teacher was scared, but she made sure all the children got out of the classroom and as far away from the school building as they could. The last he saw of her was when she went back inside the school to help some others, just before the roof sank to the ground.

What the boy could remember was the silence. At first there was noise, screams and crashes, the ground pulling apart and people and cars and buildings falling into cracks and holes. Then there were sounds of dust and debris whooshing into the air, and clouds of impenetrable fog obliterating everything. Then, as it all settled, the silence.

The children stood still for a long time, waiting for an adult to tell them what to do, to reassure them it was all going to be all right. Even at their young ages they knew instinctively it wasn't going to be anything but very wrong.

No one came for them and eventually they realised that nobody would. The older ones took control and led them carefully into Port-Au-Prince. They may as well have led them straight to Hell.

Already bodies littered the streets. Piles of rubble were as tall as many of the buildings had been. Although the first earthquake had been massive, the size and numbers of all the aftershocks added devastation to disaster and was likened to kicking a dead body for fun.

A 7.0 magnitude earthquake struck Haiti at a depth of 8.1 miles. The epicentre was located 15 miles west of Port-Au-Prince. Since then there were 59 or more aftershocks, ranging from 4.2 to 5.9 magnitude in strength.

Even before the earthquake struck, Haiti was the poorest country in the world with more than two-thirds of the people living on less than $US2 per day and with most of the people in Port-Au-Prince living in slum conditions, mostly tightly-packed, poorly-built, concrete buildings that fell like decks of cards balanced on a needle.

A large proportion of the education in Haiti was provided in often poor-quality private schools, and although the state system generally provided better education, there were far too few places. Half of the people in Port-Au-Prince had no access to latrines and only one-third had access to tap water. Before the disaster Haiti was a beggar scrambling for scraps.

Afterwards there were two million people living in the most affected areas, over two hundred thousand were dead and close to 300,000 homes damaged or destroyed, leaving one and half million people homeless. There were now nineteen million cubic metres of rubble and debris in Port-Au-Prince, and one and a half million people living in camps including places that were at critical risk from storms and flooding. There were over one thousand camps and several held over five thousand people each. After the disaster Haiti was too tired to scrabble for scraps and too traumatized to beg.

4

Alan Lancaster owned two hotels on Grand Bahama Island as well as several on the Out Islands — or the Family Islands as the government preferred them to be called these days. We'd known each other since childhood but despite this our backgrounds were very different.

Alan's house was about a mile away from my bungalow and as it was a fine summer's morning I decided to walk. Even this early the temperature was close to eighty and the humidity was high, but a breeze was coming in from the sea making the heat more bearable.

I reached the house and rang the doorbell. Elsa, the Lancasters' German maid, opened the door but didn't greet me with her usual welcoming smile.

'Mr Lancaster isn't at home,' she said flatly. 'And Madam isn't receiving visitors.'

'I think Anna will see me, Elsa,' I said.

She looked at me sceptically, shaking her head slowly.

I didn't give her time to argue. 'I'll go around the back and wait by the pool.'

The Lancasters' house was probably one of the most modern buildings on the island. It had been designed by Phillip France, the American architect responsible for designing the Blue Water Hotel on Eleuthera, the latest and most prestigious of Alan's hotel chain. The back of the house was constructed almost entirely of glass, giving a dramatic view of the shoreline.

I glanced up at the top floor window and saw Anna standing there, staring out at the sea. I waved, but she was oblivious to me. I saw her turn as Elsa came into the room and I heard her voice rise in anger. I couldn't hear what she was saying — the glass did a good soundproofing job, muffling the words — but I caught the tone and assumed that my visit wasn't the most popular event in Anna's social diary for that day. I sat down on a sun lounger and scratched my head, wondering what the hell I'd done to upset her.

Finally she came to the window and stared down at me. I threw her a salute and received a scowl in return, and then she moved out of sight. Moments later she was through the sliding glass doors to join me poolside.

Anna Lancaster was a stunningly beautiful woman. Tall and slim with chestnut coloured curls that fell to her shoulders. Her skin was flawless and she looked ten years younger than her thirty-five years. She was wearing a simple white cotton shift, a stark contrast to the Balmain and Oldfield dresses she normally favoured, but it did nothing to detract from her natural elegance. She would have looked breathtaking in a potato sack.

She stared at me with her almond-shaped, tourmaline-green eyes and said, 'What the hell do you want, Harry?'

'Is that any way to greet an old friend?' I said lightly, trying to bring a smile to lips that seemed to have been cemented into a thin grim line.

She stood over me as I sat on the lounger, regarding me coolly for a full thirty seconds, and then said, 'Have you got a cigarette?'

'Sure.' I fished in the pocket of my shirt and brought out a crumpled packet of Marlboro. I eased one out, trying to straighten the kinks so she wouldn't notice, and offered it to her. She took it abstractedly and leaned forward for a light. The sun was glaring down over her shoulder and I had to squint to focus on the end of the cigarette as I touched it with the flame from my Dunhill lighter. She stood erect once more and inhaled deeply, blowing out the smoke in a thin stream from between pursed lips. 'I was looking for Alan,' I said.

'He isn't here.' She walked past me and stared down into the blue water of the pool. 'And in another half an hour neither will I.'

'Going into Freeport?'

She shook her head and, before I could ask anything else, Sally, the Lancaster's seven-year-old daughter, burst from the house like a greyhound after a hare and leapt into my arms. She planted a wet kiss on my cheek and said, 'Hello, Uncle Harry. Guess what? Mummy's taking me on an aeroplane.'

'Is she now?' I said, staring over her shoulder at her mother.

'Yes, isn't it exciting?'

'Sure is.'

Anna turned to face us. 'Go and play, Sally,' she said.

'But Uncle Harry's here and he hasn't told me a story yet.' For some reason Sally put me on a par with Hans Christian Anderson as a teller of fairy stories.

'Sally, do as you're told,' Anna said sharply.

Sally pouted, tears moistening her eyes. I set her down on the ground and ruffled her straight fair hair. She looked up at me beseechingly. 'Next time I come, two.' I held up a finger on each hand. 'Two stories.'

'Three,' she said.

'You drive a hard bargain, just like your daddy. Okay, three.'

'Promise?'

'Cross my heart and spit.'

'Ugh!' she said, but considered the deal for a moment then said brightly, 'Okay, but remember, you promised.' She darted off around the side of the house and I turned my attention to her mother. 'An aeroplane?'

Anna threw the cigarette to the ground and crushed it petulantly with the toe of her expensive Italian sling backs. 'Stay out of this, Harry. This is between Alan and me.'

I shrugged. 'Couldn't agree more,' I said, sitting back down on the lounger and lighting a cigarette.

For a moment there was silence, broken only by the sound of the pool's water filter and the high pitched buzzing of an itinerant mosquito. She sat down on the lounger beside me and buried her face in her hands. When she took them away her palms were wet, her eyes tearful. 'I'm leaving him, Harry. I'm taking Sally and flying back to Charleston, to Dad. He said we could stay with him for however long it takes to get things arranged legally.'

'So this is permanent?'

'I think so. It depends.'

'On what?'

'You'd better ask Alan. I don't want to talk about it.'

'Try,' I said gently.

She shook her head. 'There's no point. I've spoken too many words and shed too many tears over that man, Harry. I've had enough. I just can't take any more. And it's not just me. There's Sally to consider too.'

It shook me to hear her talking like this. From what I'd witnessed of their marriage I would have rated it as one of those matches that could only have been made in heaven. Which only went to prove how little I knew.

'I don't even know why I'm talking to you. You're probably in it with him.'

'In what?'

She carried on as if I hadn't spoken. 'You two were always thick with each other. You're buried as deep in the filth as he is.'

'Anna, I haven't the faintest idea what you're talking about,' I said. I laid my hand on her arm, but she snatched it away.

'Don't lie to me. Please, Harry, don't insult my intelligence.' There was fire in her eyes as she got to her feet. 'It's funny, you know, but I always thought that out of the two of you, Alan was the bigger bastard. I always had you figured as an honest, decent man, but I should have known better, shouldn't I? Now, if you don't mind, I have to pack.'

She ran back into the house, leaving me sitting there, open mouthed but speechless, wondering what I'd said, but wondering even more just what the hell Alan had done. Whatever it was, I wasn't going to get any answers sitting here imitating a bullfrog catching flies. If I wanted answers then I had to find Alan.

Stevie had spoken with him down at the harbour. Maybe she hadn't told me everything Alan had said; not deliberately of course, but there just may have been something more, if only a clue to his whereabouts now. I really didn't fancy the idea of touring the island until I found him.

The Lancasters' house stood between my harbour and Freeport International Airport. I'd gone only a couple of hundred yards before I heard a car on the road behind me. I stopped walking and turned to see the Lancasters' silver-grey Mercedes gliding towards me, Anna at the wheel, grim faced, Sally in the back. As they passed Anna slowed briefly, and for a moment I thought she was going to stop, but she obviously thought better of it. I heard the accelerator being gunned and the car picked up speed again.

As the Mercedes drew away I saw Sally climb up onto the back seat and wave from the rear window. I raised my hand to wave back, but suddenly there was a searing, blinding flash of light and the car disintegrated into a ball of smoke and flame. The noise and shock of the explosion followed a split second later, blowing me off my feet, leaving me sprawling in the dust at the roadside.

Dazed and deafened by the blast, I pushed myself up onto my elbows and looked back down the road. A thick pall of oily black smoke hung in the air above the few chunks of twisted burning metal. All that remained of the Mercedes.

Of Anna and Sally there was no sign at all.

5

Sonny was placed in a shelter made out of canvas tent material, tree trunks and corrugated iron sheets. There were over one hundred children there and at first the humanitarian helpers that came from America and Europe fed them and clothed them and tried to keep them alive.

Then gradually people began to arrive who wanted to take them away from the horrors and look after them somewhere else. There was a scandal of sorts when some Christian aid groups tried to adopt several of the children at once. Eventually the charities operating in Haiti realized they were losing control of the situation and when Tarradon Exports approached them with impeccable credentials and arrangements seemingly in place to place large numbers of the children, orphans all of them so far as could be ascertained, with families in the USA it seemed too good to be true and an answer to their prayers.

The Dodge Grand Caravan bore a discreet logo on the side doors that revealed it belonged to Tarradon Exports, but Sonny, floating in a world of his own imagination in the rear seats, hadn't noticed it.

He had been kicking a ball around in the dirt with three or four other boys when the men came for him. He watched as the men spoke with Pierre, who was in charge that day. Pierre welcomed them, had obviously met them before, and took some paperwork from them that he put into a drawer without reading.

Sonny had a feeling that they were coming for him, but he wasn't scared. Since everything had happened he didn't really feel much of anything any more. He was looking at them as Pierre pointed across to the boys playing football, but Sonny knew he was pointing at him. One of the men smiled and waved, but the other one didn't even look in his direction, eyes hidden behind big sun glasses.

They took him that day and by the evening he was on a boat headed for Florida. He didn't enjoy it on the boat, he felt sick a lot of the time, but it was traveling fast and they made sure he was comfortable.

When the boat moored it was at a marina with dozens of similar sized yachts and launches. One more just blended in and no questions were asked about passengers or cargo.

The men were quite gentle with Sonny, though he had been used to hardship and some cruelty in his six years of life. The Grand Caravan was waiting in a parking slot in a huge car park, the engine running and a driver casually seated at the wheel.

It took hours to drive even though they seemed to be going fast and the roads were wide and long and straight. When they stopped, which they did a couple of times, they sat in booths at a diner and ate burgers and fries and drank Coke which he had only ever had once, and the can had been warm. He slept some of the way.

One of the men turned in his seat and said to him, 'You're near Disney now. Know what Disney is?'

Sonny shook his head, though he had a vague idea.

'You know. Mickey Mouse, princesses and fairy tales and all that magical shit.'

Sonny looked out the window, but all he could see were huge signs advertising food, cars and hotels. Everything was bright, the sun was high in the sky and he thought that if this was Disney he would probably like it. Then he saw the lampposts were purple and then they passed a road sign for a town called Celebration and he thought that if there was somewhere called that it must really be a magical place, though he knew enough to know that shit was a bad word.

They drove onto a wide road called the 27 and passed huge shops and housing estates with big houses and fountains. Eventually the car turned into a private drive and pulled up outside the only house that could be seen in either direction. It was large, a mansion, with manicured green grass that looked fake and probably was, and sweeping stands of coloured bushes. There were three storeys, and so many windows you could look out of a different one each day and have some left over at the end of the month.

'This it, kid, the end of the road.'

Sonny got out and was immediately hit by the intense Orlando heat and humidity.

'Bring the boy inside,' a man called from the house. It was a Southern American accent and as Sonny was ushered into the cool interior of the house he saw the man that the accent belonged to. He was dressed in a brightly coloured shirt, but it was the size of a marquee, the man was grossly fat. His eyes were small and almost hidden by the excess flesh on his face. His fingers were like sea slugs, restless and stubby.

'How old is this one?'

'We were told six, but you can't be sure.'

The fat man looked Sonny up and down but gave no sign of approval or any indication he was welcoming him into his home.

'Have you got the next one lined up?'

6

Inspector Hector Reynolds strode up and down the deck, his hands clasped behind his back, his crisp white police uniform dazzling in the late afternoon sun.

Stevie was below tinkering with the engines. When I came back and told her what had happened to Anna and Sally Lancaster she'd hardly reacted at all, though she knew Anna quite well. There was a flicker of something behind her eyes, but it was well concealed. I'd asked her the same kind of questions Reynolds was now asking me, and I could understand Reynolds' frustration.

The wife and daughter of a prominent Bahamian businessman had been blown to pieces by a car bomb. The said businessman had vanished without a trace, and the two people who had last seen the husband and wife alive could offer precious little information to throw any light on the tragic events.

'A strange name for a boat, Mr Beck, *The Lady of Pain*, if you don't mind me saying so,' Reynolds said. He said the same thing to me every time we met. Fortunately that wasn't often on his official business, but we were aware of one another. I was a law-abiding citizen, at least by my own definitions.

Maynard Sims

I was leaning against the rail, smoking, watching my hand tremble as it held the cigarette. 'You wouldn't say that if you knew the particular lady the boat was named after.' It was my stock response to his comment about the name of my boat. I was sure he knew exactly who she was named after.

Reynolds cocked an eyebrow, but I wasn't in the mood to play the games he clearly thought would work in his favour and elicit more information than I was giving him. He turned round and gripped the rail, staring across the clear blue ocean to the horizon. 'So you don't know where Mr Lancaster is, and you don't know anyone who held a grudge against him or his family?' That was pretty much the sum of all I had told him.

I was getting tired of the questions. 'Inspector,' I said. 'I've told you, I haven't seen Alan in days. And in answer to your other question, no. Alan is a very good business-man, and less ruthless than some I've known. I'm sure he hasn't reached his position without stepping on a few toes along the way, but I know for a fact he's never stabbed anyone in the back to get what he wanted. He might have business rivals, but he simply isn't the type of man to make enemies.'

'A laudable testimonial, Mr Beck, but, I fear, errone-ous. A man with no enemies does not lose his family in such a murderous manner.' Reynolds' face had the ap-pearance of black granite as he stared off into the distance.

He spent a lot of time on minor crime; drunks, low level drugs busts, domestic violence. He was more than capable of dealing with serious crime as he had shown on regular occasions with murders, drug smuggling and organised crime syndicates.

Serious crime was not a rare occurrence in the Baha-mas but car bombs were, and I could tell he was agitated by it. Luckily for him Assistant Commissioner Brooks was away at a conference until Thursday. That gave Reynolds three full days to get some kind of angle on this. Brooks was a different type of policeman entirely to Reynolds. Aloof and priggish where Reynolds was accessible and broad minded. If Brooks was here now I would probably be in custody simply because I was as good a candidate for a suspect as he would be likely to find, given such short notice.

Reynolds was Islands born and bred and that seemed to give him a doggedness which, allied to his natural Caribbean phlegmatic nature, made him effective at his job whilst not ruffling the feathers of the people he questioned. Though if you were guilty of something, and he knew it, he would cling like a barnacle and ruffle your feathers so hard you'd end up bald.

'Such a cowardly crime,' Reynolds said quietly, almost to himself. 'That poor child.'

I shared his sentiments, though my own reaction to the murders was dulled, numbed by the vicious brutality of it all. And I was worried about Alan.

After the car exploded I ran like hell back to the Lancasters' house, explained to Elsa what had happened and phoned through to the police. Poor Elsa. The news devastated her. She'd been Anna's maid for years, long before Anna married Alan; and Sally she treated as her own child. Elsa was a stockily built woman of German origin, who possessed a stolid, unflappable nature, but when I told her what had happened she seemed to crumble from within. Her erect frame sagged and she appeared to age ten years in as many seconds. The news of Anna and Sally's death somehow diminished her, and I doubted that she would ever be quite the same woman again.

After I telephoned the police I started to ring round all the possible places I thought Alan might be and, after at least ten phone calls, drew a complete blank.

I returned to the scene of the explosion, getting there just as the first police vehicle arrived. Reynolds was first on the scene, along with Sergeant Jim Henderson. I knew Henderson a lot better than Reynolds—we were drinking buddies from way back—and it was to him I gave my initial statement. After that I went back to the bungalow where I poured myself a very stiff whisky, which I promptly threw up into the lavatory bowl.

The rest of the day passed by in a blur, and it was only now, with the commanding presence of Inspector Reynolds on my boat, that my mind started functioning again.

Reynolds was built like a wrestler. Tall, well over six feet, with wide, strong shoulders and a chest that resembled a rum barrel. His skin was deep black, the features of his face strangely angular despite the size of his head, the round dome with the hair shaved very short.

Alan's disappearance could possibly be quite innocent. He may have been called away on business at short notice; it had happened before. But I was very aware that Alan had tried to contact me this morning, and I had a gut feeling that had we managed to speak to one another, the events of the day might not have developed so tragically. Anyway, we were friends, and for the sake of that friendship I had to find out what in God's name was going on.

'Was there anything else, Inspector?' I said. 'Only it's been a rough day.'

'Of course,' Reynolds said. 'But, Mr Beck, should Mr Lancaster contact you, you will let me know immediately, and I would appreciate it if you would make yourself available should any further questions arise.'

'That goes without saying. I want to catch the bastards who did this...probably more than you do yourself.'

He looked at me sternly. 'I doubt that, Mr Beck. I doubt that very much indeed. Good day to you.'

After he'd gone Stevie came up from below. 'What do you really think happened?' she said. That was Stevie, straight to the point, but for once I had to disappoint her.

'Sorry, Stevie, I told the Inspector the truth, straight

down the line. I haven't got any more idea about what's happened here than you have.'

She regarded me thoughtfully for a moment, and then said, 'Okay, I believe you.'

'That's very big of you.'

'So what are we going to do about it?'

'*We* are not going to do anything about it. You're going home and I'm going down to *Louis' Oyster Bar* for something to eat.'

'And that's it?'

'That's it, Stevie. See you in the morning.'

'You're up to something,' she said.

'I'm not. Scout's honour.'

She frowned and shook her head. 'You're a bloody useless liar, Harry.'

I gave her a tired smile. 'I know, Stevie, I know.'

7

I meant what I said to her, I was going for something to eat, but my stomach could wait. There was something I wanted to do first. I would go to the *Oyster Bar*, but the man who owned it would be somewhere else.

I went back to the bungalow, showered quickly, then drove across town to Lucayan Beach. I parked my Jeep in the small car park behind *The Jolly Tar*, a small English-style pub overlooking Lucayan Harbour. *The Tar* was popular with the tourists, especially the British, and tonight was no exception.

Jack Dylan, the owner of *The Tar*, and the *Oyster Bar*, prided himself on the authenticity of the pub and as I walked through the door I was greeted by the malty aroma of draught beer and the sound of a slightly out of tune piano hammering out the strains of *Maybe It's Because I'm A Londoner*, with a chorus of off-key voices picking up the refrain. Why was it that the British always wanted to recreate a part of their homeland when they were abroad? Was it a love of the United Kingdom or a reluctance to embrace different cultures?

The pub was crowded, but I pushed my way through and found Jack. He was in his usual position on the wrong side of the bar, making conversation with a small group of tourists, while his harassed bar staff served glass after glass of cool, refreshing beer. I walked up behind him and slapped him on the back. 'How are you keeping, Jack?'

Jack Dylan was a giant of a man; around six foot six and around two hundred and eighty pounds. He had a round, open face latticed with broken veins, giving him a permanently flushed appearance. He turned and threw his arms around me, squeezing me in a bear hug. 'Harry, great to see you, howya been?'

'Lousy.' I started to tell him about Anna, but he held up a hand to stop me.

'I already know, Harry boy. News travels fast — bad news even faster.'

It didn't really surprise me that Jack knew about it. In fact I'd been banking on it. Very little happened on Grand Bahama Island that Jack Dylan didn't get to hear about. He also knew Alan as well as I did; we'd all been friends for just over thirty years. More than friends, we'd grown up together, shared all our life experiences together. We were close, or so I'd thought. Alan's disappearance was making me doubt my own memories.

Alan had helped Jack establish *The Jolly Tar* fifteen years ago when Jack's former business venture collapsed. He'd run a high-class seafood restaurant at Chub Cay on Andros, but when a virulent outbreak of salmonella food poisoning hospitalised twenty-four of his customers, and killed three more, the authorities closed him down. They're strict about such things on the Islands, but then with two million tourists coming here each year they have to be. News of a food poisoning epidemic just isn't good PR.

Alan, a regular face at Jack's tables, had just bought *The Jolly Tar*, or *The Conch* as it was then called, and he was looking for someone to run it for him. He called Jack in to do the job, and within two years he'd made such a success of it he could afford to buy it from Alan outright. In time he'd also bought the *Oyster Bar*.

'It's bad, Harry—Anna and Sally. Tragic,' he said. He gripped my arm and steered me to a vacant booth at the back of the pub. 'Too public there,' he said. 'I guess you want to know if I've seen anything of Alan.'

'You've heard he's disappeared then?'

'I've not seen him, Harry. We had a falling out about a rum shipment a couple weeks back. He hasn't set foot in the place since.'

I couldn't keep up with all of Alan's deals, but I knew he had some kind of arrangement with Jack and several other of the island's bar owners. He'd buy cheap liquor in Cuba, bring it back to the island, where it would be rebottled, and then he'd pass it on to his outlets for a tidy profit. I'd always suspected the authorities knew about the deal but turned a blind eye to it. Alan Lancaster had a lot of clout in certain high places.

'I take it you've tried his mobile phone?' Jack said.

'Switched off.'

We sat down in the booth and Jack signalled for one of the barmen to bring us a bottle of wine. 'You know Anna was packing up and moving out when it happened?' I said.

'You're kidding me. Anna and Alan were like that.' He crossed his middle finger over his index finger.

'She was taking Sally to the airport for a flight back to the States when the car exploded.'

Jack Dylan shook his head sadly. He was a man with three broken marriages behind him. He knew firsthand the emotional strain of wives walking out on husbands and taking the kids with them. It had happened to him. 'Poor bastard,' he said. 'Who would have guessed?' He stared me in the eye. 'I reckon you've got the right idea, Harry boy. Never let yourself get tied down. Am I right or am I right?'

'I learned that lesson a long time ago, Jack. Katy, remember?'

'Little Katy, God, yes I'd forgotten about her. *The Lady of Pain*. Lucky escape, Harry boy.'

'Lucky for whom?' I said under my breath. 'Where do you think he's gone, Jack?'

'Alan? Haven't got a clue, but I'll give you a word of advice, Harry. Stay out of it.'

'So you *do* know something.'

'I didn't say that. But car bombs! That's in a different league from a little liquor smuggling. The people who operate that ruthlessly deserve to be given a wide berth, a very wide berth indeed. Take it from me, Harry. You don't want to get involved with it.'

'I've got to try to help, Jack, and so do you. We're friends, remember?'

We talked some more, just general stuff, finished the bottle between us, and then I left. Some detective I'd make. My first and only lead had ended up a blind alley. I'd thought if anyone would have an idea where Alan had got to, it would be Jack.

8

When we were kids, growing up in Port Lucaya, we'd run together. But although Alan and I were best friends, it was always Jack I'd turn to in times of trouble. It was probably because Jack was the biggest of us. Six feet tall at thirteen, he'd acted as our protector from the local bullies.

I hadn't heard about their recent argument; Alan had said nothing about it, and Jack, by nature, didn't tell you anything about his life unless you asked…and then it depended on whether or not he thought it was any of your business.

I had a theory about Jack, and it was as much centred on his success in attracting women as it was in his failure to keep them. Sure he had gone through some difficult financial times, and he had a temper that flared when you least expected it, but I think it was more about expectations and ambitions. Although Jack and Alan were very different temperamentally, my theory was that Jack wanted to be Alan.

Alan was a third generation Bahamian, his grandfather settling out here from Liverpool, England back in 1910. Henry Lancaster had built up large shipping interests during the latter years of the Victorian era and, by the turn of the century, was one of the wealthiest men in the north of England. A severe asthma attack nearly killed him, and when he'd recovered he uprooted his family, and his fortune, and transported them halfway across the globe to settle in the colony. He based the family in Nassau and quickly established himself in business once more, at first in shipping, but then, more profitably, in oil.

Sometimes it was hard to imagine the years that had passed since we'd lazed away time on the beach. Three very different boys had grown into three diverse and complex men. Tired and worried as I was, I wondered whether all we had in common was our past.

Wearily I climbed back into the Jeep and headed home. Alan and Jack falling out, Anna about to walk out on Alan. It was starting to look like I didn't know my friends half as well as I thought I did. It was a sobering thought.

But only sobering in one way. I was feeling woolly-headed. Jack's cheap wine hadn't helped, but basically I was exhausted and needed to sleep for a good eight hours. As I drove I realised I wasn't hungry anymore.

Henry Lancaster's son Robert had none of his father's business acumen. When old Henry died and Robert took over the firm, things deteriorated pretty quickly. Robert was a gambler with a penchant for the ladies on whom he liked to lavish expensive and wildly extravagant gifts. Soon the company's balance sheets were decimated, and by the time Alan was old enough to assume control of the business, the Lancaster wealth had dwindled to a few hundred thousand dollars and several pockets of apparently worthless real estate.

Alan had a shrewd head for business, and within five years—during which time Robert Lancaster died of syphilis, a return gift from one of his young ladies—he'd turned the business around, and was making use of the real estate his financial advisers had deemed only useful

Maynard Sims

as a tax loss. Hotel followed hotel and tourists flocked conveniently to the island to fill them.

Now Alan Lancaster was in the comfortable position of being one of the wealthiest men in the Bahamas, perhaps not yet in the same league as his grandfather, but getting there.

Except his wife and daughter were dead, and he had disappeared.

I pulled up outside the bungalow and the first thing I noticed was the front door. It was hanging askew, having been smashed from its hinges. It was pretty remote up here — my nearest neighbour not within shouting distance — so I'd always taken precautions against a break-in. Mortise deadlocks on all the doors, security latches on the windows.

I got out of the Jeep and approached the door cautiously. The locks had held up well, but the door looked like it had been battered with a sledgehammer. I stopped outside the door and listened carefully for the sound of movement from within. All I heard were the waves breaking down on the beach and the sputtering cough of an outboard motor being coaxed into life, somewhere down by the harbour.

I went back to the Jeep and rummaged under the seat until my fingers closed over the cool and satisfyingly heavy metal of a wheel brace. Feeling more comfortable with a weapon of sorts I approached the house again, pushed the smashed door aside and entered. I groped on the wall for the light switch and flicked it on.

The bungalow was deserted, but it was a complete shambles. The desk had been overturned, its drawers ripped out, papers scattered about the room. The couch had been slashed open exposing the white filling and gunmetal springs. The same fate had befallen my favourite armchair. I wandered through to the bedroom, tripping over pieces of the mattress, which had also been gutted. The built-in wardrobe doors were wide open and my clothes had been removed and dumped on the floor in a pile. I went across and picked up my leather aviator jacket. Someone had been busy with a knife tonight. The leather was shredded and the lining sliced open.

I didn't bother with the rest of the bungalow as I guessed it would be in pretty much the same condition. Instead I found the phone, which had been kicked under the bed, sat down on the windowsill and started to dial the number of the local police station. I was halfway through dialling when something caught my attention. I replaced the handset and stared out through the window. I could see *The Lady of Pain* moored in the harbour, but there was something else. There was a light burning in the wheelhouse.

I moved to the wardrobe and searched the top shelf until I found my binoculars. That they were still there told me this was not just a simple burglary. They were made by Leica and had cost me half a week's money. I took them across to the window and used them to look down to the harbour. Then I threw them down onto the vandalised bed and bolted from the house.

I reached the harbour, breathless, my heart racing, and jumped over the rail on *The Lady's* aft deck.

And I found Stevie.

She was tied to the aft rail, her legs dangling down into the water.

She was naked and bloody.

She'd been crucified.

9

Stevie was barely conscious, but at least, thank God, she was still alive. Her arms were outstretched and secured to the rail by thin leather straps, tied so tight they were cutting into her skin. Her naked body was peppered with cigarette burns and she'd been beaten about the face, leaving one eye red and puffy, the other blackened and nearly closed. There was a crust of dried blood where her nose had been smashed, and her lips were swollen and split. I tried untying the straps, but the knots were too tight, and as I fumbled with them Stevie moaned and opened her eyes.

'Harry?' she mumbled through her swollen lips.

'It's okay, I'm here,' I said, and stroked her hair. 'I'll get you out of this.'

'It hurts, Harry. It hurts.' A small tear trickled down her bruised cheek. It was the first time I'd seen her cry since her father died.

'Give me a second. I'm going to get my knife. I'll have to cut you free.'

She nodded in understanding and I went below to the cabin where I kept my gutting knife. The fact that the cabin hadn't been ransacked the way the bungalow was could mean one of two things. The people who'd crucified Stevie had either been disturbed before they could search it, or they'd found what they were looking for. I dragged open the door of the locker that housed my charts and log book and found the knife.

It wasn't easy slicing through the straps without cutting her, but I worked as carefully as I could, whispering words of encouragement as the knife bit into the leather.

Once she was free I eased her as gently as I could back over the rail and laid her down on the deck, took off my shirt and wrapped her in it, cradling her in my arms.

'Who did it, Stevie?'

She looked up at me, tears glistening in her eyes. 'Don't know, Harry,' she said, and then she fainted.

I got her below, laid her on the bunk and covered her with a blanket, then went to fetch the first aid box from the wheelhouse.

It was a warm clear night, the stars blinking in a sky of black velvet. There was a full moon, reflecting on the ocean, capping the waves with silver. I entered the wheelhouse feeling murderous. Whoever did this to Stevie was going to pay for it in kind. I was certain of that.

Beneath the wheel was a panel set into the woodwork; one of my few modifications to *The Lady's* structure. There was a small button, hidden from view, to the right of the wheel. I pressed it and the panel sprang open. Clipped to it were two guns. A Smith and Wesson .38 revolver, and a small Beretta automatic. I kept them there in case of emergencies.

Pirates still operated in these waters, though the fashionable term now was *yacht-jackers*. Drug-runners and smugglers would steal boats to use for making their deliveries, and they weren't too fussy if anyone happened to be aboard when they decided to make the theft. Boat owners had been known to go for a moonlight swim with twenty kilos of chain wrapped around them before now.

With the guns I was hedging my bets. They were my ace in the hole.

I unclipped the Beretta and stuck it in the waistband of my trousers. It made me feel more secure. Then I carried the first aid box below and started to dress Stevie's wounds.

I was cleaning the blood away from her mouth when she came to. She stared up at me, panic in her eyes, then, with a sob, threw her arms around me. 'Jesus, Harry, I was so scared.'

I held her tightly. 'It's okay now, they've gone.' But she held onto me for a long time.

Reynolds would want to know about this, this and the break-in at the bungalow, and I would have been happier if Stevie was being looked after at the hospital, but she was slipping in and out of consciousness, and the first time I tried to get to the radio she roused and panicked. I cleaned her up as best I could and eventually she drifted off to sleep. I left her for half an hour and tried to raise Alan on his radio. If he was on his boat it was safe to assume he'd have it switched on, but in the end I gave up went below and sat by Stevie, holding onto her hand, praying she'd suffered no internal injuries.

When dawn broke, just after four, I eased myself up from the floor, where I'd spent the night awake, sitting with my back to the bunk, and went through to the galley to brew some coffee. I'd left Stevie sleeping peacefully, but when I returned her eyes were open and she was struggling to sit up.

'Take it easy,' I said. 'Can you drink this?' I offered her the coffee I'd made for myself. She took the mug from me, holding it in both hands, sipping at it, wincing as it scalded her damaged lips. 'When you feel like travelling, I'm going to take you to the hospital. Get them to fix you up properly.'

She said something, but I didn't catch it. 'Sorry?'

She took the cup from her lips and fixed me with a fierce look from her one good eye. 'I said, like hell you will.'

'You're not going to be difficult, are you?'

'No hospitals,' she said firmly. 'I'll be all right. Doc Roberts can give me something for the pain.'

'Why do you have to be so bloody tough?' I said. 'What're you trying to prove?'

She avoided my gaze. 'Nothing,' she said. 'Hospitals give me the itch, that's all.'

I wasn't going to argue with her further. 'Okay, you win. But once I get you home I'm getting in touch with Roberts myself, and you're not going anywhere or doing anything until you've seen him, okay?'

She shrugged and finished the coffee.

'Do you want to talk about it?'

'I feel like sleeping the clock round.'

I knew what she meant. The question and answer session could wait until she felt like talking and my mind was in a fit state to make some kind of sense of her answers. I lay down on the bunk opposite hers, tucked the Beretta under the pillow, and closed my eyes. Within minutes I was asleep.

I awoke to the mouth-watering aroma of frying bacon. My first thought was that Stevie was out in the galley cooking breakfast. Then I checked the opposite bunk and saw her still lying there, sound asleep. From the galley I heard the rattle of plates. I felt under the pillow, found the gun and went to investigate.

I eased the galley door open with the toe of my shoe. The woman standing at the small cooker frying bacon and eggs turned around and smiled. 'Hello, Harry,' Katy said.

10

'What the hell are you doing here?' It wasn't one of the most gracious welcomes ever recorded, but it suited my mood, and camouflaged my shock at seeing her again.

'I see you've lost none of your natural charm,' she said acidly.

It was just over five years since we split up and the passage of time hadn't touched her at all. She was thirty-two but looked ten years younger. Her hair, once waist length, had been cut to a short bob, but it still shone like spun gold, and, if anything, the haircut made her look younger still.

Katy was one of the most beautiful women I had ever known. Her eyes were midnight blue, set in a perfect face; the type of face fashion photographers drool over. She wasn't tall, only five-three, but those sixty-three inches were perfectly proportioned; long slim legs, narrow hips, small but firm and perfectly formed breasts. She looked as elegant as ever, dressed in a pencil-slim grey skirt and a white silk blouse. On her feet were black, patent leather shoes, the heels giving another three inches to her height.

As soon as I saw her my stomach lurched, leaving me feeling hollow inside. An old familiar feeling. I repeated the question, but phrased it more politely.

'I heard about Anna and Sally. Harry, I'm sorry.'

I searched those blue eyes looking for the lie, but the sentiment appeared genuine, so I decided to take it at face value.

She turned her attention back to the frying pan but kept talking. 'I looked for you at the bungalow. The place is a wreck.'

'Someone broke in.'

'So I gathered.' She turned back and looked at me squarely. 'Harry, are you in some kind of trouble?'

I shook my head. I suddenly realised the Beretta was still in my hand, pointing directly at her. She hadn't even mentioned it — as if it were an everyday occurrence to be held at gunpoint by an ex-lover; but then maybe for Katy it was. She'd always run wild, even when we were together. Seeing her now, in such a domestic setting, was partly the reason for the sense of shock I felt. I put the gun away.

'Who's the boy with the smashed up face?' she said.

'Stevie, and she's not a boy. Tom Bailey's daughter. Remember Tom?'

Katy raised an exquisitely shaped eyebrow. 'You like them young these days,' she said.

I glared at her. 'It's not like that.'

'It's none of my business, Harry, not now.'

'Let's leave it like that then. You still haven't told me what you're doing here.'

'This is ready,' she said, forking the bacon onto a plate. 'Should I make your *friend* some too?'

'Ask her yourself,' I said and went topside for some fresh air, leaving her standing there holding the plate. On top of everything else that had happened in the last twenty-four hours, the last thing I needed was Katy Donahoe back in my life. God knows, she messed it up for me pretty well the first time around.

A short while later I heard her come up on deck. 'We don't have to be at war with each other, you know,' she said.

'Don't we?'

She sighed. It was a sound I remembered well. 'Grow up, Harry. Five years is a long time.' She walked up and stood next to me at the rail. She even smelled the same. 'I see you changed the name of the boat. What was wrong with *Island Girl*? You named her after me, remember?'

'She's still named after you,' I said sullenly.

'I thought changing the names of boats was unlucky.'

I ignored her. I could have said that meeting her in the first place had been the biggest slice of bad luck ever handed down to me, but what was the point?

She rested her hand on my bare arm. The hand was cool and smooth. 'I hurt you, didn't I?'

I didn't want to swim in those waters again. I changed the subject. 'How's Max?' Maxwell Donahoe was her father, the owner of Donahoe Holdings, and one of the richest men on the Islands.

'He's fine,' she said. 'Actually, he's the reason I'm here.'

I frowned. 'He sent you to see me?'

'Not exactly. He wants to see you. He was going to get in touch, but I heard the news and said I'd come over and deliver the message personally.'

'You shouldn't have troubled. He's got my phone number, though he hasn't bothered to use it much over the last few years.' The sun was catching highlights in her hair. She was standing close, still holding my arm, and I felt myself becoming aroused, in spite of my better judgement. I pulled away from her. 'In fact he probably breathed a huge sigh of relief when we split. Somehow I never could see me fitting into your family's social circle.'

'Then that only goes to prove how little you know him. He made my life hell for a few weeks after I finished with you.'

A few weeks! I was going to tell her that my life had

45

been hell ever since our relationship ended, but I was damned if I was going to give her the satisfaction of knowing that. 'So Max gave you a hard time. I'm sorry.'

'Liar.'

I shrugged. 'Well, you've given me the message. I'll call Max and make arrangements to see him, but tell him not to hold his breath. I might be tied up for a few months yet.'

She grabbed hold of my shirt and spun me round to face her. Her cheeks were flushed and she was breathing heavily through her nose. 'Look, your argument is with me, not my father. Don't take your childish temper tantrums out on him, he doesn't deserve it. You never got less than a fair deal from him. He liked you, Harry. Still does, though God knows why. You're one of the most pigheaded, arrogant, and selfish bastards I've ever met.' She climbed over the side of the boat, jumped down onto the concrete harbour and walked away quickly, back towards land.

'You didn't tell me what he wanted to see me about,' I called after her.

'Go to hell, Harry,' she said, without looking round. 'If you want to know then phone him.' There was a black Porsche parked at the edge of the harbour. She opened the door and climbed in. A second later she took off with a squeal of tyres, raising an ochre cloud from the dusty road.

I watched her go, then slammed my hand against the rail and swore loudly. Often in the past I'd wondered what it would be like to see her again. I'd run imaginary conversations over and over in my mind, playing out different scenarios. In all of them we'd end up reconciled, in each other's arms, making love. How different it worked in reality. I could taste the dust her car tyres had thrown up. It took away some of the bitterness, but not much.

I went below to check on Stevie. She was sitting up,

ploughing through the plate of bacon and eggs Katy had cooked for her. 'Feeling better?' I said.

She nodded and finished her mouthful. 'What did she want?'

'Just a laugh and a joke about the good old days,' I said, crouching down beside her and checking her wounds. 'I'm surprised you remembered her. I think you only met her once when we called in on your old man one evening. You'd have only been about ten.'

'Once seen never forgotten, that one,' she said. 'What did a woman with looks like that see in an old wreck like you?'

'They asked the same question when my mother married my father. I guess there must be something about Beck men that makes us irresistible to beautiful women.'

'Don't kid yourself, Harry. Remember, you're talking to someone who's had to put you to bed when you've been pissed out of your brain, and on more than one occasion.' She gave me a quick half grin with her damaged mouth. It was all she could manage, but it was an encouraging sign. The bastards last night might have busted her up physically, but they hadn't been able to touch her spirit.

'She thought you were a boy,' I said and took the empty plate from her.

'The bitch!'

I laughed and ruffled her hair. 'Do you feel up to travelling now?'

'I think so.'

'Right, I'll take you home. We can talk on the way.'

11

It had just begun to rain in the slum settlements of Haiti.

Cholera was becoming widespread, contracted through drinking unclean water. Hygiene was always difficult in the conditions the families existed in, but since the earthquakes and the temporary camps, sanitation was non-existent. The temporary camps had been in place almost a year now.

Humanitarian aid was a vast enterprise, but still thousands of people sat in their own filth, ate barely enough to survive and lived inside their heads.

To hear the orphans at play, even in the warm tropical storm, was almost enough to give people hope. The innocence was something to cling onto when nothing else had a future.

Everyone had become used to the Americans and the Europeans who lived and worked amongst them. Many of them had strange accents that made what they said unintelligible to the local people, but they recognised the kind tones in which they spoke.

Most of the foreigners were such frequent visitors that they went unnoticed, part of the landscape. Walking amongst people who were shocked and traumatised, they were like unseen ghosts, leaving a residual presence that barely dented the damaged lives they touched.

Regular visitors included three groups of two men who didn't exude quite the same kind tones as some did. The six men were never seen together, and always came in the same pairs. The patterns of their visits were random, the times of day differed and the dates in the months varied. The only similarity to their visits was when they left. Always it was with one child.

Sometimes it was a young girl, sometimes a young boy. Over the weeks they took with them babies, two-, three-, four-year-olds and upwards to children around thirteen years of age.

They talked at length with the people running the orphanages that had sprung up out of necessity. They had credentials of the highest order. Impeccable papers that were correctly completed, stamped with authority, and signed with impunity.

Children who had lost their parents didn't ask questions. If they did, and some wondered where they were going, they were told they were being taken to a better life, many to America, others to Europe, some as far as Asia and Australia.

Imagining a better life wasn't difficult for the children; their world had been hard, had fallen apart, and was now hell.

When they took the hand of the men to be taken to a new life, they thought they had a lot to look forwards to.

12

Stevie lived about half a mile away from my place, so I took the drive slowly to allow her enough time to tell it properly.

'After you left I came down to give the engines a final check. I'd been down there a while when I heard a boat approaching. It was an outboard motor, not running properly; sounded like a blockage in the fuel line. I heard it pull in close, then it thumped against the side of *The Lady* and someone climbed aboard. I thought it might be Ernie or Raoul, so I went up to check.'

Ernie and Raoul Rodriguez were a father and son who worked a small fishing boat farther along the coast. Sometimes if they got back early they'd call by and we would all go for a drink together.

'When I reached topside there were three characters standing there. One of them was holding a gun, a shotgun, short barrel.'

'What did they look like?'

'They were all dressed the same, in black, with black ski masks, y'know—covering the head, with holes cut out for eyes, nose and mouth. One of them was about six-three, built like a brick wall; the one who did all the talking was smaller, about your height.'

I was five-eleven.

'And one of them was a woman, about my height, but thick set, like a Russian shot-putter. Vicious bitch! She was the one who did these.' She pointed to the cigarette burns on her arms.

'Did they say what they wanted?'

'They didn't, not at first. The smaller man told me to strip off. I told him to go to hell. But the big one held me while the woman stripped me. I got in one punch, but I hit the big one. It was like hitting a tree. Anyway, they dragged me through to the cabin and started throwing questions at me.'

'What kind of questions?'

'General stuff at first, about you, about me. It's funny. They seemed to know an awful lot about us, and yet they didn't know much?'

'I think you'd better explain that. It sounds like someone tipped them off?'

Stevie thought for a moment. 'It was as if they'd read about us, all the facts, dates of birth and so on, but they didn't really know us. They kept calling me *Stephanie* for a start!'

She said the name Stephanie with the contempt one normally reserves for a despised relation.

'And there were a few other things, I forget now.'

'Carry on, I get the drift.'

'Then they changed tack and started asking about Alan.'

'Alan Lancaster?'

'Right. It was then I started to get really scared.'

We reached Stevie's apartment. It was one of a block of eight. Holiday apartments most of them, but Stevie and another girl, Jackie, were permanent residents. Jackie acted as the block's unofficial janitor.

I pulled up outside and switched off the Jeep's engine. 'You can tell me the rest once we get inside.'

'Aren't you forgetting something?'

I looked at her quizzically.

'The pleasure trip? The family from the hotel?'

'Shit!' I said. 'I'll have to use your phone.'

I let Stevie unlock the door, but, remembering what I'd found at the bungalow, I went in first. I didn't want any unpleasant surprises this time. The Beretta was still tucked into the waistband of my trousers. I took it out and switched off the safety. It looked impressive, even though the only thing I'd ever fired at was the occasional shark off Cat Island. If I was confronted by an armed thug, the question wasn't so much would I have the courage to pull the trigger, but more would I actually hit him if I fired?

I didn't get the chance to find out. Stevie's apartment was empty. It looked like a whirlwind had blown through it, but Stevie assured me that the clothes strewn about the floor and the jumbled pile of paperbacks in the corner was her normal habitat.

'And you accuse me of being a slob,' I said, noticing the dirty dishes in the kitchen sink.

'I never seem to get the time to clean it up,' she said defensively.

I shook my head in mock admonition, and then picked up the phone. First I called Doc Roberts, and made arrangements for him to drop by Stevie's place later in the day. I didn't tell him the nature of the problem — he'd find that out soon enough for himself — but I intimated it was pretty urgent.

Next, the hotel. I got put through to Ray Burgess, an old friend of mine who was manager there.

'Harry, dear boy, lovely to hear from you. I won't ask how things are with you. News travels fast here, as you well know.'

'You heard about Alan's family?'

'And about poor Stevie. No serious damage I hope?'

'I'm with her now. That's one of the reasons for the

call. I won't be able to make the pleasure trip today.'

Ray laughed. 'Fully understood, dear boy, and as it happens it doesn't matter, as the family you were meant to be taking for the joyride checked out that morning. They were English, and the bombing reminded them too much of home, and the random, but apparently ever present threat of *Al Qaeda* terror attacks.'

I didn't comment, but the thought did cross my mind that threats living here were different, but just as real.

'So they asked to be transferred over to one of Alan's hotels on Eleuthera. They'd heard Eleuthera was a much quieter island than Grand Bahama.' He laughed again. 'Like the excellent manager and good PR man I am, Ray Burgess granted the request, and offered them dinner in the hotel restaurant on the house.'

Ray asked about Alan. Had he been in touch, did I know where he was? I'd heard the questions before and was getting sick of them, but I answered them all patiently. Ray Burgess was a gentleman in its truest sense. He wasn't asking in an attempt to get some vicarious thrill. He asked because he had known Alan Lancaster almost as long as I had, liked him, but moreover, considered him a friend and genuinely cared about him.

It was a quality in Alan I had long admired, even envied. He had a certain aura about him that attracted other people. He made friends easily, and moved through all strata of society with ease, picking up friendships as he went. It was another quality that fitted my theory about Jack's envy of him; there was an aura about Jack as well, but it was something that put people on their guard, as if they sensed they had to stay wary around this man.

I was different from both of them. I was a loner by nature. Consequently, people often found me to be cold and distant, or so I'd been told, and they tended to shy away, or else, conversely, they found my easy going manner appealing and wanted to be friendlier than I needed.

I had friends, but could count them on the fingers of both hands…and still have a couple of digits left over.

Before I rang off a thought occurred to me. 'Ray what chance is there of having a room at the hotel for a few days?'

'Your place unfit for human habitation?'

'Something like that. It'll be just until I get the bungalow sorted out.' I didn't mention the details of the break-in; I figured Ray had enough on his plate right now with Alan out of the picture, without being burdened with my problems.

'No trouble, Harry,' he said. 'Strangely enough, a room's just become vacant.'

I laughed and thanked him.

13

After speaking with Ray Burgess I telephoned the police. Reynolds was out of the office so I was put through to Jim Henderson. I told him about Stevie and the bungalow, and he, in return, roasted me for not informing him sooner. 'And if you think I've given you a hard time, Harry, I assure you it's nothing compared to what you're going to pick up from Reynolds when he gets back. He'll have your balls on a plate.'

'He's welcome to them,' I said and rang off.

Stevie had made some coffee and I sipped at it as I punched out the number for Max Donahoe. I'd deliberately left him until last because he was the one I wanted to speak to least. I thought I'd finished with that family a long time ago, and the thought of getting enmeshed with them again didn't appeal to me one iota. But despite my misgivings, the curiosity factor needed satisfying. I hadn't spoken to Max since Katy and I split simply because I'd never had a reason to get in contact with him. Still, this seemed like it was going to be a week of surprises.

Max wasn't at home. He had a butler, Jenkins, and Jenkins told me Max was entertaining clients on the *Minotaur*, the yacht he kept at anchor off the New Providence coast.

Jenkins offered to patch my call through to the *Minotaur's* radio, but I told him not to bother. I'd radio through later when I got back to *The Lady*.

Stevie was sitting on the couch, flicking through a magazine. I glanced at the cover and wasn't at all surprised to see it was a journal on the finer points of kickboxing. I went and sat down next to her, finishing off my coffee down to the grounds. 'Any more where that came from? All that talking's left me dry.'

'Sure,' she said and took my cup.

I watched her as she walked through to the apartment's tiny kitchenette. If it wasn't for the marks on her face, hands and arms you wouldn't have guessed anything was wrong with her, let alone that she'd been subjected to a painful and terrifying ordeal.

'What's the matter?' she said as she came back to the lounge. 'You look like you're ready to strangle someone.'

I took the coffee from her. 'Thanks. Sit down and we'll pick up from where we left off outside. We should have time before your visitors arrive.'

She looked alarmed. 'Visitors?'

'Doc Roberts and the police. Jim Henderson's going to call in personally, and you know Jim, so there's nothing to be concerned about.' She relaxed a bit and sank back carefully into the puffed-up cushions on the couch. 'Still hurt?' I said.

'Pride more than anything else. Christ, I was so stupid. I know where you keep your guns. If only I'd managed to get hold of one first, instead of walking out there like a lamb to the slaughter.'

'Hindsight makes wise men of us all,' I said. 'But then if you'd come up armed, you might be talking to the fishes right now, instead of sitting here talking to me. They were armed too, don't forget. You don't want to hear it, but you were lucky to got off as...lightly as you did.'

She agreed I had a point, so she picked up the story

from where she'd left off.

'They said they'd seen Alan at the harbour that morning and they asked if he'd said where he was going. I told them no, but they didn't believe me. Then the woman asked if Alan had given me something to look after for him. A package of some kind. Again I said no. The woman hit me then and called me a liar. She lit a cigarette and then said something to the big one and he grabbed me and held me down. That's when I got these.' She lifted her arms and looked down at her burns.

'You say the woman said something to the big man. What did she say?'

'I don't know. It was foreign.'

'And you didn't recognise the language?'

'Italian, Spanish, Greek, they all sound the same to me.'

'Not a lot of help,' I said.

She glared at me furiously. 'Oh, I'm so sorry, Harry. Remind me to book up for some foreign language lessons some time in the near future, so that the next time I get tortured I can give you a full bloody translation!'

'Simmer down,' I said, and I thought she was going to take a swing at me.

'No, I won't! It's all right for you sitting there so bloody smugly, asking your stupid questions. But it was me who was strung out there on that bloody rail for an hour while they did those things.'

I looked at her sharply. 'What things?'

'There you go again. Bloody questions. Well, okay, Harry, if you really want to know I'll tell you. The big one had a blackjack. You know what a blackjack is, Harry? It's a cosh about eight inches long, made out of leather and filled with lead shot. At first I thought he was going to hit me with it. Oh, he gave me a few playful taps, just so I knew what it was and what it felt like. But he had another use in mind. They dragged me back over the rail, so I was hanging face down, then the woman grabbed my ankles and spread-eagled me.' She stopped, breathing hard, her face flushed, tears pressing out from her eyes. 'Do you want to know what he did next, Harry? Do you really?'

She didn't have to tell me. I could read it in her eyes, and it sickened me. I shook my head and reached out for her. I wanted to hold her in my arms, to comfort her, to protect her, I suppose. But I was too late, much, much too late.

She sat upright to avoid my embrace. 'No, Harry. I'll cope with this my own way. But can we stop these fucking questions?'

'No more,' I said. 'I didn't realise...'

'Leave it, Harry. Just leave it. I'll get over it, given time. I'm hard as nails, remember? Stevie Bailey, toughest broad in Freeport. Scourge of the local bars. It's the image, you see? My way of surviving since Daddy died. But I'm a woman too, Harry. I can be hurt the same as anyone else. And those bastards knew that. They knew it!'

I sat in silence. I'd never heard her talk this way before. It was an unsettling experience, like looking in the mirror and not recognising the face staring back at you.

'I think I'd better go now,' I said. It sounded pretty feeble. 'You gonna be okay?'

She looked at me bleakly. 'Jim's going to want to know about it too, isn't he?'

'Yes,' I said. There was no point lying to her. 'And now, with what you've told me, he'll probably order a full physical examination. He'll treat it like any other sexual assault.'

She shuddered. 'I'll try and get Doc Roberts to do it, at least I know him.'

I reached out and ruffled her hair. She grabbed my hand and held it tightly. 'You're a good friend, Harry. I'm sorry I let rip at you. It had to come out though, do you see?'

I put a finger to her lips, leant across and kissed her on the forehead. It was the first intimate contact I'd had with her, of any kind, despite Katy's assertions. Perhaps I was finally seeing Stephanie, the woman who hid inside Stevie, the buddy.

14

I waited with Stevie until Doc Roberts arrived, then went down to *Louis' Oyster Bar* for something to eat. I parked the Jeep outside and stepped out before I remembered I still had the gun sticking from my waistband. *Louis'* had a free and easy atmosphere, but not so free and easy that someone packing a gun wouldn't attract attention. I opened the glove compartment and slipped the gun inside, then made my way into *Louis'* under the candy-striped awning.

The place was empty and, at this time of the morning, the atmosphere was flat. Night was the best time to eat at *Louis'*. The interior was small and sparsely decorated. The tables were wooden, covered with gingham cloths, and apart from a draped fishing net and a 8x10 framed photograph of a very proud Louis showing off a one hundred and twenty pound marlin he'd caught off Bimini, the walls were bare. Three lobster pots hung from a black-beamed ceiling, and at the back of the place was a long leather-topped bar, which separated the kitchen from the dining area.

Where *Louis'* scored was the frontage, which looked out on the sea. There were more tables out here, and it was the best place to dine.

I remembered several romantic nights sitting out there with Katy, listening to the waves lapping on the white sand, serenaded by the cheerful, carefree music of the goombay band Louis employed in the high season. Sheer magic!

In the morning light the magic wasn't there, or perhaps it was simply that I was eating alone. It was something that never usually bothered me, but, today, it just seemed to make me feel bloody miserable.

Even Louis wasn't his usual self. The grin on his round black face dropped as soon as I entered the bar. He'd heard the news — it seemed like everyone on the island had heard about it — and decided that it must be a great personal tragedy for me which, to a certain extent, it was. But I didn't need to be reminded of it every five minutes. When he served me he wore a mournful expression, and kept shaking his head and muttering, 'Oh dear, oh dear.' Until, finally I could stand it no longer and went across to the jukebox in the corner, which stood in as a poor substitute for the goombay band, and put on the happiest, liveliest song I could find.

In the corner were a young courting couple who, up until the music started, were so besotted with each other I don't think they were even aware I was there. As the Latin rhythms and vibrant congas of Santana blasted out through the jukebox's powerful speakers, they turned as one and gave me a withering look. I smiled at the boy, winked at the girl and sat down to finish my lobster. Louis stared at me with open-mouthed amazement, so I winked at him too for good measure.

It brightened my day.

Louis' Oyster Bar had carried the name for as long as anyone could remember. The current Louis was the third that I knew of. It wasn't *his* bar as such. Sure, he ran it, managed it and did all the hard work, but it was Jack who owned it. My old friend Jack Dylan. Though on nights when I'd drunk too much and was nostalgic more deeply than was good for me, I had unformed ideas that the real owner was more likely to be Alan Lancaster.

The missing Alan.

I got back to my bungalow to find it had been turned into a circus.

The police were there in force with Reynolds in charge. They were swarming over the place like ants at a picnic. A forensic team were dusting every flat surface; other officers were going through my belongings, checking the damage and looking for clues to the identity of the intruders. When I looked down to the harbour I saw another team was there, giving *The Lady of Pain* the same treatment.

Reynolds finally noticed me and stormed over. I was standing outside the bathroom watching one officer who had his arm down the lavatory bowl, though what he was looking for I couldn't begin to guess.

Before Reynolds could open his mouth I said, 'I know what you're going to say, Inspector, and you're quite right. I should have contacted you straight away. And, in fact, I was halfway through dialling the number when I saw Stevie down on *The Lady*.'

'I've seen Miss Bailey,' Reynolds said. 'I have just come from there. Sergeant Henderson thought it important enough to call me in and, after speaking with Miss Bailey I have to agree with him. And despite what you say, and whatever noble motives you see in your actions, what you did was irresponsible.' He waved his finger under my nose. 'In fact, it was only a fraction short of criminal.'

I spread my hands humbly. 'I can only apologise, Inspector,' I said.

Reynolds stared hard at me. I could tell he was reining in his temper. He gave a snort, spun on his heel and went to speak with a junior officer. As he spoke to him he kept glancing back at me, emphasising the odd word by slapping his fist into the palm of his hand, which I assumed was acting as a substitute for my face. Then he walked out of the bungalow and I heard a car engine revving. I didn't see Reynolds again that day.

He was right, of course, and he had every reason to be angry with me. And if he'd known how events were going to develop he might have been more than angry.

He might have arrested me there and then.

15

The circus finally left town and I was once again on my own. I spent a few hours trying to get the place straight, salvaging what I could from the mess. My wardrobe was in a worse state than I'd thought. They'd been looking for something, sure, but I was certain that there was an element of vindictiveness about it all. Who the hell hides anything in their underpants? But they'd been ripped up too.

They'd asked Stevie if Alan had given her a package, and got very nasty when she'd said he hadn't. Whatever was in the package must be important, and it must have been what they were looking for here.

As I worked in the bungalow I tried to figure what it was Alan was involved in, but the more questions I asked myself the more questions I seemed to be left with. Whatever it was, it was enough to drive a wedge in between Alan and Anna. I tried to think back to all the conversations I'd had with Alan over the past few months, but again came up with nothing.

I was trying to make the bedroom habitable when there was a knock at the door. That had been my first job, screwing the door back into place. The last thing I needed were visitors turning up unannounced, especially if they were the type of visitors Stevie had encountered down on *The Lady*.

Jim Henderson stood on the step, his cap gripped in his hand. 'Hello, Harry. Can I come in?'

'Sure.' I held the door open for him and showed him through the lounge. 'Care for a drink?'

He sat down on the couch, turning his cap over and over in his hands. 'Officially I'm on duty, but…Yes, I will. Got any brandy?'

'That kind of day, huh?'

'I've just left Stevie. Harry, I'm sorry I gave you a hard time earlier. I can see why you didn't want to leave her on her own. She told me what they did to her. I had to call Reynolds in after that.'

'I know,' I said.

'Did he give you a hard time?'

'Balls on a plate. Sautéed.'

'Sorry. I had no choice.'

Jim had reached the age when he was nearer retirement than most and yet he did his job with a passion that put many of his younger colleagues to shame.

I poured a Remy Martin and handed it to him. His hands were shaking. He looked up at me, grateful for the brandy, but there was something else in his eyes.

'It's hard when it's someone you know, Harry. Christ, I remember taking her down to the beach to play volleyball when she was just a kid, when old Tom was alive. When I think what those bastards did to her it makes me want to…' He hesitated and gulped his brandy.

'Rip them apart with your bare hands?'

'I can think of worse things, but yeah, I'd like to get my hands on them.'

I poured myself a Chivas Regal and joined him on the couch. 'How's the investigation coming along?'

He grimaced and shook his head. 'Very little to go on,'

he said. 'The forensic boys say C4 plastic explosive was used on the car, but the type of bomb it was doesn't tie in with the MO of any known terrorist group. This looks like a more personal attack.'

'Well that doesn't surprise me. Alan wasn't into politics in any big way.'

He picked that one up quickly. 'So you think the bomb was meant for Alan, not Anna and the kid.'

'Isn't that what you think? Alan used that car every day to buzz around the island. Anna drives…drove a little Fiat to do her running around. The only reason she was driving the Mercedes that day was because she was in the process of leaving Alan, and was taking her luggage to the airport. She wouldn't have got all the cases in the Fiat. Whoever planted the bomb couldn't have been doing it on spec. They must have had the Lancasters' under observation for a time, so they would have known the Mercedes was Alan's car.'

Jim nodded. 'Reynolds agrees with you.' He'd finished his brandy. I poured another. 'I shouldn't be doing this, I'm still on duty.'

'Live a little,' I said. 'God knows, life's too short as it is.'

He shook his head and stretched out on the couch. He wasn't a big man, only about five-ten, but he kept himself in shape, and I'd seen him clear a bar full of rowdy drunks single-handed on more than one occasion. His biceps were almost as big as my thigh and his legs were like ebony tree trunks. He put his drink down on the side table and went back to torturing his cap.

'The problem is, we just don't know where to start,' he said. 'The bombing was bad enough, but then with Stevie, and the break-in here…I'd give a year's salary to know what it was they were looking for. You don't know, do you?'

'Of course I don't, and the question's been bothering

the hell out of me too,' I said.

Jim suddenly fixed me with an intense gaze, the whites of his eyes very bright in his black face. 'Alan wasn't into narcotics, Harry, was he?'

I reacted as if I'd been stung. 'What the hell kind of question is that, Jim?' I said. 'You've known Alan for years. You know what his feelings are about drugs and shit like that.' And indeed he did. Alan once called the police in when he discovered that a guest at one of his hotels on Eleuthera was giving cocaine parties. It caused a hell of a stink at the time, and for a while the hotel, and Alan in particular picked up some bad press, but he'd told me it was worth all the fuss. His mother had been a heroin addict, and had ended her days in a Miami sanatorium, burnt out and used up. With parents like his Alan knew all about the perils of drug abuse, and he was fervent in his condemnation of both the users and suppliers.

'There's no way Alan would get himself mixed up in anything like that, Jim, and you know it.'

He sighed and nodded his head slowly. 'I had to ask, Harry. Reynolds has been trying to get an angle on this affair, and he knows Alan's not as pure as the driven snow.'

'Meaning?'

He gave me what can only be described as an old fashioned look. 'You've done the liquor run from Cuba for him yourself in the past, Harry. You know exactly what I'm talking about, so spare me the righteous indignation.'

I stared at my feet. 'Liquor's one thing, Jim, but drugs are in a completely different league.'

'So you don't think there's the remotest possibility that Alan has somehow got himself tied into it? You see, if it's not drugs, what else could it be? Alan hasn't said anything to you, anything at all? '

'I'm not going to repeat myself, Jim. In fact I think it's best if you leave now.'

He raised his eyebrows. 'I don't want there to be bad

blood between us over this, Harry. We've been friends a long time. Just remember I have a job to do. Sometimes I have to ask questions, even when they hurt.' He got up from the couch and walked to the door. 'If it means anything to you, Harry, I don't happen to think Alan's involved in drugs. But the question had to be asked.' He looked sad, and it made him look older, more tired.

He let himself out and I heard his car start up. I swallowed the last of my whisky and stared at the empty glass in my hand; and then I threw it at the wall where it exploded into a thousand glittering pieces.

16

I sat morosely for a while, turning things over and over in my mind and getting nowhere. Finally, I got sick of just sitting there and went down to *The Lady*, started her engines and headed out to sea.

I found that being out there on the ocean had an immensely calming effect on me. There was something about the sheer vastness of all that water that gave me a perspective on life, and on my place in the universe. And if that sounds pretentious, that's tough. When you're out there and a storm's blowing force ten, and your boat is being tossed about like a cork in a cauldron, it's very hard to retain any sense of self importance. You are only too aware that the elemental force of the sea is all powerful. That if she wants to she can snuff out your life as easily as one snuffs out a candle.

And yet the force is also beneficent. People like my father, like Ernie and Raoul Rodriguez and, to a lesser extent myself, make a living from the sea. She gives us food to eat, puts money in our pockets, and asks for very little in return. Only that you show her some respect. And as any fisherman or yachtsmen will tell you, if you don't respect her then her punishment is quick and cruel.

Today, however, the sea was as flat and as calm as a millpond and as I cruised out I let the problems of the last two days drain away. It was good therapy.

I came from a long line of dissolutes who could trace their lineage back to Randolph Beck, a loyalist to the British Crown who'd fled America in 1784, the year after the end of the War of Independence.

My father, Lucas Beck, upheld the family line, a fisherman, smuggler and sometime gunrunner who played authority for a fool, until the day the authorities decided enough was enough and slapped him in jail for five years. Before that happened though, he'd met and married the beautiful Louisa Fletcher, who gave him a son, me. There was a daughter who followed five years later, but my mother, who, despite her beauty, was a sickly, physically weak woman, didn't survive the rigours of childbirth the second time around. My sister, Caroline, succumbed to meningitis in the first year of her life.

Being alone in life sort of became a habit.

Life with my father was a lonely existence and when I met Alan it was that shared feeling of isolation that formed the bond between us. Alan, me, Jack, and occasionally a few other kids from the island would often spend time down on my father's fishing boat, *The Majesty*, unloading the nets and generally helping out.

Those times on *The Majesty* cemented the bond between the three of us boys, but especially Alan and me, and as we grew into adulthood the cement grew stronger. When my father started his jail term and *The Majesty* was impounded by the authorities, Alan stood by me, offering help and advice, even standing me the money to buy my first boat. And as the years went by he tried to interest me in various business ventures, as equal partners, with him supplying all the capital, but some fatuous sense of pride always made me refuse.

So now he found himself not only my best friend but

also my landlord, as he owned the freehold on my bungalow and the surrounding land that included the small harbour where I moored *The Lady of Pain*. It was here we made our only deal. Alan let me live rent free and I, in return, gave the guests of his hotels first refusal on my time and on my boat.

Alan was my friend and whatever trouble he was in I had to help him.

I anchored about a mile offshore and was sitting on the deck smoking a cigarette when I suddenly remembered I was meant to call Max Donahoe. It had gone completely out of my mind. I flicked the half smoked cigarette into the sea and went to the wheelhouse and tried to raise *The Minotaur*.

Max didn't waste time getting on the radio. 'Harry, great to hear from you. Katy gave you the message then. When she suggested she come and see you I told her you'd probably send her away with a flea in her ear.'

Using quaint old expressions like that were all part of Max's charm. And he used his charm to great effect. Many business rivals were taken in by his courteous manner and his rather antiquated turn of phrase. Those of us who knew him better weren't so easily lulled into the very false sense of security. Max Donahoe had a mind as incisive as a laser and was as ruthless as they come. But I liked him. Katy was right. He'd always treated me fairly.

'It's been too long, Max,' I said, and meant it.

'So when are you coming to see me?' he said.

'I didn't know I was. Katy just said you wanted to talk to me.'

He chuckled. 'And so I do, Harry, so I do, but I don't like doing business over the telephone, let alone this squawk box. Come and see me. I'll be out here on *The Minotaur* for the rest of the week. Drop by and we'll have a drink together. There're a few things I want to discuss with you.'

I pressed him, but he wasn't giving anything away. If I wanted to know what he had to discuss then I was just going to have to accept his invitation. I fixed it for the following morning at eleven.

I went back out on deck and found it had started to rain. It rains a lot in the Bahamas, especially during the summer months, and you take no notice of it. Besides it's usually nothing more than a tropical shower, rarely lasting more than an hour. If anything the rain comes as a relief, clearing the air, cooling things down.

I pulled up a deck chair and sat back, lulled by the gentle rocking of the boat. A few gulls flapped overhead, but once they realised I wasn't fishing and there were no easy pickings to be had, they wheeled away in search of a meal. Away on the horizon a vast oil tanker was making slow progress across the ocean as if it had all the time in the world, and, as I sat there on the deck of *The Lady*, Freeport seemed like a million miles away. After the events of the last few days I was beginning to wish it was.

The peace was interrupted by the radio crackling into life and I heard my call sign being repeated. I cursed and went to find out who it was.

It was Max again.

'Harry,' he said. 'How are you planning to get over here? Plane?'

'I'll get a flight to Nassau in the morning,' I said. 'Then I'll charter a boat to get me out to *The Minotaur.*'

'Don't trouble with that, Harry. I'll have the Lear waiting on the runway at Freeport International at nine tomorrow morning. It'll get you to Nassau in a couple of shakes. My launch will be in the harbour to bring you out to the yacht. How does that sound?'

'Sounds great, Max. But don't go to any trouble. I'm quite capable of getting to you under my own steam.'

'Wouldn't hear of it m'boy. You just get yourself down to the runway at nine tomorrow, and let me worry about things from there, okay?'

'Fine, Max, and thanks. See you in the morning.'

17

I switched off the radio and stood there for a long time, thinking that whatever it was Max Donahoe wanted to see me about it must be pretty important. He hadn't got to be a rich man by making extravagant gestures, and a Lear jet wasn't the most inexpensive way to island hop. My hopes for a restful, thought free afternoon were shattered by that call. Irritably I weighed anchor and headed home.

By the time I got back to the bungalow the rain had stopped and the sun was shining again. It was going to be a glorious evening. I let myself in and went through to the bedroom to pack a bag, hoping the room at the hotel would be a quiet one. I really didn't fancy spending the night in a room above the hotel's disco.

I found my overnight bag in the bottom of the wardrobe and set about packing whatever clothes I could find that hadn't been ripped or torn. I ended up with three shirts, one pair of shorts, a pair of chinos and a pair of grey slacks. I did rather better with the underwear. Five pairs of underpants had remained unscathed. I had no idea how long it was going to take me to get the bungalow back in a habitable condition. I just hoped the hotel's laundry service was efficient.

I was about to leave when the telephone rang. It was Stevie.

'I've been trying to get you all afternoon,' she said. 'Where are you?'

'Home. What is it? Is everything okay?'

'Yeah, everything's fine. I just wanted to know what we've got on for tomorrow, that's all.'

'Nothing,' I said. 'I'm going across to New Providence to see Max Donahoe. You've got the day off so relax and enjoy yourself.'

'Oh.' She sounded disappointed.

'Are you sure everything's all right?'

'Yeah, fine, Harry. Everything's great. It's just that I didn't really want...I mean, I didn't like the idea of staying here...Oh shit! Look, Harry, just skip it, okay?'

'Do you want me to come over?' I said. 'I can drop my bag off at the hotel and come direct.'

'I said skip it, Harry. I'll be fine. Jackie's dropping by later and we're going to...'

I didn't hear anymore. My gaze was fixed on an envelope lying on the door mat. I was pretty sure it wasn't there when I came in, though I suppose I could have stepped over it without noticing. 'Hold on a moment, Stevie,' I said, and went across to pick it up. I wasn't sure why I felt the envelope was important, perhaps it was some kind of sixth sense, but when I picked it up a tingle ran down my spine. The envelope had only one word on. My name, *Harry*. But I recognised the handwriting.

Alan Lancaster had written the envelope.

I didn't open it straight away. Instead I went back to the phone. 'Sorry about that, Stevie. I had something boiling over on the stove. What was it you were saying?'

'I said, Jackie and I will probably go to the movies tonight, so there's no need for you to come over.'

'And you'll be all right tomorrow?'

'Don't worry about me, Harry. I might spend the time

tidying the place up. Just didn't want you to have to spend the day alone, that's all. If you're tied up that's fine. Give me a call when you need me again. See you.' She rang off.

I sat down in my mutilated armchair and opened the envelope. Inside was a single sheet of paper. I took it out and read it.

Like the envelope it was in Alan's hand, but what it said made no sense, no sense at all.

Harry, look where you'd least expect it, Alan.

That was all it said. I turned the paper over to see if he'd written anything on the back, but it was blank. I read it through again, but its meaning remained as elusive as the first time round.

Look where you'd least expect it.

I couldn't begin to fathom what it meant.

18

Max Donahoe's Lear jet was waiting on the tarmac at Freeport International just as he said it would be. I had no reason to doubt it wouldn't be there, as I'd always found Max to be as good as his word.

Inside, the jet was luxurious. White leather upholstery and a well stocked bar. He even had a stewardess on hand to serve drinks and minister to the comforts of the passengers, not that she had too much room to minister in such close confines. It was ironic that for all its comfort and luxury, the Lear was the only one of Max's status symbols he couldn't exactly experience firsthand. He had a fear of flying that bordered on the pathological.

The jet, like the yacht, was there to impress. Max saw himself as an international business tycoon, a self-appreciation that was pretty accurate, and his *toys*, as he liked to call them, were there because they fit the image; but it wasn't all artifice. Max had a canny enough grasp of psychology to know that first impressions counted for a lot in his world, and the Lear, with its plush interior and luxurious ambience, created a strong, and lasting, first impression.

Dark of the Sun

The flight was only a short one. It seemed that no sooner had we taken off from Freeport, than we were preparing to land at Nassau. I, like Max, though not quite so extreme, was a nervous flier, so I welcomed the journey being brief.

I was still puzzling over the letter from Alan, and remember staring down through the Lear's window at the scattering of coral cays, thinking that somewhere, down there, was the answer. Something was niggling away at the back of my mind. Fleeting and wispy, a memory so thin I could only see its shadow. When the stewardess came up and asked me if I wanted a drink the shadow vanished completely.

We landed and I stepped out of the plane. A silver Rolls-Royce was sitting not ten yards away, its chauffeur polishing the bonnet with a yellow duster. The stewardess escorted me to the car and the chauffeur opened the rear door. It seemed I was being given the VIP treatment, but I felt self-conscious because I really didn't look the part. I was wearing a loud Hawaiian shirt, hanging loose over my shorts; no socks, but on my feet were a pair of canvas shoes with rope soles. I made a mental note to raid my bank account in the not too distant future and buy myself a new wardrobe. It would be a sacrifice; I tended to use all my spare money keeping *The Lady* seaworthy and I'd recently bought a new linear drive autopilot for her, which had all but cleared me out. But I couldn't walk around looking like a scarecrow for very much longer.

The Rolls-Royce took me to the harbour where the launch was waiting, a Riva Tropicana 43'. Nice boat, and fast, but a little flashy for my tastes. The pilot was a barrel-chested man who would have looked more at home on a harbour tug. His arms were awash with tattoos, and I glimpsed another on his chest as his shirt flapped open in the breeze. He welcomed me aboard with a grunt and ignored me for the rest of the trip out to Max's yacht. I couldn't really say it bothered me that much, as I wasn't really in the mood for making polite conversation. Instead I sat back, closed my eyes, and let the spray wash my face.

The Minotaur was a beautiful boat. A one hundred and twenty-foot Picchiotti in steel and aluminium. Two 625hp diesels and two 80kw Caterpillar generators. She would cross the Atlantic with ease if Max had a mind to take her that far. I hadn't seen her for a while and from what I remembered she was impressive.

A ladder was thrown down for me to board her. Standing at the top of the ladder was a handsome young black man in a uniform so white it hurt the eye. For a moment I thought he was going to pipe me aboard, but that was sheer fancy. Although he did salute, and say, 'This way, Mr Beck. Mr Donahoe will receive you in the stateroom.' All very proper. You had to hand it to Max; he certainly knew how to impress his guests.

Max received me like a father welcoming a son who'd been away at war. He was positively beaming as he wrapped his arms around me and said, 'Harry, bloody wonderful to see you again!'

'Good to see you too, Max,' I said, though I was a little taken aback at the warmth of his welcome.

Like his daughter, Max Donahoe was not very tall, but what he lacked in height he made up for in girth. He must have topped the scales at two hundred and thirty pounds, and he was quite bald except a trimming of white fuzzy hair that covered his ears. He wore gold half-rimmed spectacles, on a round pleasant face. It was only when you looked at his eyes you realised that behind the cherubic features lurked a very sharp mind. The eyes were blue and they flicked over you rapidly. It was quite disconcerting. As if a microcomputer was controlling them, feeding the information they took in back to the mainframe for analysis and evaluation. Which, I suppose wasn't too wide of the mark, as anyone who'd had dealings with Max would ruefully tell you. In business Max Donahoe was a shark.

He released me and held me at arm's length, looking me up and down. 'You must give me the name of your tailor,' he said with a chuckle. Then quickly, 'No offence, Harry, we don't stand on ceremony here.' Which, coming from him in his ten thousand dollar Savile Row suit and Gucci loafers, made me feel even more like a bum.

'My bungalow was broken into,' I explained. 'They gutted my wardrobe.'

'Then they did you a favour,' he said with a chuckle, draped an arm across my shoulders and led me across to a burgundy leather chesterfield. 'Sit yourself down, Harry. Drink?'

The stateroom was about as big as the lounge and bedroom of my place combined. The chesterfield dominated, but there were also two matching club chairs, a low, marble-topped coffee table, and, against one wall, a bar that would have brought tears of envy to Jack Dylan's eyes. 'What are you drinking these days,' he said, planting himself behind it and reaching for a glass. 'Still malt whisky?'

'That'll be fine.'

'I like that in a man. Consistency. It shows a man content with himself, who doesn't have to keep chopping and changing, just to keep up with fashion or trends.' He produced a bottle of Chivas Regal from a shelf behind him and started to pour a very stiff measure into the glass.

'Used to have a business partner, Jake Goodwin,' he said as he poured. 'Solid type, no frills, bloody good polo player, but a bit unimaginative. Typical beer drinker really. Now old, solid, stick-in-the-mud Jake met this girl; a pretty little thing, but without too much upstairs, if you follow my meaning. Anyway, old Jake was so besotted by her he set about trying to live up to what she expected him to be. Started going to fancy nightclubs, dressing like a teenager, you know the sort of thing? Made a right bloody fool of himself, all for the sake of a piece of fluff. We ended up falling out and I dissolved the partnership. The last time I saw him was in a bar in Miami, sat at a table, still dressed like a teenager. He was alone. The girl had left him for a lifeguard. I said to him, 'Can I get you a beer, Jake, for old time's sake?' And do you know what he said to me? 'I'd rather have a pineapple daiquiri, Max." Max hooted with laughter. 'A pineapple daiquiri for Christ's sake! I wonder what his fellow players down at the polo club made of that!'

I smiled at the story, more out of politeness than anything else.

'Consistency, Harry. An admirable quality.' He poured himself a gin and came round the bar to sit opposite me in one of the club chairs. 'It's a quality in you I admired when you were courting Katy.'

Ah, Katy. I'd been wondering when we were going to get round to her. Strangely though, he showed no desire to continue from that point. In fact he changed tack completely. 'Your place was burgled then,' he said. 'Did they get away with much?'

'Nothing of any value. They just messed it up; busted up the furniture, that sort of thing.'

'Probably kids, skylarking. No bloody discipline.' And that was enough of that topic of conversation. 'Well, how are you keeping these days? Still got that boat of yours?'

I said I was keeping well, and yes, I still had the boat. I was waiting for Max get to the point of why he'd asked me out here. He hadn't laid on jet, Rolls and launch just to tell me a story about an old friend and to enquire after my health. The cogs were turning in that sharp old mind of his — I could tell by the way his eyes danced around — and I wanted to know what he was thinking.

19

He took a leather cigar case from his pocket and offered me a hand-rolled Havana. When I declined he lit one for himself and puffed on it contentedly for a few moments. Finally he spoke. 'I suppose you're wondering why I asked you to come out here,' he said.

'It had crossed my mind.'

'What would you say if I told you I was planning to open another casino?'

I said it wouldn't really surprise me at all. Donahoe Holdings controlled four casinos in the US; one in Vegas, two in Atlantic City and one, the showpiece of the chain, *Boothe's* in Miami. I'd visited *Boothe's* once, and had never forgotten my evening there. It was decked out like an old colonial Gentlemen's club. There was no glitz, no neon — even the slot machines had a special soundproofed room all to themselves. I went there not long after it opened and thought at the time that it was just too conservative for American tastes. Which only went to prove what lousy judgement I had. *Boothe's* took off and quickly became the most exclusive gaming house in the state of Florida, patronized by movie stars, rock singers, oil sheikhs, in fact anyone who was vaguely anyone. If they had a taste for gambling, they made *Boothe's* their first stop when visiting Miami.

As well as his American casinos, Max also owned two on the Islands. *The Diamond* in Nassau and *The Lucayan Star*, which was a neighbour of Jack Dylan's *Jolly Tar* pub.

'So where do you intend to build this one, Max?' I asked, still trying to work out what all this had to do with me.

'Oh, it's built already, Harry. My design team is there at the moment fitting it out. I tell you, it's going to be one of the finest casinos in the world by the time we've finished with it. It'll make *Boothe's* in Miami look like a gin palace.'

I found that hard to believe, but I urged him to go on. I was intrigued to know how I figured in this. Though I was beginning to have a suspicion. I wouldn't have been at all surprised if Max wanted the same kind of arrangement that I had with Alan. First refusal on *The Lady*, pleasure trips for his punters. I could imagine what Max was thinking. *Poor old Harry Beck, still puttering around on that old barge of his, perhaps I'll toss him a few commissions, just for old time's sake.* Or perhaps Katy was behind it and had been priming Max to deliver my final humiliation. Wasn't it enough that she'd screwed around with half of the male population of Freeport behind my back, without this?

'So how does your new casino concern me, Max?' I said.

He took a long pull on his cigar and contemplated the glowing tip for a moment. Then he met my gaze and held it. I started to bridle in anticipation and the refusal was already half formed on my lips. If he asked I'd tell him to shove it. I didn't need charity, especially Donahoe charity.

'It's quite simple really, Harry. I want you to run it for me.'

My jaw must have dropped open, judging from the amused look on Max's face. I swallowed his whisky in one gulp and sat there staring down into the empty glass, until Max plucked it from my fingers and went across to the bar to replenish it.

'Could you repeat that?' I said.

He did.

'But why, Max? Why me? I know nothing about running a casino. Besides, I've got the boat. I've got *The Lady*.'

'And *The Lady's* going to make your fortune, is that it?'

'It's a living,' I said defensively. 'Besides, there must be hundreds, thousands of people you could ask who'd be better qualified for the job than me.'

He sat back in his chair and appraised me over the rim of his glass. 'Yes,' he said. 'I dare say you're right...'

'I know full well I am.'

He held up a restraining hand. 'Quite. But I want someone in there who's a little bit different from the normal run of the mill managers I employ. I like you, Harry, always have. What's more I trust you. And that's what I want from you. The other things, experience of running a large casino, knowledge of the intricacies of gambling, its laws and conventions, they're all things that any intelligent man can pick up, providing he's given the right tutelage. And I'll provide excellent backup. Your second in command will be Mike Somers and he's been in the game since he was weaned.' He leaned forward and stabbed the air with the glowing tip of his cigar. 'Believe me, Harry. I'm a good judge of people, and I think you'll do just fine.'

Which was more than I did. I'd never heard a more ridiculous suggestion in my life. Me, running a top-flight casino? It was enough to give any hardened gambler hysterics.

With a shake of my head I stood up. 'Thanks for the drink, Max,' I said sourly. 'Quite a piss take. How long did Katy take to put you up to it?'

He frowned and said, 'Sit down, Harry, before you make a complete bloody fool of yourself. I don't think you're another Jake Goodwin, do you?'

I glared at him and sat down.

'Right, that's better. Now let's get one thing straight. No one has any intention of humiliating you. Not me, not Katy. I'm a businessman, Harry, and even if I do say myself, a bloody good one. Do you honestly think I'd jeopardise such an important investment as the casino, for a piss take? Credit me with more common sense than that, please.'

'Okay,' I said grudgingly.

'Christ, you're stubborn! Mind you, that's another reason I like you. You're a hard man, Harry...tenacious, that's the word.'

'So okay, I'm tenacious, I'm stubborn, I'm honest and I'm trustworthy. That still doesn't make me the ideal candidate for casino manager. At least not in my eyes.'

'Yes, but you're not sitting where I am. You can only have a subjective view of yourself, and, if you don't mind me saying so, you put a pretty low value on your attributes. Give yourself a little time to think about this, before you dismiss it out of hand. Besides, I haven't finished.'

'You mean there's more?'

'Harry, if I'd just wanted to offer you a job I could have done it over the phone, or by letter. I wouldn't have gone to the trouble of flying you over here.' He chuckled again. It was beginning to get irritating. Like he was enjoying some private joke at my expense.

'All right,' I said. 'What else is there?'

Max rested the cigar in a bronze ashtray and swallowed the last of his gin. 'The deal is this, Harry. You come to work for me. Your salary is negotiable, but I had in mind a figure in the region of five hundred thousand dollars per annum, to start. You get a seat on the board of Donahoe Holdings, and five per cent of the stock. You'll have the title of vice-president. How does that sound?'

I opened my mouth to speak, but nothing came out.

Dark of the Sun

Five hundred thousand dollars, a year! I doubted I could make that kind of money in ten years running *The Lady* on pleasure cruises, even with the occasional fishing trip thrown in. But the sticking point was still, why me? Why had Max Donahoe decided to play fairy godfather to Harry Beck, the ex-fiancé of his daughter, a man he hadn't set eyes on for the past five years? There had to be a catch. Things like this just don't happen to people like me without there being some massive scam involved.

'Let's get this straight, Max. You're offering me five hundred thousand a year. A vice-presidency with Donahoe Holdings, and five per cent of the stock...voting shares?'

'Of course.'

'And for what? Just so I'll come and work for you. No, I'm sorry, Max. It just doesn't hang together. How many other people have you started at Donahoe Holdings on such favourable conditions? I bet the answer is none. You'd start them at the bottom, unless of course, you'd poached a top executive from a rival company. In which case I can understand you giving them the red carpet treatment. But not me, Max. Not me. I've only ever been to a casino twice in my life, and I lost my shirt both times.'

'Which makes you rather an expert. There's nothing quite like losing a fortune to cure you of the desire to gamble. It's the first lesson I teach my prospective managers. Gambling's a mug's game. Fortunately for us there are thousands of mugs out there. But yes, yes, I quite agree with you, Harry. I wouldn't offer anybody else such terms...but then I wouldn't allow my son-in-law to join my company with anything less.'

'Your what?'

His eyes glittered. 'My son-in-law, Harry. You're going to marry Katy.'

I knew then what had happened.

Max Donahoe had gone absolutely, stark staring mad.

20

The *Miami Post* offices were air-conditioned, but the small cramped office Sam Goldberg was working in somehow always seemed hotter and more humid than any other part of the offices. The air conditioning unit was noisily buzzing away, there was no doubt it was switched on, but it seemed to fan out only warm air.

Goldberg was young, but he had a persona about him that suggested someone much older. He had little interest in his appearance, had a clothes-style that screamed charity shop chic, and his interests were limited to research for whatever story he was working on and eating fast food.

His current story was being written as a series that was building up a head of steam. It had started as small pieces lost around page twelve, but as interest grew so did the length he was allowed for the articles and the pages got closer to the front page; not there yet, but with every paper they appeared in the emphasis was greater.

He was five hundred words into the latest article when the door to the cramped office opened.

'Sam,' Larry Osler said. 'Got a minute?' Larry was deputy editor.

'Sure.' Goldberg knew what was coming.

'Hot in here. You should tell someone.'

'Who?'

'I'll get maintenance onto it. Or we'll get you moved.'

This was a worrying development. Very little concern had been demonstrated towards him in the year of so he'd worked here. Osler showing this amount of interest, when he'd never even visited the room before meant he was softening Goldberg up.

'I've got another couple of hundred words to do and the story is written for this week.'

Osler found the view from the grime-covered window suddenly fascinating.

'Is there a problem, Larry?'

'I guess you've been irritated about the changes we've had to make the last week or so.'

Irritated didn't begin to cover it. As a journalist basically working freelance for the one paper, with occasional magazine articles sold where he could, he was used to having his work edited, changed, revised, until he sometimes felt that what was left shouldn't have his name on it. But it went with the territory.

The changes that had been made, without any reference to him, to the last two or three pieces he'd done for the *Post* had been unacceptable and he was using the story he was writing up today as a way of putting back in the facts that had been removed. That was what they had done; not just re-written, but factually altered his work so it had a different meaning.

Larry took his silence as agreement. 'You know how we're funded. You know we need the advertising revenue. There's been complaints.'

'Complaints?'

'The stuff you're writing, it's unsavoury.'

'Unsavoury...are you are fucking joking?'

'Fact is, tone it down.'

Goldberg stood, his fingers moving as if they had a

life of their own.

Osler was already turning away and the door was ready to close behind him. 'Don't bank on the heat getting turned down.'

21

'You must be out of your mind,' I said. 'Me and Katy, married?' I laughed, but it was harsh and brittle, and sounded strange to my ears. Despite the air-conditioning, the stateroom seemed as hot as an orchid house, and I dabbed at my sweating brow with a handkerchief.

Max Donahoe, however, looked cool, completely unruffled. 'I assure you, Harry. I'm perfectly sane; though I know what I'm suggesting may sound a little unusual.'

'Unusual, it's fucking ludicrous!' I got to my feet. 'Thanks for the drink, Max. I'll see you around.'

Max didn't move from the comfort of his armchair as he watched me walk to the door. I'd grasped the handle and was pulling the door open before he spoke. 'Can you look me in the eye and tell me you don't still love her?'

I froze. Turning slowly I said. 'My feelings for your daughter, Max, are none of your bloody business.'

He put his glass down and leaned forward, clasping his hands together as if in prayer and resting them between his pudgy knees. 'Just tell me you don't love her, Harry, and I'll drop the subject and get the launch to take you back to Nassau.'

'Look, Max,' I said, walking across to where he was sitting. 'Remember something. It was Katy who finished with me, not the other way round. Throw the pitch at her and see what response you get.'

'Oh, I know the silly little bitch threw you over, but don't you think she hasn't regretted it? Don't forget, she did come to see you to arrange the meeting between us and that wasn't my suggestion, Harry, it was hers. She still loves you, you know.'

'Bullshit!' I remembered the visit only too well, and how acrimoniously it had ended. Her actions were hardly those I'd expect from someone who was looking at me as a prospective husband. I told Max in detail what had happened.

'Well what do you expect? My God, you young people, sometimes you can be *so* blind. Katy told me all about it, and if it's any consolation to you, she was in tears when she told me. What did you expect her reaction to be? She comes all the way to Freeport, holding out an olive branch, you hold her at gunpoint...'

'I explained that.'

'Don't interrupt!' His voice was suddenly loud, authoritative. His boardroom voice, no doubt, the shark shedding its disguise of affability. 'You hold her at gunpoint, and if that's not enough, she finds you're shacked up with a girl young enough to be your daughter. What the hell did you expect her reaction to be?'

'I didn't ask her to come to the boat, and I'll tell you what I told her. My relationship with Stevie is strictly platonic. She works for me, and I, in return, watch out for her welfare, just as I promised her father I would when he died in my arms. She's just about young enough to be my daughter for Christ's sake.'

'You don't have to explain yourself to me, Harry. Just put yourself in Katy's shoes for a moment. Think about what it must have looked like to her.'

'And I'm supposed to give a shit?'

'Ah, but that's it. Harry. You *do* give a shit.'

'Go to hell!' I said, but stayed standing there.

Max stood. 'Let's go for a walk on deck. The sea breeze will cool us both down.' He took my arm and led me to the door.

'Look, Harry,' he said as we stepped out into the open. 'I know Katy hurt you. Her behaviour when she was with you was despicable, and I'm not saying any of it was your fault. You were trying to build a business for yourself, and that takes time. Believe me, I know. No, if anyone's to blame then it's me.'

We were walking towards the stern. *The Minotaur* was rocking gently on the waves, tethered by her anchor. I looked across the ocean and saw no other vessels. It felt as if we were the only two people left alive, having a bizarre conversation that was doing nothing but dredging up memories that were best left submerged. Max stopped walking and stood by the rail, staring down at the water, letting the breeze fan his face.

'Katy was only five when Mary died, and I found it difficult raising her on my own. Not that she wanted for anything, except perhaps a mother's love and, more importantly, a mother's counsel. That was something I just couldn't give her. And she was a wild cat, always in one scrape after another. When she met you and fell in love, I noticed a difference in her. She calmed down, seemed more contented. I had high hopes for the pair of you, but then…Well, I suppose her wild nature got the better of her. Oh, I know she had other men, but they meant nothing to her. You were the one she really cared for.'

'So why did she do it?' I said, though I knew the reason, deep inside.

22

I'd not long bought *The Lady*, though at the time I christened her *Island Girl*, after Katy. I'd been trying to establish the business, and that, inevitably, led to long hours spent at sea. I was working day and night, trying to build up a reputation on the Islands, trying to secure commissions from the various hotels. Alan helped, of course, he helped a lot, but he alone couldn't provide me with all the work I needed if I was going to build a future that included a wife, possibly children. The truth was, I neglected Katy, neglected her badly, and no matter how much I tried to justify my absences by telling her I was working for her, for us, I knew the bottom line was that I was doing it for myself alone.

I needed to be successful, to triumph where my father, and his father before him, had failed. *The Beck Curse*, they called it. It was something I was determined to beat. When Katy sought comfort in the arms of other men, I reacted badly. I blew my top. Unforgivably I slapped her. Yet I knew it was my behaviour that had driven her to it. Perhaps it was more than jealousy that had made me react the way I did.

She walked out on me after that fight. She said something to me as she left that came back to haunt me over the following years. 'You'll never be successful, Harry. Do you want to know why? Because you want it too bloody badly, and you don't give a shit who you hurt trying to get there.' And then she was gone, out of my life.

The worst thing about it was that she was right.

Max was still talking. 'After you two split up she went completely off the rails. I lost count of the number of men she had. And then there were the parties; wild parties, and she'd invite the dregs of society along. I'd bought her a house by this time, in the mistaken belief that if she had somewhere to call her own she'd perhaps settle down.'

He gripped the rail, his knuckles white, and a pained expression in his eyes. 'It was like trying to put out a fire by dousing it with gasoline. That house became a haven for every dropout and junkie who lived on, or visited, the Islands. It was only a matter of time before Katy got sucked into that scene. She started like they all do, smoking a little dope, the occasional snort of cocaine. I tried to keep tabs on her, but all it did was to alienate her further. Before long she was into heroin. It broke my heart, Harry. It broke my heart to see her that way.' His voice caught in his throat and I turned to see tears coursing down his cheeks.

'I knew that if I didn't do something about it, she'd be dead within months. You hear such terrible stories about what that stuff does to people. So I took the only course of action I could. I had her committed.'

'You what?' I said, stunned.

'Oh, it was all very discreet. A private nursing home, on Andros. Not many people know of its existence, and the owners like to keep it that way. They treated her well there. They put her on methadone, gradually weaning her off the heroin. I went to visit her once, but it was a mistake. She was a savage, Harry. Quite out of her mind. She'd obtained scissors from somewhere and cut off her hair, right down to the scalp, all her lovely hair. I remember Mary sitting on the bed, with Katy on her lap, brushing her hair for her until it shone…

'I visited my daughter at that clinic, and was confronted by a wild animal. She kept screaming over and over, 'I hate you, I hate you!' He stopped talking and wiped his eyes with the sleeve of his jacket.

I reached out and laid a hand on Max's shoulder. 'When was this?'

'She came out six months ago. She's better now. And I want her to stay that way.'

'And you think marrying me will keep her on course?'

'Her only hope, Harry. Her only hope. She needs the security that only you can provide.'

I fumbled in the pocket of my shirt for my cigarettes and lit one. 'I can't do it, Max. I can't marry her.'

His shoulders sagged. 'I was afraid you'd say that.'

'I'm sorry.'

He looked up at me bleakly. 'You know, Harry, I think you are. And I'm not going to change your mind, am I?'

I shook my head.

'Just promise me one thing.'

'No promises, Max.'

'All right, no promises. But, please, give what I've said to you today some thought. Don't just banish it from your mind. She needs you, Harry. And I meant what I said about the job too, although I realise it sounds like a bribe. Regardless of whether you marry Katy or not, the position's yours if you want it.'

I held his gaze for a moment. A sadder, more pathetic man I couldn't imagine. 'Sorry, Max. I like my life the way it is now. I've got *The Lady*. It isn't much of a living, and certainly she'll never make my fortune, but it's what I enjoy doing. Understand?'

He managed a smile. 'Yes, I suppose I do. I'll get the

launch to take you back. But I *will* make you promise one thing. Don't leave it so long before you come to see me again, okay? Come and shoot some skeet with me. There's nothing quite like standing on deck, blasting things out of the sky to get the adrenaline flowing through the veins.'

Skeet shooting was one of Max Donahoe's passions and I had shot with him from the deck of *The Minotaur* a number of times in the past, usually with Katy sitting there, bored out of her skull, while the two main men in her life behaved like little boys, trying to outdo each other and hit as many targets as possible. Without Katy there acting like a wet blanket it would be even more enjoyable.

'Sounds like fun, Max,' I said. 'I promise I'll come back soon.' We shook hands on it.

'And if you change your mind about the job...well, you know where I am. Now, let's get you to the launch.'

23

I woke the next morning with a hangover to end them all. I felt as if I'd been fired from a cannon head first into a brick wall. I lay there for a long time, just staring at the ceiling, trying to bring my eyes into focus, and when I attempted to get out of bed, my legs folded underneath me and I sank to my knees with a groan.

I hadn't felt as bad as this for a long time, probably not since the morning after the break up with Katy. I'd gone on a bender then too, with similar aftereffects.

When the Lear landed me back at Freeport I started drinking almost immediately, first at the hotel, and then, when I'd got heartily sick of my own company, I toured the local bars. In one of them, can't remember which, I bumped into Ernie Rodriguez, and spent a forgettable hour with him putting the world to rights, and although I couldn't now remember what we talked about, it had a lasting effect, because shortly afterwards Ernie passed his boat on to his son, Raoul, and gave up the sea entirely.

That I'd end up at *The Jolly Tar* had an inevitability to it that I hadn't been able to resist. Where Jack Dylan had always turned to Alan in times of crisis, I had always sought out Jack.

Jack had an easy manner about him that almost seemed to invite you to sit down and pour out your troubles, and he'd Dutch-uncled me often in the past. The reason I turned to him and no one else was that Jack never sat in judgement. He'd let you talk, sometimes to the point of incoherency, and he'd always be open-minded. Oh, he'd slip in the occasional, 'don't be so bloody stupid,' or a 'for God's sake pull yourself together,' but he'd never ridicule your feelings, or try to take advantage from whatever you might tell him.

That night I walked, or rather, staggered along to *The Tar*. Once there Jack found us a booth, set a bottle of scotch down on the table, and slipped into the seat opposite mine. 'Okay, Harry boy, tell Uncle Jack all about it.'

And I did. I told Jack everything, even to the point of baring my soul and admitting that Max was right. I was still in love with Katy.

I wasn't seeking advice from Jack, and he, thank God, didn't offer any; but I needed to speak to him, if only to get things straight in my head. By the time the bottle was finished I was falling asleep on the table and I vaguely remember strong arms hauling me to my feet and dragging me from the pub. I had a dim memory of the car, Jack's Daimler, pulling onto the side of the road so I could be sick. After that nothing until I woke up on *The Lady* just as dawn was breaking over Freeport.

The hangover wasn't shifting and there was only one way I knew to get rid of it. I stripped off and dived over the side, letting the ocean soothe away the headache. I swam for half an hour, by which time the hangover had gone. But one thing had become clear as I swam in long lazy circles around the boat. I needed to get away to think things through. Too much had happened in too short a space of time, and my reactions were becoming knee-jerk, not at all rational. I needed to be away from Freeport for a while. I climbed back over the rail and started to prepare

The Lady for a trip. Twenty minutes later she was ready.

I cast off the stern line, went back to the cockpit and pressed the starter. *The Lady* coughed once then the engines roared into life. Someone was calling my name. I glanced back and saw a man in a lightweight suit running towards me, waving his arms and yelling. Feeling antisocial, and a little bloody minded, I eased the throttle forward and *The Lady* moved gently away from the quayside. The man drew level. His face was red from exertion and there was desperation in his eyes. *The Lady* was eight feet from the jetty when he jumped. He made it over the side rail, landing on a coil of rope. He pitched forward and hit the deck in a tangle of arms, legs and rope. I swung the prow round, pointing her out to sea, leaned on the throttle and we surged forward. Whoever he was he was going on an ocean voyage whether he liked it or not.

I'd lit a cigarette and was sitting at the wheel smoking when he finally untangled himself and joined me in the cockpit. 'Sam Goldberg,' he said extending his hand.

'Congratulations.'

'What, on being Sam Goldberg?'

'On not breaking your neck.'

'Oh, sorry. I was calling you. I thought you'd heard me.'

'I heard you.'

He nodded slowly, understanding. He was about thirty with a pinched face and small inquisitive eyes. There was a fluffy moustache resting on his top lip like a small sleeping animal, and his dark, thinning hair was plastered to his pink, sunburnt scalp with sweat.

'Where are you going?' he said, settling himself on the seat next to me.

'I'm going to Abaco. Unless you explain what you're doing crashing aboard my boat you'll be swimming back to Grand Bahama.'

He laughed uneasily, then he realised I meant it. 'I

need to talk to you, about Alan Lancaster.'

I said nothing, just kept my eyes focussed on the ocean. I drew the last from the cigarette and flicked the smouldering end out to sea. *The Lady* glided through the crystal-green water, raising a white frothy wake. For a while the only sounds were the throb of the twin Penta engines and the slapping of waves against *The Lady's* hull.

'You're not saying very much,' I said. 'I thought you wanted to talk about Alan.'

He was swallowing loudly. I looked round at him. His face had turned grey and waxy, and the sheen of perspiration on his brow had nothing to do with his earlier exertions. 'If you're going to puke then do it over the side,' I said. There was a small sea running, but nothing to get excited about. It would get worse however before it got any better.

'I'll be all right,' he said.

I shrugged.

'I'd heard you were a hard bastard.'

'You heard wrong. My parents were married.'

'You were Alan's best friend?'

'Were?'

'Were, are, who knows?'

'How does he know you?'

'I used to work for the *Miami Post*. Alan contacted me because he had some information relating to an investigative piece I was working on.' He paused and inhaled deeply three times, wiped his sweating brow on the sleeve of his cream suit and took another deep breath, just for luck. 'That's better,' he said, and then threw up on the deck.

I swore softly, throttled back and went to fetch a mop and bucket. 'Your mess. You clean it up,' I said, handing them to him.

24

Some time later *The Lady* sat at anchor. She was rocking gently on the swell, but not enough to bring about another bout of vomiting from my uninvited guest. I brought some beers up from the cold locker below and sat drinking one. I wanted to know what Sam had to say and I did not want his conversation interrupted by constant visits to the side rail. Working seemed to be doing Goldberg good. He finally swilled the last of the water over the deck and came aft to join me.

'All cleaned up,' he said. 'Sorry, I'm no sailor.'

'So I gathered.' I tossed him a beer. He looked at it doubtfully for a moment then popped off the top and put the bottle to his lips. 'You said you used to work for the Post. You don't now. Why?'

'I left to write a book.'

'Is this book connected with the story Alan's helping you with?'

'*Was* helping me with. I came out to the Bahamas to interview him. Now he seems to have disappeared.'

'So why track *me* down? You surely don't think I can help you with your book?'

'I don't know. Possibly, though I doubt it. What you will be able to do though is to give me some background on Alan.'

'Why should I?'

He swallowed some more beer. The colour was returning to his face. 'I can't offer you money, if that's what you're getting at. I haven't got the resources of a major newspaper behind me now. Everything comes out of my own pocket. I even had to pay for my own flight out here.'

'You're breaking my heart. And I can't believe you haven't got a publisher in tow to bankroll you.'

'That's not how it works...not this time anyway. This book I'm writing deals with a very controversial issue. I haven't even approached a publisher yet. I need more facts to corroborate my findings so far. Alan was going to provide some of those facts.'

'So what's the book about?'

He took a final swallow of his beer and pitched the bottle over the side. 'Child pornography and paedophilia. It's a delicate area.'

'Are you saying Alan Lancaster is a paedophile? Because if you are you'll be joining that bottle over the side.'

'I'm not saying anything. I was writing a series of investigative pieces for the paper. When they started spiking my stories I decided I'd have to leave and carry on with it as a book. Alan called me the day after I left. He said he needed to talk to me. He said he'd been following the series and he had some facts and figures that would help me, and more importantly he had names.'

'Names?'

He ran his fingers through his thin hair. 'It's difficult if you haven't been following the stories, but in précis this is it. Child pornography is one of the criminal growth areas of the twenty-first century. Magazines, books, DVD's, even computer software. I've been investigating it for the past three years, trying to find out where most of it originates. It's fairly global. Eastern Europe is a major source; to a lesser extent the Scandinavian countries, some from France and Germany, Holland and Britain. At the end of 1999 our Government blitzed these sources as they tried to export the filth into the US, and for a while it seemed to be a success. Then in 2001 a new supplier entered the scene.'

'The Bahamas?'

'No. The stuff doesn't originate from here. We know that most of it is produced at home. The FBI has been instrumental in closing down some of the manufacturers, but you close down one operation and two more spring up in its place, like a fucking hydra.'

'Have you spoken to anyone in the FBI about this?'

'Sure. I have my sources,' he said proudly. 'But they admit themselves that what they're doing is about as effective as pissing up a tree when you're trying to put out a forest fire. The main problem is how it's all financed. At first they thought there was Mafia money behind it, and there was an element of truth in that, but only as far as the distribution was concerned. But now they believe differently. The current intelligence is that there is a cartel made up of some of America's rich and finest who get their jollies from watching very young girls and boys being sexually abused. Although that intelligence is soft. So far they haven't been able to get on the inside track of the cartel.'

'By *cartel* you're talking about a paedophile ring.'

'In essence, yes.' He reached for another beer. 'They're not only dealing in pornography, but also sex slaves; children being bought and sold to paedophiles who want to do more than just watch.'

I opened a beer for myself and lit another cigarette. I was starting to feel nauseous myself as I thought of Alan and his seven-year-old daughter, Sally. How could he…

'Okay, you get the picture so far?'

'I'm following you.' I found I couldn't meet his eyes.

Dark of the Sun

Afraid, I suppose, of betraying my thoughts about Alan.

'So far I've managed to trace everything back to Florida, and that also ties in with another important aspect. The raw materials. The children themselves. Twenty years ago the porn merchants used kids from their own cities and towns, but in the last three or four years the majority of pornography emanating from the US features Cuban and Haitian children. We know this because some of the kids have turned up on the streets. Usually they're drugged out of their minds and they're stealing and mugging to support their habits; some are working the streets as prostitutes—girls and boys. They're the lucky ones. Others have turned up dead, usually murdered.

'We've managed to build up some of the background by talking to a few of them, but most of the kids we encounter are just too shit scared to say anything.'

'So you think the children are being routed through the Bahamas.'

'Historically it makes sense. The Bahamas have always been a gateway into the US for all types of contraband. Liquor during and after Prohibition, cocaine, marijuana. Why not children?'

'And you're asking me to believe that the Cubans and Haitians are just selling their kids to paedophiles to be used in pornography?'

'Harry, these are poor countries, their economies are shot to shit. Haiti was all but destroyed by the earthquakes. Their birth-rates are forever increasing. I'm not saying that they're told what the fate of the children will be. They're probably fed a line about desperate American couples, ready and willing to adopt children. Christ, it's always in the papers how some rich, bored actress or whatever has adopted a foreign baby to give it a chance to grow up in the Land of the Free. Imagine a young couple with half a dozen kids living in a tin shack in Havana, approached by some smooth talker offering them hard US currency to take one of their kids back to the States, with the promise that the child will live with an affluent family, have a college education, all the trappings. They're hardly likely to turn around and say, 'no shove it up your ass; my child enjoys poverty,' are they? They're going to have that kid's bag packed before you can say Viva Castro!'

I got up from my seat and weighed the anchor. 'We're moving on. I can smell a storm in the air.'

'You're the captain. I'll try to keep the contents of my stomach to myself.'

As *The Lady* raced the thunderheads to Abaco, Goldberg said, 'Now you've heard what it's all about will you co-operate?'

'I need to think about it some more. How long are you staying in the Bahamas?'

'For as long as it takes.'

'Just one question.'

'Sure.'

'How were you so sure I wasn't involved in all this too? After all, Alan Lancaster is my best friend. It would make sense to assume I'm just as involved as he seems to be. His wife certainly did,' I added, still stinging from Anna's tirade.

'You checked out, Harry,' he said, his cheeks flushing slightly.

'Who checked me out?' I said coldly.

'The FBI has been on to the Bahamas connection for some time.'

'So the FBI has a file on me and you know what's in it, is that what you're saying?'

'Sorry, Harry, that's the way it works.'

'Are you FBI too?'

'The FBI has no jurisdiction in the Bahamas, Harry, as you well know. I'm writing a book. I co-operate with them and they help me out when they can.'

I'd heard enough. There was a white-hot ball of fury

burning in my stomach and I wanted nothing more than to punch Sam Goldberg in the mouth. Instead I opened *The Lady* up to full throttle and let her bounce over the choppy water, giving Goldberg one of the most uncomfortable rides of his life.

25

Barracuda Cay lies three miles south of Great Abaco and is probably the ugliest and most inhospitable island in the whole of the Bahamas. Eighty-five per cent of the interior is swamp and marshland. There is only a thin shingle beach littered with conch shells and other oceanic debris. The harbour is flanked by mud flats and mangrove. Bonefish, snappers and shark have made their home in the mangrove roots, as well as the barracuda from which the cay takes its name.

The harbour itself is a mistake; a misguided venture by a North American property developer called Wesley Morgan who bought a parcel of land on the cay and built Barracuda's one and only hotel. The money ran out half way through building the harbour and now it sticks out into the sea like a decaying tooth, a testament to the man's folly. What is left of it is crumbling away year by year, eroded by the tides. The hotel didn't fare much better. It did not see a single guest and now it stands dilapidated and boarded up in a town ironically called Morgan's Pride.

The hotel was a brave venture, but doomed to failure because, apart from the twenty or so inhabitants who make up the entire population of Barracuda—of which my father is one—the cay's only other residents are mosquitoes. There are millions of them and they're said to be the most voracious mosquitoes this side of the equator.

I dropped a protesting Sam Goldberg off at Marsh Harbour on Great Abaco, but not before he'd scribbled his hotel number on a card and pressed it into my hand, imploring me to contact him when I was ready to talk. He was like an oversized child, eager to talk but too ill from the sea journey to insist.

Then I took *The Lady* over to Barracuda Cay. It was always a tricky crossing because in the three miles between Great Abaco and the cay the depth of the ocean rarely drops below twenty-five feet, sometimes even shallower. There is only a narrow channel you can follow if you don't want to risk ripping the bottom out of your boat on the razor sharp coral reefs that hug the ocean floor. I had made the crossing many times now and knew the channel well, but I was still cautious, rarely letting our speed go above five knots.

I pulled into the harbour and spotted Julius Flood sitting in the shade of a palm tree mending a fishing net. He looked up from under the wide brim of a battered straw hat and his black cherubic face split into a huge grin of welcome. 'Harry, man! How the fuck are you? It's been too long.'

'Grab a line,' I called and threw him the stern rope. He caught it deftly and tied *The Lady* to the quayside. I jumped ashore.

'*Island Girl's* looking good, Harry,' he said. He never called the boat by anything other than her original name. I figured it was because he was quietly superstitious, but he would never admit to it.

'It's all thanks to Stevie,' I said. 'She keeps her in shape.'

'She okay?'

'Fine,' I lied.

He put his arm around my shoulder. Julius Flood was a big man, six foot six in bare feet and not an ounce of fat on his two hundred and eighty pound frame. He eked out a meagre existence from the ocean, catching crawfish and selling their tails. He was the only local, apart from my father, who actually made his living on the cay. The others commuted across to Great Abaco to work. My father kept his head above water now by wood carving and making coconut shell jewellery.

'How is he, Julius?'

'Dry. Has been since the last time you seen him.'

Julius was my father's unofficially adopted son. Their houses were next to each other and Julius watched out for him.

The last time I'd seen my father was in a small room at Nassau's Princess Margaret Hospital, where he had been airlifted to after collapsing on Barracuda with acute alcohol poisoning. One of my father's many weaknesses was pineapple rum, which he drank like water. By the time I reached the hospital they had pumped his stomach and connected him to a glucose drip, drying him out slowly and trying to restore some nutrients to his emaciated, drink sodden body. They saved his life that time, but the doctor treating him took me to one side and told me that my father's liver was so enlarged and his general health so poor that another bender would probably kill him.

Two days later the old man discharged himself from the hospital and begged a ride back to Barracuda on one of the local bonefishing boats. I thought then that the next time I saw him it would probably be in a coffin, but I hadn't counted on Julius Flood, who obviously decided that my father's life was worth saving. I felt slightly guilty that I had left his well being to Julius, but I knew that if I tried to interfere the old bastard would probably drink himself to death just to spite me.

'Are you here to see him?' Julius said as we walked towards the settlement.

'Would he like me to?'

Julius shook his head sadly. 'You two are blood-tied, man. It's a tragedy you don't see eye to eye.'

'Both strong willed,' I said.

'Pig-headed is what I call it.'

26

The houses on Barracuda rest on two acres of dry land in the middle of a swamp. There is no main road to speak of, and the only way across the marshy ground is by way of a wooden bridge that always seems to be in a state of imminent collapse. As we approached, Julius was constantly slapping at his bare arms, swatting mosquitoes as they landed to feed. The insects never bothered me. There was something in my blood they didn't like. Whatever it was I had inherited it from my father who claimed to have lived on Barracuda Cay fifteen years and never once been bitten.

All the houses were New England-style; clapboard painted in pastel shades, pinks, yellows, blues and greens, with russet red shingle roofs. They all had wide verandas and shutters on the windows to protect them against the tropical storms that occasionally swept through the cay. Apart from my father's place all the houses had insect screens on the doors and windows; not attractive but very necessary.

My father's house was the most run-down house in the settlement. The paint was peeling from the boards in leprous flakes and the boards themselves were starting to warp and twist. The veranda was a cluttered workspace with a bench made from an old mahogany dining table, and littered with discarded tools, silver wire and half-sewn pieces of coconut shell. There was a cane chair in the corner with a sagging seat and from a beam above the bench hung a rusty but usable hurricane lamp. A few lizards had made their home in the eves and a colony of spiders nested in an empty beer crate that doubled as a foot stool. It was a depressing sight and as usual gave me a hollow, empty feeling in my stomach. As they normally were during the day, the windows were heavily curtained to keep out the sunlight. My father was nocturnal, preferring to sleep away the daylight hours and emerge at twilight and work on through the night by the light of his lamp.

I walked past the place and up the steps to the house Julius shared with his wife, Nona. 'Can't face it yet, Harry?'

'He's probably still asleep. Anyway I could use a drink first.'

The big man smiled. 'You might even be in time for dinner.'

Nona Flood greeted me like her long lost son, even though she was only five years my senior. The hard life on Barracuda, though, had taken its toll on her looks. Her hair was liberally flecked with grey and there were deep lines at the corners of her eyes and mouth. She hugged me for a long time, all the while calling instructions to Julius who was checking on the meal she'd been in the middle of preparing.

'It's so good to see you, Harry,' Nona said, finally letting me go. 'I'll kill that man of mine for not telling me you were coming. I could have cooked something special.'

'He didn't know,' I said. 'And I don't expect to be fed.'

'Nonsense. You'll eat with us. It's just cracked conch and grits, but I'm sure Julius has got a bottle of something to sweeten its way down.'

The food when it came was wonderful. Nona Flood could do things with conch that would have a gourmet's mouth watering. It was simple fare, the conch seasoned with lime juice and dipped in egg and cracker crumbs, but the taste was out of this world.

'This is superb, Nona,' I said. 'You're a witch.'

'I'm no witch,' she said. 'But my mama was. She came from Haiti. She had the gift.'

'*Obeah*,' Julius said, raising his eyes to the heavens. 'Hokum, woman, that's all it is. Voodoo mumbo jumbo.'

There was a fierce look in Nona's eyes. 'You want dessert, man? 'Cos the way you're bad mouthing *Obeah* you ain't likely to live long enough to eat it.'

'I'll take my chances. What is it anyway?'

'Guava duff.'

'Quick, Harry man. Give me the name of some *Obeah* high thing so's I can pray for forgiveness. Nona's guava duff is the food of the gods. Ambrosia.'

And it was.

After dinner Nona put a Bob Marley tape into the tiny battery powered cassette player that made up their sound system and they sat back in their shabby but comfortable easy chairs, listening to reggae and sipping coconut rum. It suddenly occurred to me that this was the real reason for coming to Barracuda. The Floods were the closest thing to a functioning family I'd ever had and, sitting in their relaxing company making small talk, it was a relatively easy task to put the events of the last few days out of my mind for a while and to enjoy the simple pleasures of family life. It was Nona who brought me back to reality with a jolt.

'Your papa's becoming the most popular man on Barracuda. All these people dropping in to see him. Your friend Alan the other day, those men last night. He's developing quite a social life.'

Julius noticed the look of alarm in my eyes. 'What is

it, Harry?'

'The men, last night, who were they?'

'Cubans,' Julius said. 'Two of them came to talk to your pa about his jewellery. I took them to the house myself.'

'What were they like? Describe them could you?'

'Young, black, very polite. One was about my height. The other one was shorter; about the same size as you. He did all the talking. Is there a problem, Harry?'

'Was there a woman with them?'

'No,' Julius said.

'Yes, there was,' Nona said. 'She stayed on the boat. I saw her when I went down to the harbour later.'

I'd heard enough. I bolted from the chair and out of the house, Julius at my heels. I hammered on my father's door, but there was no response.

'He can't have gone anywhere,' Julius said. 'Nona would have seen.'

'We'll have to break down the door.'

27

Julius elbowed me to one side. 'Let me.' He lifted his great, size fifteen foot and kicked the door open. It crashed inwards, slamming against the wall and rebounding back. The stench was appalling; a mixture of vomit, shit and booze. Inside it was dark and Julius went across the room yanked the curtains apart and threw open the window. My father was lying on the floor, unconscious in a puddle of filth.

'How the hell…' Julius said and crouched down beside him, listening to his breathing. I looked around the lounge, counting three empty rum bottles scattered about the room. There were pools of vomit and damp patches on the threadbare carpet. Julius turned to me, his face taut with anger. 'There wasn't a bottle in this house. I check it every day. And there's nowhere on the cay he could have bought it.'

'Then it looks like his guests brought it in.'

'But they weren't carrying…shit! They both had briefcases. They must have carried the bottles in those. But why? Why do this to the old man?'

'I've got a pretty good idea,' I said. 'But it's a long story. We'll get him cleaned up and into bed and I'll tell you all about it.'

We carried the old man up to the bathroom, took off his stinking clothes and sponged his body down from head to feet. I was shocked at how emaciated he looked. His arms were withered and stick-like, and you could count his ribs through his sickly, translucent skin. He'd lost his dentures somewhere along the line and his face looked sunken, emphasised by a few days growth of grey bristle on his chin. He looked like a very old man; much older than his sixty-five years. And slowly, as I washed him, all the old bitterness I'd felt for years towards him seemed to drift away.

Julius stooped down to lift him up and carry him to bed. I shook my head. 'I can manage, thanks.'

A brief smile flickered on Julius' lips. 'Sure thing, man.'

I slipped one arm under my father's knees, the other under his neck and lifted. He was light. It was like lifting a child. I carried him through to the bedroom, and as I lay him gently down on the bed his eyes opened and he looked up at me. He said nothing, but for a long moment his eyes locked with mine and there was no drunken confusion in his expression. He seemed totally aware of what was happening to him. His mouth was working and he mumbled something I didn't catch, then his eyes closed and he fell asleep.

I asked Julius if he'd heard what the old man had said.

'He said, "Thanks, son."'

It felt as though a ring of steel was tightening around my throat and I found I couldn't speak. Julius slapped me on the shoulder. 'Come on, Harry. Let him sleep it off.'

I pulled the sheet over my father's frail, naked body, acutely aware that someone somewhere was systematically hurting the people closest to me.

And I knew then that I was going to kill them.

When we went back to the lounge we found Nona clearing up the mess. I gave her a shaky smile but didn't trust myself to speak. Instead I went out and sat on the veranda to smoke. From inside I could hear the Floods' murmured conversation. I leaned back in the cane chair and closed my eyes, overwhelmed by fatigue.

28

Julius was shaking my shoulder. I opened my eyes surprised to find the daylight had gone and night had arrived, filled with the sound of cicadas.

'He's awake, man. He wants to see you.'

I walked into the bedroom to find my father propped up on his pillows. He motioned me to a chair at the bedside.

'Never been much of a father to you, have I?' he said, his voice as rough as gravel.

'No,' I said. 'You haven't.'

'Too late to change now.'

'Yes, I suppose it is.'

His tongue flicked over his cracked lips. 'Could use a drink.'

Nona had put a carafe of water and a glass on the nightstand. I poured some into a glass. His hands were shaking too much to take it so I put the glass to his lips. Water trickled down his chin and I wiped it away with the corner of the sheet.

'Alan's in trouble,' he said. 'Those Cuban bastards were after him. Thought if they got me drunk enough I'd tell them where he was.'

'And did you?'

'Didn't tell them a damned thing.'

'Do you know where Alan is?'

His fingers plucked at the blanket, peeling off balls of fluff. 'He was a bright kid, Alan. Always ambitious. Always trying to touch the sun. I used to worry that one day he would and he'd get more than his fingers burnt.'

'Looks like he has.'

He carried on as if I hadn't spoken, gazing at the wall as though a movie of the past was playing there. 'You remember Jenny Lancaster, Alan's mother?'

I did, but vaguely. She rarely came to the Islands, preferring instead to stay at her family's house in Boston. I remembered her mainly for her beauty. A willowy, blue-eyed blond with a face and figure that could start barroom brawls.

'She was class. Too good for the likes of Bobby Lancaster. She had brains. Alan takes after her.'

I asked him again, 'Do you know where he is?' And again he ignored the question.

'Her brains, my spirit. That's what made Alan a success.'

It took a few seconds to register what he'd just said, and then hit me like a hammer blow. 'You and Alan's mother?'

'You always were slow on the uptake.' A slow smile spread across his face. 'Alan's your brother.'

Suddenly my past and my relationships with both Alan and my father began to make sense. Long days aboard *The Majesty*. Father taking the time to show Alan how to navigate, how to steer, how to recognise the cays and channels that made up the Bahamas. Leaving me to find everything out for myself. Me telling myself that he was only taking special pains with Alan because he was my friend. I also remembered how conversations between the two of them would dry up as soon as I approached.

'Alan knows you're his father.' It wasn't a question; it was a statement of fact.

'Has done for years. Why do you think he's looked after you so well? You could have been a rich man by now if you'd taken advantage of every opportunity Alan put your way.'

Yes, and I'd probably be up to my eyes in the child pornography business as well.

'But you always were a fool. I watched you two grow up together and I never had any doubts which of you would be a success. Alan's proved me right.'

I walked across to the window. Outside the stars were blinking in a black velvet sky and Nona Flood was playing her Bob Marley tape again.

I couldn't bring myself to say anything to the old man lying in the bed. I could no longer think of him as my father. It seemed now he was just as a person I once had a fleeting acquaintanceship with. I could not even hate him for all the slights and the lack of love he showed me; nor even for the astonishing lack of sensitivity he'd just shown. Surprisingly I found it easy to hate Alan Lancaster, my brother, for all his lies over the years.

'Why tell me now?' I said finally.

'Because I'm dying, slowly I know, but I'll get there sooner rather than later. Alan needs your help, and you, as his brother, are honour-bound to give it to him.'

I wheeled on him then. 'That only goes to prove that you've never really known me at all. I've been trying to help Alan for the past few days. I held his child in my arms moments before she died. Did you know that? Your granddaughter died because of Alan and what he's mixed up in, or hasn't that fact sunk in yet.' He didn't even flinch. 'You must be really proud of him, selling kids to perverts. You probably applaud his entrepreneurial spirit. Until I walked into this room I was still going to try to help him if I could, but now, after what you've just told me, I wouldn't cut him down if he was hanging.' I walked to the door and opened it. 'And you'd better pray that the Cubans find him before I do.' I walked out, slamming the door behind me.

I was almost at the harbour before Julius caught up with me. 'Harry!' He caught my sleeve and spun me round. He saw the anger in my eyes. 'You going somewhere, man?'

'Home, Julius. I'm going home.' I shrugged him off and carried on walking.

'But your pa, Harry.'

'What about him?'

'He needs you, man.'

I climbed aboard *The Lady*. 'No, he doesn't. He needs Alan, he needs you and Nona. He certainly doesn't need me. Untie me.'

Julius reached down and untied the stern rope. 'I know you're upset, Harry, but running away isn't the answer.'

I looked at him sharply. 'You knew?'

He shrugged. 'It's history, man.'

I said nothing. I started the engines and switched on the navigation lights.

'I know how you feel,' Julius shouted over the noise of the engines.

I eased away from the mooring.

'Don't do this, Harry. Don't just sail away. *He needs you!*'

Julius Flood's voice was a thin sound drifting over the water as I broke from the harbour and found open sea. I didn't look back at Barracuda Cay. I had come to here to rediscover my family. I was leaving having gained a brother I never knew I had and certainly didn't want, and lost everything else.

29

The channel was impossible to navigate in the dark and not even the canopy of stars could help me. To find your way through the channel you need to see the water. The colour of it; dark green in the deeper areas, lightening to a pale blue over the shallows. The wave patterns, sudden white eyes betraying rocks and reefs, hiding beneath the surface. In the darkness I had to admit I was lost. I switched off the engines and dropped the anchor, preparing to wait out the night. I went below and lay flat out on my bunk, letting the gentle swell lull me to sleep.

*   *   *

I was standing on a flat disc of limestone watching a thirteen-year-old Alan hop bare-footed from rock to rock as deftly as a gazelle. He was dressed in his summer uniform of cut-off denims and a baggy black T-shirt, this one bearing the legend *Surfer Dude* in fluorescent yellow. His pale hair was long and flopped in front of his eyes, and after every jump he'd sweep it away with his hand. As he moved the hair away from his brow you could see the sunlight reflecting from the tiny droplets of water trapped in the fine silk hairs on his arm. He reached the edge of the rock-pool and stared down into the water, watching the small shoals of fish darting away from his shadow. Beneath them multi-coloured anemone and coral swayed in the currents made by the fish. The bay never attracted tourists. There was no room for sunbathing on the narrow slash of sand between the sea and the rocks, but it was the perfect playground for two thirteen-year-old boys with adventure in their hearts. Jack wasn't with on this occasion. I can't remember why.

It was here we played out our summer scenarios. We were both huge fans of espionage books and films, and spies were our heroes. James Bond, Harry Palmer, Adam Hall, even George Smiley all had roles to play in our adventures, with Alan leading the charge against the red menace.

I was usually cast as the hapless sidekick, mere cannon fodder, destined to die at the height of the game, justifying Alan's bloody vengeance. *You're dead. You've been shot, stabbed, poisoned, bitten by a deadly spider* — it depended on the book we'd just read or film we'd just seen; and I would dutifully fall to the ground, clutching whichever part of me that had been targeted. I never questioned the hierarchy. It was the natural order of things.

In the next scene he was in the water, swimming lazily across the rock pool, rolling over onto his back, floating there, shielding his eyes from the sun and squinting up at me. 'Going down!' he called, then twisted, jack-knifed, and swam down beneath the surface. I watched him swimming through the crystal water, exploring the cracks and fissures of the rock wall of the pool. A moray eel stuck a curious head out of one of the cracks as Alan approached. He reached out and stroked the head before darting lower into the pool.

Finally he surfaced, sweeping a curtain of wet hair away from his eyes. 'I've found it.'

'Found what?'

'The perfect dead letter drop. A crack in the wall and I can get my whole arm into it. Perfect. We can leave secret messages for each other and no one will ever find them. Come on in. I'll show you.'

The crack opened out into a smooth-sided chamber about eighteen inches deep and about four inches in diameter. I turned to Alan who was grinning widely, tiny air bubbles escaping from his nostrils and the corners of his mouth and eddying up to the surface. I gave him the thumbs up. Perfect.

Perfect!

*   *   *

I jerked awake, the memory of the dream as clear as the crystal water of the rock pool.

The dead letter drop—Look where you'd least expect it?

It was possible my subconscious had solved the riddle that had been bothering me since I received Alan's note. Long forgotten childhood memories drifting up to the surface after being submerged for decades.

I started *The Lady's* engines. Dawn had broken and the channel was visible again. I headed back to Freeport.

*   *   *

The bay looked no different from the memory of it. It was still deserted. A few crabs were sunning themselves on the strip of sand, but there were no people. The rock on which I'd stood to watch Alan swimming in the rock pool was still there, though a little more weed-strewn. I stripped off my shirt, donned a mask and snorkel and eased myself into the water. It was colder than it looked. I drew in a deep breath and swam down.

It took a while to get my bearings, to remember where

the crevice was, but eventually I found it. It was a smaller than I remembered, but that was simply because I had grown a lot in the ensuing twenty years. It took an effort, but I still managed to slip my arm inside.

I found it almost immediately.

My fingers closed over a small, polythene-wrapped package no bigger than my fist. I would never get my hand out again clutching the package so I hooked my finger through the tape securing it and withdrew it carefully. Once I had it in my hand I surfaced and climbed back onto the limestone disc. I hadn't thought to bring a towel, but the sun was high in the sky and my skin was dry within minutes. My shorts took a little longer.

I sat crossed-legged on the rock and peeled back the layers of polythene, almost holding my breath as I unwrapped the parcel.

Finally I was left with a small self-sealed polythene bag, the type drug dealers use to distribute their wares. Inside the bag was a computer memory stick, a small black plastic capsule with a USB plug on one end; and contained within the capsule, I hoped, were all the secrets Alan wanted me to know.

I slipped it into the top pocket of my shirt and sat for a little longer watching the crabs moving across the sand. I had another problem. I didn't own, and had never owned a computer, so accessing the information on the stick was going to prove problematic. I knew people who did own the infernal machines, but I didn't want to get any of them involved in this. I was left with only one option.

30

Sam Goldberg had told me he was staying at the Princess hotel in downtown Freeport. I knew the hotel and the street in which it was situated by reputation. It was a hang-out for pimps and pushers, whores and petty criminals. The fact he was staying there told me he was speaking the truth when he'd said he had no publisher's money to finance his project. The Princess hotel was little more than a flop house and was not the kind of place anyone in their right mind would choose to stay.

I pushed my way through the revolving door and was immediately confronted by the mixed odours of marijuana and cheap booze. There was a bell push on the stained wooden reception desk. I leaned on it and a few moments later an elderly black woman hobbled out from a back room. She was wall-eyed and looked as old as Methuselah. She fixed me with her one good eye and snapped, 'Yes?'

'Is Sam Goldberg staying here?'

She reached under the desk and pulled out a heavy-looking faux-leather-bound register. It seemed to take all her strength to open it, but once she had she ran a wizened finger down a column, stopping at Goldberg's entry.

'Room 408,' she said, then slapped the book shut, replaced it under the desk and returned to the back room without so much as a backward glance.

The elevator had a hand-written OUT OF ORDER sign taped to the partially open door. I shrugged and took the stairs.

I found 408 and rapped on the door with my fist. It was opened immediately by a young woman with bobbed chestnut hair, slim physique and the most kissable mouth I had ever seen. Even that improved when she smiled.

'Sam Goldberg?'

'Nice try,' she said. 'Billie-Jean Martinez. Billie to my friends. Who are you?'

'Harry Beck.'

'Ah, the man who kidnapped Sammy and took him on a cruise out to Abaco, only to leave him to find his own way home. He still hasn't recovered from the crossing, you know? Sammy's no sailor.'

'He's told you about me then?'

She smiled. 'You'd better come in. He's on the phone.'

I accepted the invitation and found myself in a squalid little hotel room that smelled badly of stale smoke and sweat.

Sam Goldberg looked round as I entered the room, gave a small wave with a hand clutching a cigarette, and then turned away, lowering his voice.

'He won't be long,' Billie said. 'Talking to his agent. Can I get you a coffee?'

I could have used something stronger, but doubted the room possessed a mini-bar. 'Yeah, coffee's fine.'

There was an electric kettle perched precariously on the edge of a cluttered table under the window. She shook it to see if it contained enough water then flipped the ON switch. She then crossed to the bed where an array of camera parts were strewn across the counterpane. She sat and drew her legs underneath her, picked up a cloth and started polishing a lens.

'Do you live in Freeport?' she said.

'Born and bred in Port Lucaya,' I said. I pulled up a hard chair, reversed it and sat astride.

'Lucky you. I love it here.'

'And you?'

'Hong Kong. My mother's Chinese. My father was an airline pilot. Irish American by all accounts, but I never met him.' I could see her heritage in her eyes. They were almond shaped with a slight Asian cast, but were also quite a startling blue.

'Quite a mixture,' I said.

She chuckled. 'Oh, it gets worse. My paternal grand-father was Spanish. When I was growing up I didn't know whether to dance the Irish jig, the dragon dance or the flamenco.'

'Tough choice.'

'Tell me about it. So what about you? Were both your parents born here too?'

I nodded.

The kettle started to boil. She uncurled herself and padded across to make the coffee. 'Sugar?'

I shook my head. At that point Goldberg hung up the phone and turned to me. 'I didn't expect to see you so soon,' he said. He was scowling. The trip to Abaco Island had obviously affected him deeply.

'Likewise. But I need you to do something for me.'

He exchanged a glance with Billie. I couldn't say what was communicated between them in that look, but there was definitely something. The scowl slipped away from his features to be replaced by a look of curiosity. 'Go ahead,' he said. 'Shoot.'

I fished the memory stick out of my shirt pocket and tossed it across to him. 'Will your computer read this?'

He caught it deftly and turned it over in his palm. 'Possibly. Possibly not. It depends on file formats.'

'Can you try?'

His laptop was in its case, lying on the bed. He slid it out and opened it up. A few seconds later the screen came alive. 'We'll give it a moment to boot up, and then we'll try it.'

A few moments later he inserted the stick into a USB port at the side of the laptop and hit a few keys.

Billie put a cup of coffee down beside me and went across to the bed, looking over Goldberg's shoulder at the screen. The pair were close, but not a couple; the body language was all wrong. Friends then. Perhaps she was helping him with his book.

He turned to me. 'Well, there's something here, but I can't tell you what.'

'Oh.'

Billie read the disappointment in my eyes. 'There are lots of files there, but they're encrypted.' She tapped a few keys. 'And it's quite a sophisticated encryption. It's going to take me ages to crack it.'

'Do you think you can?'

Goldberg smiled at me. 'If Billie can't get us in there nobody will. She's good.'

'Just good?' Billie said and punched him in the arm.

I picked up the cup and took a swig. 'Makes a mean cup of coffee too,' I said.

'There's no end to my talents.' she said and pushed Goldberg out of the way. Then curled herself into the lotus position on the bed and started hitting keys.

31

An hour later Billie was still sitting there tapping away at the keyboard, swearing occasionally and jotting down notes on a pad lying on the bed beside her.

'No luck?' I said.

Her lips were pressed into a hard, thin line and her brow was creased into a frown of concentration. She gave a barely imperceptible shake of her head.

'So this memory stick,' Goldberg said. 'Where did you get it?'

'Alan,' I said.

His eyes widened. 'You've seen him?'

'No,' I said. 'He sent it to me.'

'But I thought…' Goldberg began but Billie interrupted him with a triumphant 'Yessss!' and punched the air with her fist. 'We're in,' she said.

'I told you she was good,' Goldberg said with a smile. 'Come on, let's see what we've got.'

Billie was still hunched over the computer. 'Just a minute,' she said. She was running the cursor over directories and opening them. 'There's not much here…oh, wait a minute. This is interesting.' She spun the computer round on the bed so we could see the screen.

It was filled with small, thumbnail images of children. Head shots mostly, but there were a few more graphic images there too. They turned my stomach.

'What is this?' I said.

'At a guess,' Billie said with a small shrug. 'It's a market place. These kids are for sale. Look.' She let the cursor hover over a thumbnail image of a boy. As she clicked the touchpad the full-sized image appeared, filling the screen. He could have been no more than six years old. Large, innocent eyes set in a smiling, black face.

Underneath the picture was a small white box. *Nathan, 5yrs, Haitian, $10,000.*

Billie closed the image and opened another. This time a girl, again black, her hair plaited into cornrows. *Michelle, 8yrs, Cuban, Experienced, $15,000.* I didn't have to guess what *Experienced* meant. It was written there on the stony, unsmiling face, and echoed by the dead expression in her eyes.

'This is sick,' Sam Goldberg said. 'It's a meat market.'

'Are these the only ones on there?' I said. I didn't want to look at any more pictures of children.

Billie closed the directory and opened another.

The next thing to appear on the screen was a list of names and addresses. Billie scrolled down the list.

There were names I recognised instantly. A US Senator, two prominent members of the British government, one from the Commons, one from the House of Lords, a popular TV newsreader and his wife, two reasonably famous actors. The list went on. The only common link between them was wealth. They all had money; lots of money.

Billie scrolled down as I scanned the names. And then one jumped out at me; a name that announced it's presence with an explosion in my mind and a sucker punch to my stomach. For a moment I thought I was going to throw up, experiencing nausea similar to that suffered by Sam

Goldberg on the trip across to Abaco.

Sam Goldberg noticed my reaction. 'Someone you know?'

I reined in my emotions. 'There're a lot of names I recognise,' I said non-committaly.

He studied me for a moment then let it go. 'This is a client list,' he said after a while. 'A database of all the sick fucks in the market for this filth.'

I agreed. It was also the reason my bungalow had been trashed, why Stevie had been tortured and why they had forced my father to drink himself close to death.

The memory stick was two inches of pure dynamite; a career and life wrecker for so many people. It was small wonder that those behind it were desperate enough to do anything to stop the stick and the data contained in the silicon falling into the wrong hands.

I wondered about Alan. It was obvious now he was deeply involved in this, but what had happened? A change of heart perhaps? A sudden realization that he was into something so sick and so depraved that his moral compass had finally steered him away from it?

He had entrusted the memory stick to me. The question was, what the hell did he expect me to do with it?

'Can you print the list out for me?' I said.

Billie looked up from the bed, her face serious. 'You realise that there are people out there who will kill to stop this becoming public knowledge.'

'They already have.' I thought about Anna and Sally.

'And you still want to walk around with a printout of this list in your pocket? You're mad. We need to hand the memory stick over to the authorities.'

Goldberg butted in then. 'For them to do what? It's just a list of names. There's no proof linking anyone on it to anything criminal. Did you see some of the names on there? Between them they have enough money to buy silence in every country of the world. With enough cash dropped into the pockets of the right people they could make this go away. It might inconvenience them for a while, and maybe cost them the down payment on their next chateau or yacht, but ultimately money talks.'

'So,' Billie said. 'Suggestions?'

'This is just the springboard I needed for my book,' Goldberg said.

'And you've got your photographs now so there's no point me hanging around anymore,' Billie said, an edge to her voice.

'Don't take it like that,' Goldberg said. 'I told you before you came out here there were no guarantees. Besides, if I remember correctly you invited yourself.'

"Yes, I did.' She scowled at him, but turned her attention to me. 'What about you?'

'I don't need photographs either,' I said. It didn't improve her mood.

'Don't be facetious,' she said. 'What are you going to do now?'

'I need to find Alan Lancaster,' I said.

'You think he's still alive?'

I nodded. 'He was alive enough when he sent me the message about the memory stick. There's every reason to think that he still is. Alan knows these Islands as well as I do. There are hundreds of places to hide yourself away. If you don't want to be found you won't be.'

'So that's what you think he's done,' Billie said. 'Hidden himself away until it all blows over?'

'I suspect so.'

'Even though his wife and daughter have been murdered?' Goldberg said.

'There's one thing you should know about Alan,' I said. 'He's a survivor, first and foremost. There's only one person he'll be looking out for now and that's himself.'

'Nice friends you have,' Billie said.

'Alan is my oldest friend,' I said. 'It doesn't mean I

like him very much at this precise moment. But I need answers, and he's the only one likely to provide them.'

32

Ten minutes later I left the hotel room, the database printed out, folded and slipped into the pocket of my shorts along with the memory stick. I took the stairs down to the lobby, and had almost reached the bottom when I heard voices.

'Look again. Do you recognise this man?'

The voice was harsh, laced with a Cuban accent. I stuck my head around the edge of the stairwell and drew back quickly. The three of them were there, the big man, the smaller man and the woman; the three who had attacked Stevie on *The Lady*, and who had plied my father with liquor until they rendered him unconscious. I felt my muscles bunching, my hands balling into fists.

They were talking to the wall-eyed old lady behind the desk and showing her a photograph.

'I'm not sure.' Came the querulous, ancient voice.

'Show her again,' the Cuban woman said.

There was a pause, followed by a cry. '408...He's in 408...Don't!'

I didn't hesitate. I took the stairs three at a time. A few seconds later I was banging on Goldberg's door.

'It's Harry! Let me in!'

Billie answered the door again, an expression of curiosity mingled with alarm on her face. 'Harry, what...'

'We have to get out of here. The Cubans. They've found us.'

As Goldberg scooped up the laptop Billie was bundling camera parts into a leather holdall.

'Leave them. We haven't got time,' I said, standing by the door and holding it open. I could hear footsteps thudding on the thinly carpeted staircase.

'Fuck you!' she snapped at me. 'This is my livelihood.'

Finally they were ready. I bundled them onto the landing and shut the door behind them. The footsteps were louder. They were nearly on us. 'This way,' I said and started to run in the opposite direction to the stairs. 'Is there a fire escape?'

Goldberg shrugged.

'Think!'

'I don't know!'

Billie ran ahead of us and stopped at another door.

'What are you doing?' I said as we reached her.

She had a key in her hand. She opened the door and pushed it wide. 'In here,' she said.

I didn't argue with her. I followed them into the room and closed the door. The room was a neater, less smelly version of the one we'd just left.

'My room,' she said with a smile.

The footsteps had reached the landing. I put a finger to my lips.

For a second there was silence then a loud crash as a foot made contact with the door to room 408, smashing it in. There was a second or two of shouting, then silence as they realised we weren't in the room; and then footsteps thudded down the landing, past our door and we heard the window at the end being opened. The sound of the footsteps changed; became harsh, metallic. It sounded like they'd found the fire escape and decided we'd escaped that way.

We waited in silence, barely daring to breathe.

Finally Goldberg said, 'Do you think they've gone?'

Billie was at the door before I could stop her. 'There's only one way to find out.' She opened the door and stepped out onto the landing, pulling the door closed behind her.

I put my ear to the door, listening. She was either very brave or completely mad. I suspected the latter. A second later Sam Goldberg joined me, pressing the side of his face against the door.

'Hi there. Can I help you?' Billie's voice rang out. She was speaking loudly, obviously so we could hear the conversation.

There were more footsteps then a man's voice said, '*Estamos buscando para alguien.*' The language was Spanish.

'*¿Alguien que conozco?*' Billie answered in the same tongue.

'*Mire esta foto. ¿Le reconoce?*'

Goldberg was whispering to me offering a translation. 'They told her they're looking for someone; she asked who. Now they're showing her a photograph.'

'*¿Cómo se llama?*'

'*Harry Beck. ¿Le reconoce?*'

'*Nunca le vi en mí vida. Y seamos sinceros, una cara como esa es difícil olvidar*'

'It's a photo of you. She's telling them she's never heard of you.'

'Do they believe her?'

Goldberg shrugged. 'Why shouldn't they?'

There were more sounds of movement. The man barked an order, '*¡Vamos salir de aquí!*'

'*Buena suerte. Espero que encontrarle.*'

'They're going,' Goldberg hissed. 'Billie's wishing them good luck. Says she hopes they find you.'

'Great,' I muttered.

A full minute passed before the door opened and Billie stepped back into the room.

'What the hell do you think you were doing?' I said.

Billie Martinez smiled broadly. 'Well I figured they weren't looking for me. I've only been here a day. Not long enough to piss anybody off. You, on the other hand… By the way, it's a terrible photograph of you. Makes you look ten years older.'

'Have they gone?' Goldberg said.

'Watch the street.'

I went to the window and inched back the blind. I could see the three Cubans across the street. The smaller of the men was talking into a mobile phone and gesticulating wildly. Finally he threw the phone down on the pavement and stomped on it.

'Yeah,' Billie said, looking over my shoulder. 'I'd say you've pissed him off.'

It was obvious they couldn't stay at the hotel. The Cubans would be back and the next time there was every chance that Billie would be targeted, and I couldn't allow that to happen. I still had vivid memories of cutting Stevie down from the rail of *The Lady* and her description of what they'd done to her. I couldn't let anyone else go through that just because these bastards were looking for me.

'So what do you suggest?' Sam Goldberg said.

'Let me take you to somewhere safe. I know a place you can hide out for a while, at least until the immediate danger has passed.'

'And how would we get to this safe haven?' Billie said knowingly.

'On *The Lady*,' I said, shooting a glance at Goldberg. He reacted much as I'd suspected he would.

'No fucking way!' he said. 'Cars, planes, fine. I can handle those. Your boat, no way. Not after the last time.'

Billie laid a comforting hand on his arm. 'Sammy, we don't have much of a choice,' she said gently. 'Harry's right. We can't stay here.'

He looked at her steadily, and then ran his hand through his thinning hair. 'You're asking a lot of me,' he said. 'I can't remember ever feeling as ill as I did on his boat.'

'I can promise you a gentler crossing, if that's any help,' I offered.

'And what will you be doing while we're hiding away?' Billie said. 'Hunting down the bad guys I suppose.'

'Something like that.'

'Hmm. I can almost smell the testosterone.'

'It's not like that,' I said. 'Three days ago I was enjoying my life. It was calm, fairly boring and predictable and easy. Then a bomb went off and blew my easy life to hell. People I care about have been killed, beaten up and violated. And this is all because I happen to be friends with a man who it turns out is a total piece of shit. I want to get back to my boring, predictable life, but until I find Alan Lancaster and get to the bottom of the mess he's in I won't be able to, and that pisses *me* off.'

'So all we've got to do now is to get out of the hotel,' Goldberg said. He was standing at the window peering out through the blind. 'Look.'

The larger of the Cuban men was leaning against a wall on the opposite side of the street, watching the doorway of the hotel. He didn't look like he'd be leaving his lookout post any time soon.

'There must be a back way out here,' I said.

Billie was at the door again. 'I'll go down to reception and ask the old woman.'

She was back five minutes later. 'Right, let's get packed up and get out of here. There's an exit that gives on to an alley at the back that will bring us out farther up the street. We can bypass him.'

'How's the old girl?' I said, guilty that I hadn't intervened when the Cubans were showing her my photograph; but it would have been madness to do so.

'She's okay,' Billie said. 'She's got a nasty cigarette burn on her arm, but no other damage.'

'Who burnt her? The woman?'

Billie nodded.

'It figures.' I said.

Billie looked at me quizzically, but I didn't elaborate. 'Okay. Get packed and we'll get out of here.'

Sam Goldberg didn't look happy, but he went back to his room, and when Billie and I emerged from hers he was standing outside in the hallway, a packed holdall sitting at his feet and his laptop bag slung over his shoulder.

We bypassed the Cuban thug easily.

Before we left the hotel I pressed a hundred dollar bill into the old lady's hand and thanked her for her help. She said nothing but stared down at the cigarette burn on her arm, then spat on the floor. Words were unnecessary.

I'd left the Jeep some way from the hotel. Once we reached it we threw the luggage into the back and I headed across to the main part of town.

'What if they're watching the boat?' Billie said as we drew near.

It had crossed my mind too. I called Stevie on her mobile phone. 'Where are you?'

'Who's calling please?'

'Stevie, don't piss about. I need you to get down *The Lady* and take her out.'

'Then I'm still crewing for you. I mean, how long is it since you bothered to check?'

'I've been tied up,' I said. 'I'll explain when I see you.'

'*You've* been tied up? That's rich.'

'Poor choice of words,' I said. 'Sorry.'

'My God, is that an apology?'

'Yes.'

There was a pause. 'Must be serious then. Where do

140

you want me to take *The Lady*?'

'Nowhere special. Just head out to sea. When it gets dark head back to the harbour. We'll be waiting. And then we're going on a little trip.'

'*We'll* be waiting? Who's *we*?'

'Friends.'

She thought about this for a while. 'Okay. See you later.'

33

It had just turned nine when I saw *The Lady's* lights approaching the harbour.

'How do you know it's your boat?' Goldberg said as we sat in the darkened interior of the Jeep and watched *The Lady of Pain* approach.

'Listen,' I said.

Carried in on the breeze was the gentle throb of two Penta engines, working in unison, powering the twin screws that drove *The Lady* forward through the waves. It was a sound that still raised gooseflesh on my arms. 'I'd know the sound of those engines anywhere,' I said.

Stevie brought her in to the harbour and eased her up alongside the dock. As the three of us climbed aboard, she emerged from the wheelhouse.

'This is Stevie,' I said to Billie and Goldberg. But before I could say anything else there was a squeal of tyres and a black SUV hurtled round the corner at the top of the road leading to the harbour and began bearing down on us.

'Shit! It's them. Stevie get us out of here.'

She didn't need telling twice. Within a blink she was back in the wheelhouse, gunning the engines and taking us back out to sea.

As the SUV screeched to a halt by the harbour wall the Cubans leapt from the vehicle, weapons in hand.

'Get down!' I yelled and threw myself at Goldberg and Billie, dragging them down onto the deck. 'Keep your heads down,' I said, as bullets ripped through the air above us. One of them shattered the side window of the wheelhouse. I glanced up. Stevie was holding tight to the wheel, her mouth set in a determined line. She saw me glance up and raised a hand. *I'm okay.*

Moments later we were out of range. They were still shooting, but their bullets were missing by miles. I left Billie and Goldberg still sprawled on the deck and climbed up into the wheelhouse.

Stevie was grinning. 'That was fun,' she said. 'Just like the old days.' There was blood on her cheek where a fragment of glass from the shattered window had sliced through the skin.

'Remind me, when were we last shot at?' I took a handkerchief from my pocket and wiped away the blood. 'It's not serious,' I said. 'Probably won't even leave a scar.'

'Damn!' she said. 'Nothing to show for it.'

She was a good little actress, but not that good. The sweat that was trickling down her face had nothing to do with heat or excitement. She'd been badly scared but was determined not to let it show.

I pulled out a chart and spread it on the table, switching on the map light.

'So where are we heading?' she said, craning her neck over my shoulder.

'Watt's Cay,' I said, pointing to a small cay in the Berry Island chain. 'I know someone there who can shelter us, and won't ask too many questions.' I jotted down the coordinates then fed them into the autopilot. It was going to take us a good few hours to reach the island and I wasn't taken with the idea of spending half the night at the wheel, plus the fact I needed to sleep.

Dark of the Sun

The ocean was calm and there were no hidden dangers lurking under the waves waiting to surprise us. Stevie could keep an eye on things while I slept, but the autopilot would do all the hard work. That was why I'd spent so much money getting a good one. 'Time for proper introductions,' I said.

'She's beautiful,' Stevie said.

'Who?'

'The woman you brought on board. Stunning.'

'I hadn't noticed,' I said.

Stevie muttered something I didn't catch.

'Pardon?'

'None of your business,' she said.

'Fair enough,' I said.

34

Watt's Cay is one of the Bahamas' best kept secrets. A privately owned island of over one thousand acres with beautiful silver sand beaches and verdant vegetation. Named after Benjamin Watt, an American print magnate who settled there in the late 1800's, it's off the tourist route simply because Kim Weaver who now owns the island is rich enough to do without that form of income.

I'd known Kim for years. She'd come to the Islands twenty years ago with her husband Ted, a wealthy financier from Baltimore, who despite being nearly thirty years her senior, loved his wife with a passion that bordered on the obsessive. The island was his gift to her. He'd retired and chose this idyllic spot to see out the rest of their life together, but his grand plan was thwarted by the onset of a very aggressive form of pancreatic cancer and he died just eighteen months after settling on Watt's Cay, leaving Kim with a fortune but a very lonely existence. She'd loved her husband dearly and his death left a huge, gaping hole in her life.

I'd filled the vacuum for a while until we realised that we worked better as friends rather than lovers. In more recent years she had developed a gift for writing fiction. Her romance novels now filled the shelves of airport book-shops across the world, and the royalties she received swelled her already not inconsiderable fortune.

There was no harbour at Watt's Cay. Instead there was a simple wooden jetty. As we were tying up at one of the stanchions. Kim came down to the jetty to meet us. To my alarm she was carrying a twelve-gauge shotgun, broken across her arm.

Her face split into a grin. 'Harry! I thought I recognised the boat.'

'Expecting trouble?' I said, nodding toward the shotgun.

She glanced down. 'This old thing? God, no. I would be in trouble if I relied on this. It hasn't shot straight since Ted dropped it down the stairs and that was, oh, too many years ago to remember. No, Harry, rabbits. They've decimated my vegetable patch. I fire at the buggers to scare them off. Haven't hit one yet though.' She laid the gun down on the jetty and opened her arms wide. 'Give me a hug,' she said. 'It's been ages.'

We embraced while Stevie, Sam and Billie looked on, all three wearing slightly bemused expressions.

Kim's body still felt the same, still smelled the same. There was more grey in her hair and perhaps the laughter lines around her eyes had deepened slightly, but mostly she hadn't changed at all.

'You're looking good, Kim,' I said. Which was true.

Kim Weaver had always been a beautiful woman, and the passage of time had done little to diminish her looks. Her brown hair was cut to an elegant chin-length bob which made the most of her delicate bone structure and her startlingly intense grey eyes. I could see why I had fallen for her, despite there being a twenty-year age gap between us. The magazines nowadays would call me her boytoy.

As an inexperienced young man barely out of my

teens, I'd found her regal, unassuming beauty irresistible. But it was more than just her looks. Kim was fun. Losing Ted was the *great trauma* of her life, but once he'd gone she made a conscious decision to embrace life and wring as much from it as she possibly could. I was just the first of a string of much younger lovers.

Finally she ended the embrace and held me at arms length. 'Let me look at you,' she said, scrutinizing me. 'Yep, as I thought. Your age suits you. You've become rugged.'

I laughed. 'You mean I look worn out.'

'No, I mean you looked rugged. Ruggedly handsome. I could see your potential all those years ago. Are you going to introduce me to your friends?' She looked beyond me to the others on the boat.

'Of course,' I said.

As I made the introductions Kim scrutinized each of them in turn, paying special attention to Stevie's beaten up face. 'My word,' she said. 'You've been in the wars,' she said. 'Did you win?'

'You should see the other guy,' Stevie said.

Kim laughed and turned to me. 'I like her. Tom Bailey's daughter, right?'

I nodded.

'I knew your father,' she said to Stevie. 'A good man.'

'One of the best,' I said.

I couldn't be sure, but I could swear Stevie was blushing.

'Okay,' Kim said. 'Let's go back to the house.' She threaded her arm through mine and we walked together along the sandy path that led to her house.

'You're in trouble,' she said quietly as we walked along. We were ahead of the others and out of earshot.

'Is it that obvious?'

'To anyone who knows you and, let's face it, Harry, I know you better than most. Why else would you come and see me?'

'It's not like that, Kim,' I said.

She snorted. 'Of course it is. Don't worry. I'm not offended. So are you going to tell me about it?'

'Later. When we're alone.'

'That works for me.'

'I do have a favour to ask you though.'

'You want to stay for a few days?'

'Not me. Them. I jerked a thumb back over my shoulder at Goldberg and Billie. They need to lie low for a while. I'm afraid I've put them in danger.'

Kim frowned. 'This sounds serious, Harry. It's nothing illegal, is it?'

'Not as far as we're concerned. But there are others to whom the law doesn't matter a damn. Which is why I have to protect them.'

There was a pebble on the path in front of us. Kim kicked it and sent it spinning into the irrigation ditch that ran alongside the path.

'Okay,' she said decisively. 'They can stay.'

'Thanks.'

'But I want the whole story, Harry. And by that I mean complete, unexpurgated.'

'You got it,' I said.

We breasted a small rise as Kim's house came into view; a large, low building, all white walls and plate glass. It was ultra-modern and quite ugly, sticking up out of the landscape and shouting its presence. Ted Weaver had spent a million dollars having it built to his own design and I'd always thought he should have spent his money more wisely and hired an architect. The ugliness was confined to the outside. The interior was a luxurious, air-conditioned palace with long, white leather sofas, terracotta floor tiles and palms set in huge stone urns. It could have been cold and sterile, but Kim's sheer ebullient presence made it homely enough.

As we entered there was a young man standing at the cooker in the open plan kitchen rustling up a stir-fry in a stainless steel wok. Apart from a blue and white chef's apron he was stark naked; his body lean and well muscled and tanned to the colour of teak. He turned and smiled.

'This is Philippe,' Kim said, completely un-fazed by the young man's lack of clothes.

'Right,' I said, glancing at the others whose faces registered a mixture of confusion and amusement. Kim strode across to the young man, planted a kiss on his cheek and whispered something in his ear. Philippe glanced down at himself, smiled and hurried from the kitchen. When he returned a few moments later he was wearing a garishly coloured pair of Hawaiian shorts.

Kim returned to us, smiling broadly. 'You'll have to excuse him. He's French,' she said, as if that explained everything. 'Have you eaten?'

We'd had a light breakfast on *The Lady* of coffee and muffins, but I could feel my stomach rumbling, encouraged by the mouth-watering aroma coming from Philippe's wok. I said as much.

She turned to Goldberg and Billie. 'Ok, I'll show you to your rooms and then we'll eat.'

'Sounds good to me.' I said.

*   *   *

Later, once we'd sampled Philippe's excellent stir-fried chicken, Kim persuaded the young man to take Billie, Goldberg and Stevie on a tour of the house and grounds. Kim and I settled ourselves in the comfortable cane chairs on the terrace with glasses of ice cold lemonade.

'So,' she said. 'What's going on?'

'A long story,' I said.

'Well, you have the time to tell it. I told Philippe to keep them out of the way for at least an hour.'

I smiled. 'You haven't changed,' I said.

'Oh, I have, my darling. In ways you couldn't possibly imagine.' She looked at me sharply. 'Begin,' she said. 'And don't leave out any details.'

35

I wasn't able to give her the complete and unexpurgated version of the story that she wanted — there were too many uncertainties in my mind for that; too much I didn't understand — but it was as close to it as I was willing to go.

'Harry Beck,' I deliberately started by referring to myself in the third person, it helped me focus. 'Harry has a carefree, almost idyllic, life in the Bahamas. The owner of a small charter company, he enjoys a laid back lifestyle with few responsibilities and fewer commitments.'

'Sounds like the man I know.'

'Exactly. I couldn't have asked for more. Anyway. His peaceful life is shattered when his best friend's wife and small daughter are brutally killed in an explosion and his friend, Alan Lancaster goes missing. On the same day, his home is ransacked and Stevie Bailey, the girl who crews for him on *The Lady of Pain*, his boat, is tortured and left for dead.'

'Anna and Sally? No…' Tears were welling in her eyes. She blinked and dabbed with her sleeve.

'I was there. I saw it happen.'

'And that's where your friend, Stevie, got her obvious injuries?'

I nodded. 'I haven't seen hide nor hair of Alan.'

'I can't believe it, poor Anna, that sweet child. Alan thought the world of both of them.

What's he got himself involved in this time?' She shook her head and sniffed back more tears.

'Harry comes to realize that the people responsible for torturing Stevie are the same as those who planted the bomb in Alan Lancaster's car that killed Lancaster's wife and child, and that the bomb was intended for Alan himself.'

Kim shrugged. 'That sounds logical. The Islands can be a bit lively, but car bombs and torturing young girls sounds like someone who's pretty organized.'

'Harry receives a message he believes to be from Alan which leads to the discovery of a computer memory stick. Contained on the stick is evidence of a paedophile ring, a cartel of rich and influential people, who are a using the Bahamas as a gateway through which to traffic children from Haiti and Cuba.'

'You have to be fucking with me.'

I drained my glass of lemonade. I wished it was something stronger.

Kim had hardly touched hers. 'I don't know Alan anywhere as well as you, but what I do know doesn't lead me to think he'd be mixed up in anything like that. What names are on this list?'

'It's a long list. There's not a lot more to tell. My father's life has been put in jeopardy, the same people tried to kill him with kindness.'

'What are you going to do now?'

'The only way to keep me and everyone around me safe is to find Alan Lancaster and, somehow, through him, bring down the cartel behind all this.'

'Sounds laudable,' she said. 'Except for one thing.'

'Which is?'

'Alan could be the one behind all this.'

Which sentiment dangerously echoed my own thoughts. What was becoming obvious to me was that everything I had always known and believed about friendship was turning into murder, and betrayal. It was the only way any of it made any sense. Alan had betrayed the people he professed to love; his wife, his daughter and his friend. Except that if my father was to be taken seriously Alan wasn't just a lifelong friend, he was my brother.

I was being forced to re-evaluate my life, and I clearly had some difficult choices to make about the future and, let's face it, for the first time in my life, I had to take responsibility and get some control.

When it was obvious I'd finished, Kim stared off into the distance. The terrace had a view down to the sea. From where we sat we could see *The Lady* tethered at the jetty.

'I knew you were in trouble as soon as I saw the bullet holes in *The Lady's* superstructure.'

'It's going to cost me a month's money to get those repaired.'

'You could have been killed.'

'But we weren't.'

She sipped at her lemonade and gave me a long, hard, appraising look. 'So what's next?'

'I have to find Alan.'

'Alan Lancaster may be many things…but a paedophile?' She shook her head. 'No. I don't buy it.'

'The evidence is pretty conclusive,' I said.

'Bullshit! It's all circumstantial. Why won't you give him the benefit of the doubt? You two have been friends a long time.'

It was my turn to stare off into the distance. I couldn't answer her. I was dealing with a whole raft of emotions as far as my best friend was concerned, and I was unable to articulate any of them.

'I think Stevie should stay here,' she said.

'I agree,' I said. 'But she won't.'

'And if something happens to her? How will you be able to live with yourself?'

'Something has happened to her, and I'm having a hard enough time getting my head around that. Believe me it gnaws away at me.'

'And if she's killed?'

'Then I'll find a way to carry on,' I said with a certainty I didn't feel.

The conversation was curtailed with the arrival of Philippe and the others.

Billie was effusive. 'Kim, it's a wonderful place to live. You're so lucky.'

'Yes,' Kim said. 'I am. That's what my husband Ted thought until his pancreas exploded.'

Billie flushed. 'I'm sorry. I didn't mean to cause offence.'

'None taken,' Kim said lightly. 'You weren't to know. Ted and I had a wonderful marriage and I don't regret a moment of it...except maybe the end. That was difficult. But the times we spent together here were the happiest of my life.' She changed tack suddenly. 'Stevie, I was wondering if you'd like to stay on for a while, rather than sailing the high seas with this old reprobate.' She jerked a thumb in my direction.

'Thanks,' I said. 'Reprobate?'

'How else would you describe yourself?' Kim asked with a smile. 'Well, Stevie? What do you think? It might be fun to get to know each other better.'

Stevie was hesitant, shifting from foot to foot, glancing first at me, then at Billie and Sam. Finally she said, 'Yes. I think I'd like that.'

She must have noticed the surprise register in my eyes. She added quickly. 'That's if you don't mind, Harry. To be quite honest, with everything that's happened over the past few days, I could use the down time.'

'Sure,' I said. 'I think it's a great idea.'

'But I'll hold you responsible if anything happens to *The Lady*. Oh, and watch that bearing on the starboard drive shaft. It needs some TLC. Be gentle with it.'

'I will,' I promised.

They all came down to the jetty to wave me off. Stevie cast off the stern line and stood, scuffing the toe of her trainers on the wooden slats. There was a hint of regret in her eyes as I pulled away from them, but not as much as I expected to see.

As they became dots in the distance I had to shake myself out of a melancholy that was settling over me like a shroud. For the first time in years I felt totally alone. I felt like I had a mountain to climb and it was very much a solo ascent. I tried to focus my mind back on the job in hand. Until this mess was cleaned up I could no longer have the luxury of the laid-back lifestyle I had enjoyed up until now. I set a course and headed back to Grand Bahama.

36

'I'm sorry, Harry. Jack won't be back 'til tomorrow.'

Pilar, the barmaid at the *Jolly Tar*, finished drying a beer glass and set it in line with the thirty or so others on a shelf behind her.

'Where's he gone?' I said.

'He didn't say where. Just said he had some business to attend to and asked me to hold the fort.'

Pilar was in her early forties and married to her job. She was more than capable of running the bar and Jack knew it and exploited it. 'You're too good to him,' I said. 'Jack takes advantage of your good nature.'

She smiled and picked up another glass, began drying. 'Quite the reverse, Harry. Jack was there for me when I needed him most; when that lowlife of a husband ran out on me for that blond slut from Abaco. If he hadn't offered me this job I would have probably blown my brains out. So I don't mind if he takes liberties now and then.'

It was obvious from the way she spoke about him that Pilar's affection for Jack Dylan ran deep.

'And he didn't say where he was going?'

She shook her head.

I left *The Tar* and set off back to the hotel.

*   *   *

Ray Burgess met me in the foyer. 'Ah, the wanderer returns,' he said. 'You're getting very popular. People in and out here all the time asking for you, dear boy.'

'Oh?' I said. 'Who exactly?'

'Reynolds for one, breathing fire. He was ranting about the illegal discharge of firearms down at your harbour last night. Seems to think you had something to do with it.'

'Only in as much that we were the targets. Go on, who else?'

'Well, there were three of them. Cubans, I think. They seemed very keen to find you. They even wanted to search your room.'

'And of course you let them,' I said with a smile.

'Normally, Harry, I would have done,' Ray said with heavy irony. 'But Reynolds arrived just as they were making the request — quite forcibly, I might add — and they ran out of steam and seemed to melt into the walls. One minute they were there and then they'd gone. Great disappearing trick. I might sign them up for the Saturday cabaret. My guests could do with something new to watch.'

'Anyone else?' I said.

'I saved the best 'til last. *The Lady of Pain* herself.'

'Katy?'

'Correct. In fact you've not long missed her.'

'How long?'

'Ten minutes. No more.'

'Did she say if she'd be back?'

Ray shrugged. 'She may have done. I was called away before she left. You could ask Jill on reception. She was talking to her last time I looked.'

'No, I'll pass. It's not important.'

I made my way to my room feeling even gloomier than I had on *The Lady*. The Cubans were still after me;

Reynolds would probably arrest me the next time he saw me, and now Katy was back. She was the last person I wanted to see, and yet I couldn't suppress a stab of disappointment that I'd missed her.

I took an ice cold shower. It didn't help.

I'd told Ray Burgess that as far as anyone else was concerned I wasn't here. I'd found a mooring for *The Lady* in the Port Lucaya Marina, tucked between a 70-foot Vitech and a Lagoon 620 catamaran unimaginatively named *Ocean Spray*. I hoped the larger hulls would hide *The Lady* from view, even though the bullet holes were something of a talking point, but I'd take my chances. Mooring her at my private harbour would have been the equivalent of announcing my presence back on the island with flashing neon lights and a marching band.

I rummaged through the clothes I had left and found a pair of dun-coloured chinos and an ancient *Guns n' Roses* T-shirt. I dressed quickly and left the hotel by the rear exit. My route took me via the kitchens and I had to endure some curious stares from the staff as I made my way through, but I was out of there soon enough and heading down to *Louis' Oyster Bar*.

I hadn't gone there to eat, but I knew *Louis'* was the hang out of Leo Diamond, a one-time business associate of Alan's until they had a falling out over money. I'd never liked Diamond and suspected the feeling was mutual. These days he was little more than a petty criminal; acting as a fence mostly for many of the other petty criminals on the Islands, but his intelligence network was huge. It needed to be to keep him one step ahead of the authorities.

37

I spotted him at once, standing at a slot machine, feeding in coins and hitting buttons, his face illuminated by the flashing lights. He had a thin, bony frame and a pointed, weasel face with eyes that were never still, flicking this way and that, always alert, always on the lookout for the next angle, the next scam, or the next knife in the back. I came up beside him. 'Hello, Leo. Can we talk?'

'What have *we* got to talk about?' he said as he slid another coin into the slot.

'This and that. What are you drinking?'

'Scotch,' he said. 'A large one. And a real one, not one of those God-awful blends.'

'Okay. And then can we talk?'

He turned his weasel-face towards me and smiled thinly. 'Yeah. Why the hell not?'

I managed to peel him away from the money-hungry machine and found us a booth at the back of the bar. When a waitress approached he called her over and ordered clam chowder. 'He's paying,' he said, nodding in my direction.

Alice, the waitress, scowled. 'Is that right, Harry?' she said, not taking her eyes off him for a second.

'It's okay, Alice. I'll get this.'

'You eating, Harry?' she said.

'Not this time.'

As she wheeled away from the table she leaned into me. 'He'd put me off *my* food too,' she whispered.

'You don't seem very popular around here,' I said when we were alone again.

Diamond took a sip of his whisky and shrugged. 'Do I give a fuck?' he said. 'So, what do you want to talk about? As if I couldn't guess.'

'Then you heard about Alan Lancaster's family?'

'I heard.'

'Any thoughts?'

'Anna Lancaster was a bitch. She had it coming.'

'And did their seven-year-old daughter "have it coming" as well?'

He didn't look in any way repentant, but he kept his tongue.

'And Alan?' I said.

'What about him?'

'Any idea where he might be?'

Diamond shrugged. 'Who the hell cares?'

His whisky arrived and he took a sip. 'Good scotch,' he said.

'You and Alan used to have quite a close working relationship. You must have known him well.'

Diamond smiled. 'Better than most.'

'Then what can you tell me about him that will help me track him down?'

He stared deep into the bottom of his whisky glass. 'You two have been the best of friends for years,' he said. 'Why are you asking me?'

'You have contacts. You hear things.'

He took another mouthful of scotch, savouring it for a moment before swallowing, and then he drained the glass. 'I'll have another,' he said.

I called Alice over. She took his glass and scowled at him.

'Yeah,' he said. 'I hear things; useful things. Things that can make me money. All information has a price.'

'So you *do* know something.'

He leaned back in his seat, narrowing his eyes to look at me. I could almost see the wheels of his crooked little brain spinning, calculating how much I was prepared to pay for what he knew.

'I know lots of things,' he said. 'But why the hell should I tell you any of them? I'll put my cards on the table for you. I've never liked you. In fact I'd go so far as to say I hated your guts. When I was doing business with Alan I got sick of hearing your name. The great Harry Beck, Alan Lancaster's moral compass. I lost count of the number of deals that either went belly up or never got off the ground in the first place, all because he didn't want to do anything you might disapprove of. Saint fucking Harry! I would have made a fortune if it wasn't for you.'

'My heart bleeds,' I said. 'But you overestimate my influence. Alan would use me as a sounding board sometimes, that's all; but all the decisions he made were his own.'

'That's a crock of shit, and you know it,' Diamond said.

Alice brought the chowder and another scotch. 'Sure I can't get you anything, Harry?' she said.

'No. I'm fine.'

I watched him eat. 'How much?' I said.

The spoon hovered at his lips for a moment, and then he shook his head and took another mouthful of clam. 'Not for sale,' he said once he'd swallowed. 'Not to you anyway.'

'A hundred dollars,' I said.

He smiled and dabbed at his lips with a napkin.

'Two?'

He dropped the napkin on the table and took another mouthful of the chowder.

'I know things about Alan Lancaster that would take your breath away. You think you know him? I tell you; you know squat. You know fuck all about the great Alan Lancaster.'

'But you're not prepared to tell me?'

'I'll eat your food; I'll drink your liquor. But don't think you've entered into some kind of contract with me. I owe you nothing...less than nothing.'

'The other day,' I said. 'I watched a young girl and her mother blown to bits in their car.'

'What would you like me to do? Weep? Tear my hair out? It's your problem. Deal with it.'

I picked up a fork from the table and rammed it into the back of his hand, pinning it down. 'Tell me what you know,' I said, bringing my face to within inches of his and leaning down heavily on the fork.

Leo Diamond squealed, like a pig rutting.

'You crazy fuck!' he gasped.

I pressed harder.

Louis was at the table in seconds, summoned by the noise.

He looked at Leo Diamond's face contorted in agony, and then at the fork, drawing blood now from Diamond's hand. Finally he looked at me.

'Do you want fries with that, Harry?'

I nearly laughed out loud,

'Leo here seems reluctant to talk to me.' I twisted the fork. Diamond squirmed in his seat and squealed again.

'Do you want to take this outside, Harry?' Louis said. 'He's upsetting my customers.'

'In a moment. Once he tells me what he knows about Alan.' I could feel the tines of the fork grinding against bone.

Leo stared up at Louis, tears moistening his eyes.

'Make him stop, man.'

'If I were you I'd start talking,' Louis said.

Sweat was beading on Leo Diamond's forehead and trickling down his face. 'Serena Carr,' he gasped.

'The singer? How does she figure in all this?'

'Alan's mistress.'

I felt the blood rushing to my face. 'No,' I said. 'That's crap.' I pressed down harder.

'It's true,' Diamond said, his hand clamping on mine, trying to pull it away. 'He was fucking her. She'll know where he is.'

I held on to the fork for a few seconds more, pressed it as hard as I could, before finally letting it go. It pinned his hand to the table. Leo Diamond threw himself back in his seat, holding his bloodied hand with his good one. His eyes were wild and curses were flying from his lips in a torrent.

I got to my feet. 'Sorry about that, Louis,' I said.

Louis shrugged.

'He might need a Band-Aid.'

'I'll deal with it, Harry.'

I pulled out a couple of bills and pushed them into the pocket of Louis' shirt. 'For the food and drink,' I said.

Once outside I leaned against the wall of the bar feeling nauseous, but I couldn't say now whether it was because of the damage I'd inflicted on Leo Diamond's hand, or because I'd unearthed yet another revelation about Alan. I lit a cigarette and smoked it through before pushing myself away from the wall and heading back to the hotel. I needed to sleep on this.

38

The next morning as I walked through the thrumming streets of Freeport, I thought about Serena Carr.

I had seen her perform a couple of times when she was providing the cabaret at Alan's *Blue Moonlight* hotel. She was a striking-looking woman, almost six feet tall and built like a gazelle. Her parentage was mixed which showed in her coffee-coloured skin and the tight black curls of her hair, and she had a voice that dripped honey. Her style when performing was that of a nineteen-thirties torch singer; the way she moved around the stage and caressed the microphone stand was lazily seductive. When I met her off stage she was completely different; warm and open, with a ready laugh and a very quick wit. If it was true that she was Alan's mistress then I could certainly understand the attraction.

Tracking her down was fairly easy. She had a residency at the *Scarlet Parrot,* a nightspot on Count Basie Square in Port Lucaya. I grabbed a taxi to take me there. I didn't want to be a target out on the streets any more than I had to be. I had no idea if it was just the three Cubans that were after me, or if there were others.

The *Scarlet Parrot* was set in a colonial-style building

overlooking the square, with décor that really only came into its own at night. During the daylight hours it looked too bright and garish.

A piano was playing a jazzy rendition of *Night and Day*. Serena Carr was draped across the piano dressed in a khaki T-shirt and green shorts, a crimson bandana covering her hair. A cigarette was smouldering in an ashtray at her elbow, next to it a long glass half filled with ice and rum. Any of her fans used to seeing her in the sophisticated, slinky silk outfits she wore for her act wouldn't have recognised her. Until she started to sing, which she did a few seconds after I entered.

I sat down at one of the empty tables and let her run through the song. My questions could wait until she had finished. Even in rehearsal she was a mesmerising performer, moving smoothly through the key changes. Finding a new interpretation of the lyrics to such an old standard seemed effortless and she made the song her own. When she finished I applauded. Two hands clapping in an empty club during the day was probably not the ovation she was used to. She looked across at me sharply. 'This is a private rehearsal,' she said.

'Sorry,' I said. 'I didn't mean to intrude.'

The piano player got to his feet. He was huge, biceps bulging through the thin cotton of his white shirt. 'Want me to get rid of him for you, Serena?'

Serena was looking at me closely. 'It's okay, Jerry. I think I know him. Harry, right? Harry Beck?'

'I didn't think you'd remember.'

She stepped down from the stage and crossed the room in three quick strides. She was not only built like a gazelle but she moved like one as well. She pulled out a chair and sat down at my table, crossing her long legs.

'What can I do for you, Harry?' she said.

'I'm looking for Alan.'

She didn't ask which Alan I meant. She knew. She

glanced back at the piano player. 'Take five, Jerry. And can you get me another rum? What are you drinking, Harry?'

'Too early for me,' I said.

'Club soda? I don't like drinking alone.'

'Yeah, fine.'

She relayed the order to Jerry who strolled across to the bar, went behind it and helped himself to the drinks.

Once he'd set them down on the table and made himself scarce she focussed all her attention on me, the chocolate brown eyes boring into mine. 'So what makes you think I know where he is?'

'Someone told me you two were an item.'

'*Were* being the operative word in that sentence.'

'You mean you're no longer together.'

She picked up her glass and raised it to her lips, taking a sip of the rum. 'This is really none of your business you know.'

'He's in trouble, Serena.'

'Serious?'

'About as serious as it gets. I think some people are trying to kill him.'

'You're kidding me.' She pulled a packet of cigarettes from the pocket of her shorts, lit one and let the smoke trickle out of her nostrils. 'Tell me about it,' she said.

I told her everything that had happened so far. When I'd finished there were tears in her eyes. 'That poor child,' she said. 'He adored Sally. He always carried a picture of her in his wallet. She meant everything to him.'

'How long were you two together?'

'Four years. Since I worked at the *Moonlight*. Understand, Harry, I didn't set out to have an affair with him, or him with me for that matter. It just sorta happened.'

Jerry was back, sitting at the piano vamping a few chords and laying some lead lines over the top of them. He kept glancing across at us, glaring daggers at me, softening his gaze when he looked at Serena.

'So when did you split up?'

'Two weeks ago. It came out of nowhere. I thought we were happy. Oh, I knew he was a married man and there was never going to be any long-term future in the relationship, but I wasn't expecting it to end quite that suddenly. I remember it was a Thursday night. He arrived here and went straight backstage to my dressing room. That was unusual because he'd normally sit and watch the set. Afterwards we'd go for dinner somewhere or maybe just grab a drink before heading back to my place. But this night, this Thursday, I saw him come in to the club, and then saw him disappearing out back. I suppose I knew then something was wrong. I found it hard to focus after that and I cut the encore and went back to see what was wrong.'

She lit another cigarette. This time I joined her.

39

'He'd been drinking. I found him in the dressing room, sitting in a chair, his head in his hands. He told me he'd had a blazing row with Jack Dylan and the two of them had parted on very bad terms. I asked him what the argument was about, but he wouldn't say. When he took his hands away from his face I saw he'd been weeping. That image burned its way into my mind, Harry. I'd never seen Alan cry before. He was always so fun-loving, so tough. He never seemed to have a care in the world. And then he dropped the bombshell. He told me it was over, him and me, over. Then it was my turn to cry.'

She reached across and grabbed my hand, squeezing tightly. Jerry at the piano noticed and fired a couple of thermo-nuclear missiles at me with his eyes. I flinched involuntarily and gave all my attention to Serena.

'Did he give a reason for the break up?'

'Yes, but it made no kind of sense at all. He just kept repeating that he wouldn't be able to protect me anymore. I tried telling him that I didn't need protection, that I was more than capable of taking care of myself, but he wouldn't listen. I asked him who he was protecting me from, but he just said I didn't want to know. He kissed me goodbye and left.'

'And have you seen him since?'

She shook her head and wiped a tear away from her eye. 'This thing you told me; the kids, the photos...I can't believe Alan's involved in anything like that. It's just not him.'

'Yeah,' I said. 'That's what people keep telling me. So why is he missing and why did he leave me the memory stick with all that damning information on it? If he's not involved, then how did he get his hands on it in the first place?'

'Come on, Harry, you know him, probably better than I do. Do *you* think he's capable of such a thing?'

I looked her directly in the eye. 'I've been asking myself the same question for the past few days and the answer is, I don't know. I really don't know anymore. The Alan I grew up with has vanished and all I'm left with are doubts and uncertainties. The question is, do you ever know anyone as well as you think you do?'

Serena finally managed a smile, though it was a rueful one. 'In my case, probably not. But you, Harry, it's different. You've been friends for years. He left *you* the evidence, not Jack or his wife, or the police for that matter. He left *you* with it, so he must believe in you, even if your faith in him has been shaken. He must trust you to do the right thing. He gave you the memory stick. I think it was a cry for help.'

She squeezed my hand. Even tighter this time. 'Help him, Harry. Find him and help him.'

I squeezed back, ignoring Jerry and his lethal looks. 'I'll try, Serena. I'll try. I just seem to be running around in circles and getting nowhere. Are you going to be all right?'

She shrugged. 'I'll be okay.'

'Maybe you should keep a low profile for a while. Until this gets resolved.'

'That's difficult in my line of work, and a girl's got to eat. Besides I've got Jerry. He has a rather protective attitude towards me.'

I glanced across at him. He glowered back. 'I'd noticed.'

'He likes to look out for his kid sister.'

Understanding dawned. I smiled. 'Yes,' I said. 'I can see that.' I got up to leave. She walked with me to the door. 'Who told you?' she said. 'About Alan and me?'

'A piece of scum called Leo Diamond. You know him?'

She shuddered. 'Pond life,' she said. 'He saw us together once. I never did trust him to keep his mouth shut.' She pulled open the door. 'How much did you have to pay him for the information?'

'Nothing,' I said. 'I found a way to persuade him to part with it.'

She read between the lines. 'Then watch your back, Harry. He's a vindictive little slug. I know how his mind works. He'll try to get even with you.'

'I'll be careful,' I said.

'Yes, do,' she said and kissed my cheek. 'I have a feeling Alan's depending on you to come through for him.'

'I'm staying at *The Lucayan Star*,' I said. 'If you need me, or if you hear from Alan, you can reach me there. But I'd appreciate it if you'd keep that piece of information to yourself. There are certain people looking for me that I'd rather avoid for the moment.'

'Of course,' she said. 'I understand.'

I walked out of the *Scarlet Parrot* feeling like the weight of the entire world had suddenly decided to roost on my shoulders for a while. *Thanks for that, Serena*, I thought as I hailed a cab and climbed inside.

Another dead end.

How many more would I hit before I finally found my friend?

40

I arrived back at the hotel to see Katy waiting for me in the lobby. I'd entered the hotel the same way I'd left it, through the kitchens, so she didn't see me. She was sitting in the reception area, ankles demurely crossed, skimming through a copy of *Vogue* and, at the same time, watching the front doors. I came in behind her and took the elevator straight up to my room.

I kicked off my shoes and flopped down onto the bed, pulling out the list Billie had printed off for me. I propped myself up on the pillow and began to run through the names again.

The name I had spotted before leapt off the page at me again. I still found it hard to believe it was there. It was the reason I didn't want to see Katy. If I saw her and I told her what had been going on since Alan disappeared, I would have to tell her that her father, Max Donahoe, was a paedophile, signed up as a client of a child pornography ring. As much as I was still angry with her, she didn't deserve that. If she was as psychologically damaged as her father had said, the news could break her, and I didn't want that on my conscience.

There was a tap at the door.

'Who is it?'

'Ray.'

I let him in.

'She's here again,' he said as he walked in. He obviously disapproved of my trying to avoid her. He was delightfully old fashioned about courtesy, was Ray.

'I know. I saw her when I arrived.'

'Are you sure you don't want me to send her up? You can't avoid her forever.'

'Ray' I said. 'You're a good friend, but you're not my moral guardian.'

He looked slightly hurt. 'I don't mean to interfere, Harry...but you and Katy, you just seemed so right together.'

'I never had you figured as a romantic, Ray.'

'I'm not. If I was I'd still be married. But I let Jane slip through my fingers, and I can tell you now, it was the biggest bloody mistake of my life. I'd hate to see you make a similar one.'

'Katy and I are finished, and have been for years. You remember the hell she put me through?'

'Yes, I do. I also remember a very stubborn man who was so determined to build up his charter business that he became single-minded to the point of obsession. I didn't say it at the time, but you couldn't really blame Katy for finding comfort in the arms of other men.'

He'd touched a nerve and I wheeled on him. 'No, I *could* understand that. I could even understand that I had neglected her, badly. What I couldn't understand was the sheer volume of men it took to make her feel better. If someone had told me she had slept with the entire Boston Symphony Orchestra I wouldn't have been surprised. It was humiliating.'

'Ah,' Ray said. 'So it was your pride more than anything else that was damaged.'

I shook my head. 'You don't get it, do you?' I went to

172

the mini-bar and took out of miniature of scotch, unscrewing the cap and swallowing the lot in one gulp.

'That's a lot of names,' he said.

I turned. Ray was standing by the bed, the list in his hand.

'There're some very heavy rollers on here. What is it?

'My Christmas card list,' I said and held out my hand.

'In other words, it's none of my business.' He handed the list back to me.

'No, Ray, it's not,' I said as I folded it and dropped it onto the nightstand.

'I saw Katy's father on the list. Is this anything to do with Alan's disappearance and the bomb that killed Anna and poor little Sally?'

'Ray, I'm going to give you the same advice that someone gave me the other day. Stay out of it. You really don't want to get involved.'

'And did *you* take that advice?'

I said nothing.

'I thought not. Tell me about it, Harry. I'm watching you chasing your tail, driven out of your home, the police wanting to interview you, nasty looking characters demanding to search your room. No man's an island, Harry.'

'And no man should be allowed to spout clichés like that,' I said.

He smiled ruefully. 'Point taken,' he said. 'But talk to me, Harry. Tell me what's going on.'

With a sigh I sat down on the bed. 'Okay. But for the moment you keep it to yourself. What I'm about to say doesn't leave this room.'

'You have my word.' Ray pulled up a chair and I went through the story again. To be honest I was sick of repeating it, because every time I did it reminded me that I knew so little about everything. It made me feel inadequate.

Once I'd finished, Ray leaned back in the chair and closed his eyes. As if digesting what I'd just told him. Finally he sat forward. 'Well, the answer's obvious. You go and see Reynolds and lay it all out for him. Tell him everything you've just told me. That way you relieve yourself of the burden and you put this into the hands of people much better equipped to investigate it.'

I shook my head. 'That would be the sensible thing to do, Ray, but I can't do it. At least not until I've spoken to Alan.'

'Then that tells me everything I need to know. There's still a part of you that believes in Alan's innocence. You're not prepared to throw him to the wolves.'

'Until I've heard his side of the story then no, no I'm not.'

He rose from the chair and went across to the mini bar, helping himself to a Coke. He popped the tab and took a long swill. 'Let me help,' he said.

'I don't see there's much you can do. Besides, you *are* helping me; letting me stay here, protecting my anonymity. Just keep the wolves at bay for me a little longer. That would be a great help.'

'Yeah, yeah, I'll do all that as a matter of course. But I can help in other ways. I know a lot of people both here on the Islands and in the US. You'd be amazed at the number of people that pass through this hotel. Important people, people of influence. I've met these people, got to know them. I facilitate their stay in the Bahamas. I provide certain services and I cover up their indiscretions.'

'You're making yourself sound like a pimp.'

'And to a certain extent I am. A very highly paid one though. At least let me make a few phone calls. Pull in a few favours. I can't promise anything, but you never know.'

'I don't see how that's going to help me find Alan. He's gone to ground. He could be anywhere on the Islands. He could have gone to Cuba, Haiti, Florida…anywhere.'

'So you haven't got the resources to hunt him down.

The people I know have, and they can do it discreetly.'

I looked at him for a long moment. Another revelation, another shock to my belief system. I had been friends with Ray Burgess for the best part of twenty years, but now I was slowly coming to terms with the fact that I really didn't know anyone very well at all, and the reason for that was mostly down to me. I had been too absorbed in my own life to really look into the lives of those around me to see what was going on under the surface.

'Okay,' I said. 'I'll keep your offer in mind. If I need to take you up on it I will. And thanks.'

He smiled. 'At last! A breakthrough. You don't have to fight the world on your own, you know? Sometimes it pays to reach out to others.'

'Okay, okay, don't labour the point. It doesn't mean I've gone soft.'

'Perish the thought,' Ray said. 'Perish the thought. Now I'm going to go downstairs and send Katy up.'

I opened my mouth to protest, but he silenced me with a wave of his hand. 'You need a clear head if you're going to resolve this, and you can't do that with your past love life hovering in the background ready to floor you when you least expect it. See Katy and get it sorted out once and for all.'

41

A short while later there was a knock at the door. Katy stood there looking radiant and I felt my stomach lurch. I tried to keep control, but it was a fight I was always going to lose. From the moment we first met I discovered that Katy Donahoe had the ability to turn me to jelly without even trying. She was a powerfully sensual woman and my body, if not my mind, responded to her sensuality every time.

'Come in,' I said.

She wafted past me in a cloud of *Eternity*, a scent that roused even more memories from their graves.

'I've come to apologise,' she said without preamble.

'Really? What for?'

She dropped to the bed and sat, legs crossed. 'Any chance of a drink?'

'Sure.' I crouched down in front of the mini bar and opened the door. 'Gin and tonic?'

'Yeah, fine.'

'I can't run to ice and a slice,' I said. 'But it's pretty cold anyway.' I poured the contents of a miniature gin into a glass and handed it to her along with a small can of Indian tonic water.

Maynard Sims

'So' I said. 'What are you apologising for? I should be apologising to you for holding you at gunpoint the last time we met.'

She waved that away. 'I need to apologise for my father and that ridiculous offer he made you.' She poured a small amount of tonic water into the glass, took a sip, shuddered and poured more tonic.

'Oh?'

'I mean, it's ridiculous. You? Running a casino? Can you imagine? I don't know what he was thinking.'

I pulled up a chair, flipped it round and sat astride it. It was obvious she had more to say. 'Go on,' I said.

'I mean, you're Harry Beck, man of the sea, the Hemmingway-styled adventurer. Can you imagine yourself dressed up like a penguin tending to the needs of high rollers and blue-rinsed slot junkies? I can't. I can't ever remember seeing you in a suit. The whole concept just doesn't gel in my head.'

'Well, thanks for the vote of confidence,' I said.

She took another mouthful of gin and shook her head. 'Oh, don't get defensive, Harry. You know the idea is patently dumb.'

I went back to the mini bar and found myself a tiny bottle of rum. I poured it into a glass and went back to my seat. 'Is that all you came here for, to tell me how inept you think I'd be running one of your father's casinos?'

A frown crossed her pretty forehead. 'Well, yes. What other reason would I have to be here?'

'I thought your dad might have mentioned the other part of his proposal. The bit where we married and I made an honest woman of you.'

She'd just taken another swig of gin, but it exploded from her mouth in a spray and she coughed. 'He suggested what?'

'That we get married. I don't think running the casino for an obscene amount of money and a seat on the board

177

was dependent on it, but I kind of figured it might be a factor in my long term association with his company.'

She placed her glass down on the nightstand and stood, crossing to the window and staring out. 'The conniving old bastard,' she said, almost to herself. 'What else did he say?'

She saw my shrug reflected in the window. She wheeled round. 'Come on, Harry, don't be coy. You might as well tell me because if you don't I'll squeeze it out of him when I get back to *The Minotaur*.'

'Very well,' I said. 'He told me how you had a breakdown when you finished with me and how he had you committed.'

That got to her. Two spots of colour appeared at her cheeks and her nostrils flared. 'How dare he? My breakdown had nothing, nothing whatever to do with you.'

'He told me you were hooked on heroin as well. Maybe that had something to do with it.'

Katy then did something that surprised and shocked me. She started to cry. As the tears rolled down her cheek she spun back to the window. 'Don't look at me,' she said. 'Don't look at me!'

I came up behind her and slipped my arms around her waist. I felt her tense. 'I'm sorry,' I said. 'I didn't mean to make you cry.'

I kissed the back of her neck. I just couldn't help myself. It was the perfume and old memories conspiring against my better judgement. She turned in my arms and her lips found mine. The next few minutes were an exquisite mixture of passion, urgency and comedy as we fumbled like excited teenagers with each other's buttons and tried to divest each other of our clothes. We tumbled backwards onto the bed and lay there semi-clothed, laughing hysterically. Finally we kissed again and then made love.

The years seemed to slip away as we rediscovered each other's bodies, remembering all the sensitive areas, all the erogenous zones that turned us on.

We climaxed simultaneously, a feat I'd only ever achieved with Katy, and lay there, spent.

Eventually she said, 'That shouldn't have happened. I'm going to regret it.'

'Thanks.'

'No, seriously, Harry. So will you.'

'I doubt it.'

She shook her head. 'Do you have a cigarette?'

I rolled from the bed and found the pack in my shirt. I lit two and handed one to her, then I lay back beside her, stroking her hair and smoking my cigarette. The room, like the rest of the hotel was non-smoking, but we'd just burst through so many taboos it hardly seemed to matter.

We ground out our cigarettes in a saucer and then she kissed me again. It was a kiss of such gentleness and tenderness it took my breath away. The moment, as we lay there, was perfect, absolutely perfect.

So why I decided then to blow the moment to bits I'll never know.

42

'We have to talk about your father,' I said, all my good intentions to spare her the truth disappearing like snow in a furnace.

'I've apologised for that.'

'No, not the job, or the marriage thing. There's something else.'

'What?'

I fished for the list on the nightstand where I'd dropped it earlier. I unfolded it and let her see it.

'What is this?'

'It's part of the reason why Alan's disappeared. It's a list of names that have one thing in common. They have all purchased children for the purpose of sex. Children who have been taken from their homes and turned into sex slaves.'

'That's disgusting.'

'Read the names,' I said.

She ran a slim finger down the list and stopped suddenly. 'But my father's name's here.'

'Yes,' I said. 'I know...and I thought you needed to know too.'

She said nothing for a moment. She dropped the list on the bed, sat up and swung her feet to the floor.

'Do you know something, Harry?'

I looked at her expectantly.

'You are the biggest piece of scum I've ever had the misfortune to meet.'

She started to pull her clothes on.

'I thought you had a *right* to know,' I said as I watched her button her shirt.

'But you thought you'd fuck me first before dropping the bombshell. Christ! I can't believe you suckered me.' Tears pressed out from her eyes again. She wiped them away impatiently with the back of her hand. 'No, I'm not going to cry again. I refuse to let you get to me like this.' She pulled on her jeans and walked to the door. 'Let me tell you one thing, Harry before I leave. I love my father very deeply and I know him well. Very well. Whatever you think you have there on that list, you're wrong. You're so wrong it's almost laughable. He would never, ever be involved with something like that.'

'So how did his name get on this list?'

'I don't know and I don't particularly care. But get this through your head. I never want to set eyes on you again. Ever.'

She yanked opened the door and stepped outside. Without even looking back she slammed it behind her.

I lay back against the pillow. Sometimes I didn't like myself very much. In fact, sometimes I hated myself.

With a sigh I got up and dressed.

A moment later there was a knock at the door.

Ok, I thought, she's calmed down and has come back to talk about this reasonably.

As I pulled it open a huge fist hurtled in behind it, connecting with my chin and lifting me off the floor. I tumbled backwards landing in an undignified heap a yard away from the foot of the bed. I fought to stay conscious although every instinct I possessed was screaming at me to close my eyes and sink into the beckoning black chasm of unconsciousness. A shadow passed in front of my vision. I blinked and looked up into the unsmiling, coffee-coloured face of Jerry Carr.

'Get up, Mr Beck,' he said.

'Why? So you can knock me down again?' I tried to look around him, still ridiculously hoping to see Katy in the doorway, but he was too big, too broad. Perhaps if she were here it might be an antidote to the tension I could see bunching in his shoulders.

'Just get up, or I'll pull you up.'

His voice was educated, cultured, not what I was expecting.

I struggled to my feet. 'What's all this about?' I said, and he hit me again; this time in the stomach, knocking all the wind out of me. I thought I was going to vomit, and then I thought I was going to pass out. Maybe I'd do both. Anything to avoid being hit again. Jerry Carr had fists like club hammers and they hurt.

I put my hands up in a gesture of surrender. 'Just tell me what you want,' I said, still glancing around him; still no Katy. Christ! What did I expect? I'd just told her that her father was a paedophile. Did I really expect her to forgive me and come running back to my arms?

What Jerry Carr said next drove all the thoughts of my argument with Katy from my mind.

'They've taken Serena,' he said, balling his fists, ready to strike again.

'Who's taken Serena?'

For a second something flickered in the big man's eyes. Uncertainty? Fear? I couldn't pin it down. 'The men who were looking for you. They arrived at the club fifteen minutes after you left. Cubans. One of them, the smaller one, kept me talking and the big one blindsided me. They took Serena. Said if I wanted to see her alive again I had to bring you to them. You for her. That's the deal. So, get on your feet. We have an appointment.'

'I don't feel like travelling at the moment,' I said.

'You don't have a choice,' he said and pulled a gun from the waistband of his pants. 'I'm getting my sister back. Now, get on your feet!'

I was looking for something smart to say; something to buy me a little more time. There was a noise that sounded like a baseball bat hitting a melon. Jerry Carr's eyes rolled in his head and he sank to his knees. He swayed there for a moment before pitching face first onto the carpet.

Ray Burgess stood in the doorway, a fire extinguisher in his hands. 'Is he dead?' he said.

I reached across and felt for a pulse in Jerry's neck. It was there, strong and steady. 'He's alive.'

'That's a relief. I thought I'd killed him.' He set the fire extinguisher down on the floor. 'I saw Katy storming out of here in tears. I figured the reunion hadn't gone well and *you* might need a shoulder to cry on.'

'Perfect timing, Ray. Perfect timing. Now help me tie him up.'

43

We tied Jerry Carr to a chair. The bonds were not particularly tight and I had a feeling that if he used all of his considerable strength he could have broken them; but Jerry looked defeated. He sat slumped in the chair, hopeless tears coursing down his cheeks.

'I love that girl so much. She's an angel...*my* angel. When she was just thirteen years old she was singing in concerts and do you know what she did with all the money she earned from her singing? She put it into a fund to help put me through college. She believed in me. She thought I had the talent to go all the way, to become a concert pianist. She used to say I'd be the first black Arthur Rubenstein, and man, she used to sing her heart out at those concerts. How could they just take her like that?'

'We'll get her back,' I said with a confidence I certainly didn't feel. 'Where were you meant to take me?'

He sniffed, trying to stifle the tears. 'A warehouse down by Freeport Harbour.'

'I don't understand why they just didn't come here and take you themselves,' Ray said. 'They were here yesterday. They knew this was where you were staying. Why go though this performance?'

'I think you'll have to ask the person employing them that question,' I said. 'How did they know I was here in the first place? I certainly haven't advertised my presence.'

'Well you haven't exactly made a secret of it either,' Ray said. 'Reynolds knew you were here after all.'

I walked across to the window and stared out. From here I could see the ocean and I longed to be out on it. I yearned for the freedom of that empty expanse of blue. I was beginning to wonder if I'd ever experience that peace and quiet, that solitude again.

'You've got to help me,' Jerry Carr said. 'You have to help Serena. She doesn't deserve this.'

'No,' I said. 'She doesn't.' I turned to Ray. 'Untie him.'

Ray was standing in the corner of the room, examining Jerry's gun. He tossed it on the bed. 'It's fake,' he said. 'A replica.'

'You're not very good at this, are you?' I said to Jerry.

He lowered his head. 'The gun isn't mine. *They* gave it to me. I protect Serena the best I can. My size is usually enough. People have told me I look intimidating,' he said. 'But I'm a piano player. I'm not a fighter. Never have been.'

'You pack a mighty punch though,' I said, rubbing my aching chin. 'So how come you never made it to the concert platform? Why are you slumming it in night clubs when you could be at Carnegie Hall?'

'Arthritis in the hands. It hit me in my third year at Julliard. Every time I had a recital I had to have a bucket of ice next to the piano. Every chance I had I'd plunge my hands into the ice to kill the pain. I realised then that I could never make it to the level Serena wanted for me. I'd never make a living on the concert stage. A couple of forty-five minute sets a night is about all I can manage before my fingers start to burn.' Ray had finished untying him. He stood and stretched his arms and legs. Then he lunged at me, catching me off guard. His heavily muscled arm was around my throat, constricting my windpipe.

'Oh, crap,' Ray said.

'I'll break his neck, I swear,' Jerry said.

'Okay, okay,' Ray said. 'Calm down.'

Meanwhile my face was slowly turning blue as the air was cut off by Jerry's forearm. I felt my head start to spin and lights were flashing in front of my eyes. I let my body sag, making him support my entire weight. It made the choking worse for a second, but when I heard him grunt with the effort of holding me up I drove my elbow into his stomach. The air gushed out of him in a rush and he relaxed his grip on my throat. I hit him again and managed to break free.

My first instinct was to turn and smash him in the mouth, but I knew he wasn't thinking straight. He was driven by the desperate need to save his sister, and I couldn't really blame him. I pushed him in the chest and he sat down heavily on the bed, blowing hard.

'Right,' I said. 'We're going to get Serena back, okay?' I wasn't sure he was hearing me. 'Jerry!' He looked up at me with a dazed expression on his face. 'We're going to get her back. Understand?'

He nodded his head slowly.

'Good. Now listen, we'll play this as if everything's gone according to plan. You'll take me, at gunpoint, to the warehouse and hand me over to the Cubans. Then you take Serena and get the hell out of there.'

'And you really expect the Cubans to let Jerry and his little sister walk away?' Ray said to me.

'Why shouldn't they? It's me they want.'

'Oh grow up, Harry,' he said tiredly. 'They're not just going to let them stroll out of there. They're material witnesses. They've seen their faces.'

'So what's *your* plan?' I said.

'I don't have one. I'm just pointing out the flaws in

yours.'

'Thanks,' I said. 'That helps a bunch.'

'But there is a way out of this.'

'Enlighten me.'

'I tried earlier, but you blew that suggestion out of the water.'

'I'm not involving Reynolds.'

'Harry, it's the only way. This isn't just about you and Alan anymore. Innocent people are at risk. The longer this goes on more and more people are going to get hurt, or worse, killed. Speak to Reynolds. Tell him what's happened to Serena. Let the police hit the warehouse and clean up this mess.'

I shook my head; not to dismiss Ray's suggestion, but to clear away the cobwebs. So far in this whole affair I'd been reacting to things being hurled at me. I had no plan, no strategy. I was letting other people call the shots and in doing so was running around in ever decreasing circles. I was no closer to finding Alan; no closer to making the world a safer place for those I cared about. With the Cubans off the streets I had one less thing to worry over. Ray was right. Reynolds was my only real option. I went to the phone and asked the operator to put me through to the police station.

'Mr Beck,' Reynolds said. 'I'd just about given up on you. I have a lot of questions. Are you going to come here or shall I come to you at the hotel?'

'There's been a development. I need your help,' I said.

There was a long pause on the other end of the line. Finally Reynolds said, 'Interesting. That's the last thing I expected you to say. Would you care to tell me what this *development* is?'

I took a deep breath, a very deep breath, and told him.

44

I could almost hear Hector Reynolds thinking on the other end of the line; weighing up his options, working out which course of action would provide him with the most advantageous outcome. I heard him take a breath. 'Well obviously Ms Carr's safety has to be paramount,' he said. 'How long do we have before you're due at the warehouse?'

I glanced back at Jerry, sitting on the bed, still staring into space, looking into his own personal hell. 'What time are we expected at the warehouse?' I said to him.

He jerked back to reality. 'Eight o'clock. They said to be there at eight.'

I checked my watch. 'We're due there in two hours,' I said.

'It doesn't give us much time,' Reynolds said. 'Still it should be enough for me to get this organized. Give me thirty minutes and I'll call you back. Where can I reach you?'

'I'll call you,' I said.

I thought I heard him chuckle quietly. 'As you wish, Mr Beck. Thirty minutes.'

'Well?' Ray said as I cradled the receiver.

'I think he's going to help. He needs half an hour to organize things. I'm ringing him back.'

The mini bar was calling again. I felt in need of something alcoholic, but knew I had to keep a clear head for what was to come, so I ignored the mini bar's siren song and made us all some coffee instead.

When I called Reynolds back he picked up the phone on the first ring. 'Okay,' he said. 'I've run your story by Assistant Commissioner Brooks and he's given it the green light. We have the resources of the entire department to draw on.'

'Good,' I said. 'That's good.'

'So what I suggest is this. I will get a squad of armed officers down to the warehouse. You carry out the plan the Cubans outlined to Mr Carr. Once we've confirmed that Ms Carr is alive and well our officers will enter the building and effect a rescue.'

He made it all sound so simple. I wasn't so sure. 'What's to stop them shooting Serena, or us for that matter, when your men burst in.'

'There won't be any *bursting in*, Mr Beck. We're not in a Hollywood movie. My men are trained for exactly this kind of situation. They are equipped with state of the art digital listening equipment and thermal imaging cameras. We will be able to see and hear what's going on in the warehouse almost as clearly as you. We already have a schematic of the building and have pin-pointed the various entrance and exit points. You will be covered at all times. We won't let anything bad happen to you.'

'I'm reassured,' I said, though I felt anything but.

'And please don't worry if you don't see my men when you arrive at the warehouse. They are trained to be invisible. We don't want to alert the Cubans to our presence.'

'So *we* go ahead with the plan...'

'...and let us worry about the rest.'

'Very well,' I said.

'And, Mr Beck, when this is all over and we have liberated Ms Carr and locked away the bad men, we talk. Agreed? As I said earlier, I have questions for you. Lots and lots of questions.'

'Agreed,' I said and hung up. I turned to the others and told them the plan.

'You're happy with this?' Ray said.

'I don't know,' I said. 'But I don't think we have a choice.'

'Reynolds can be a pain in the ass,' Ray said. 'I've had dealings with him in the past. But he's very up front and as straight as they come. He won't let you down.'

'You may be right. But I'm not going in there without some kind of insurance.' I went over to my bag and took out the two pistols I'd brought with me from *The Lady*. The Beretta I slipped into my pocket. The other gun, a Smith and Wesson automatic I weighed in my hand. 'Have you ever used one of these?' I said to Jerry Carr.

He shook his head. I handed it to him. 'Be careful. This one's real,' I sat down on the bed next to him and showed him how to use it.

'Do you want me to come with you, to watch your back?'

'No, Ray. Thanks for the offer, but I'm not involving you in this any more than I have already.'

The relief was there in his eyes.

'So what now?' he said.

'Well, Jerry and I are going to kill some time. You? You have a hotel to run.'

He smiled. 'Yeah, I suppose I do.'

45

The Cubans had chosen their spot well. The warehouse stood in an isolated plot in Freeport's industrial area. A chain-link fence topped with razor wire surrounded the building, a rectangular, steel-walled building the size of an aircraft hangar. Surrounding cover was minimal; a few low buildings to the left of the plot, behind us another warehouse, blank-walled and windowless. The area was deserted. At that time of the evening, with the sun falling from the sky and with twilight painting everything a dull grey, it felt like we'd entered a ghost town.

We sat in Jerry's car, the motor idling. 'We're here,' Jerry said.

'I guessed as much,' I said and opened the car door.

There was a gate in the chain link. It was ajar. We walked towards it; me in front, Jerry at my back, the automatic pressing painfully into my spine. We had to make this look convincing. As we walked I glanced around looking for any sign of Reynolds and his men, but there was no trace of them. He'd said not to be concerned if we couldn't see them, that they were very good at concealing themselves, but despite his assurances I was starting to feel very uneasy; I couldn't see a single place they could be hiding. 'I'm not sure about this,' I said quietly.

'Keep walking.'

'Perhaps we should wait...'

There was a soft click as Jerry flicked off the safety on the automatic and pressed it harder into my back. 'I said, keep walking.'

I kept walking, cursing myself now for giving Jerry a loaded gun and worse, for showing him how to use the weapon properly. All I hoped now was that he wouldn't do anything rash and get us both killed.

'Just keep calm,' I said. 'Let me handle this.'

We reached the door.

'Open it,' he said.

I stretched out my arm, pushed and the door swung inwards. Jerry urged me forward with the gun.

It was dark inside the warehouse; so dark I could see nothing. I realised I was holding my breath. I let it out slowly and took a few tentative steps forward. Jerry pressed the barrel of the Smith and Wesson harder into my spine. 'Keep walking,' he whispered into my ear. 'Don't stop.'

I put one foot in front of the other, moving deeper into the warehouse. My eyes were slowly becoming accustomed to the darkness, but not enough to make out anything significant. We were about ten yards inside the building when a light was switched on; a single spotlight shining a thin beam of light down from the ceiling. It illuminated a solitary figure, bound and gagged and tied to a hard chair in the centre of the concrete floor.

We'd found Serena.

I heard Jerry give a small gasp, and the gun twitched at my back.

The Cubans had tortured her. There were livid bruises on her face and her lips were swollen and split. The Cuban woman had been busy with her cigarettes and both of Serena's arms were pock-marked with small, round burns.

When Jerry took in the damage that had been done to his sister he gave a half-strangled cry and lurched forward.

There was a small cough and a bullet kicked up concrete dust in front of his feet.

'That's far enough,' said a voice from the darkness.

For a moment I thought I was hearing things and it took several seconds to digest what I'd just heard. I recognised the voice; and with that knowledge a wave of nausea threatened to sweep me away.

'That's better.' The voice spoke again.

A moment later Jack Dylan stepped into the spotlight.

46

Jack stood, lit from above, his huge frame casting a black puddle of shadow at his feet. In his hand was a silenced automatic, aimed at the gap between Jerry Carr and me; a twitch of an inch right or left and he could take out either of us.

'Drop the gun, Jerry,' he said.

Jerry Carr's eyes were focussed on his sister, and hers on his. The gun was hanging loosely at his side. I could see the indecision on Jerry's face. It was as if he was silently asking Serena what to do. Serena gave an almost imperceptible nod of her head and Jerry uncurled his fingers and let the Smith and Wesson clatter to the concrete floor. In the chair Serena relaxed a little and she turned her attention to me. The plea in her eyes was obvious. *Help us.*

'Kick the gun over to me, Harry,' Jack said.

I did as I was told. The gun skidded across the concrete, coming to a halt at Jack's feet.

He stared down at it. 'The Smith and Wesson,' he said with a thoughtful smile. 'That means *you* probably have the Beretta.' He turned the smile on me. Jack had been on *The Lady* many times over the years of our friendship. He was always a welcome guest. We'd sit on deck, sometimes until the early hours of the morning, drinking rum and getting drunk together. He knew the boat almost as well as I did myself, and he knew about the secret compartment where I kept the guns. He had a good memory.

'If you would, Harry,' he said. 'Finger and thumb only. I'd hate to shoot you, but you know I will if necessary.'

I pulled the Beretta from my waistband and dropped it onto the floor. Jack mimed a kicking action with his foot. I kicked the gun across to him.

'That's better,' Jack said. 'I hate surprises.'

Well, he'd be in for the biggest surprise of his life once Reynolds and his men arrived, I thought, but kept my face neutral. I was worried they were taking so long, but I imagined they were listening to what was going on in here and picking their moment. I glanced around to see if there was anyone else here, but my vision still couldn't penetrate the gloom in the corners of the warehouse. For all I knew there could be a dozen of Jack's men standing in the shadows, all training their guns on us.

'So, Harry, I suppose you're wondering what's going on.'

'It had crossed my mind,' I said.

'Well, you're here because I need you to do something for me.'

'And why the hell should I do anything for you?'

'Friendship?' he said, then laughed. 'No, I suppose I've blown that now. Though to be fair, Harry, I *did* tell you not to get involved. I warned you to stay out of it, but you always were a stubborn bastard.'

'So you're the one behind all this,' I said.

'You flatter me,' he said. 'No, I'm merely a player in this particular game…a very highly paid one, but a player nonetheless. The people who are running the game are much more important and much more powerful than me, and to them you've become a royal pain in the ass. You're asking way too many questions, Harry, and drawing too much attention. You're stirring up the mud, and the wrong people are starting to notice. My employers want me to stop you. In fact they want me to take you out, to dispose of you permanently.'

'Then why don't you? You're the one holding the gun.'

Jack Dylan frowned. 'Harry, I like you, always have. I won't kill you unless I absolutely have to. Besides, you can still be useful to me and the organization.'

'In what way?'

'We really need to speak to Alan, and you're the one man who can bring him to us. He trusts you, Harry. He'll do as you ask.'

'There are two problems with that,' I said. 'One, I don't know where he is, and secondly, after today, I wouldn't piss on your boots if your feet were on fire.'

He laughed. 'Perhaps this will change your mind.' He swung the gun up and fired twice. The first shot hit Jerry Carr in the chest; the second bullet punched a hole in his forehead and blew out the back of his skull, spattering me with blood, bone and brain. He gave a small groan and then Jerry Carr's legs crumpled. He sank to the floor and toppled forward, his face hitting the concrete with a sickening thud.

Serena gave a muffled cry and rocked in her chair, pulling against her bonds. Tears were coursing down her ruined cheeks

With a casualness that was almost inhuman, Jack swung the gun round, put it against the side of Serena's head and pulled the trigger.

47

I stood there paralysed, watching as Serena slumped forward, dead in the chair. Jack then turned the gun on me. 'You don't want to be next, do you, Harry?'

I looked from Jerry's body to Serena's, scarcely believing what I had just witnessed. 'Why?' I said, my voice choked with emotion.

'Loose ends, Harry. I hate loose ends.'

Reynolds, I thought. *Where the hell was Reynolds?*

Jack was talking again. I watched his lips move, heard the words on the air, but my brain wouldn't process them. I kept getting flashbacks to the *Scarlet Parrot*, Serena leaning on the piano while her brother played. I'd brought them into this. I was responsible for their deaths.

At that moment I wanted Jack to pull the trigger. I would have welcomed the bullet; but then something Jack was saying penetrated the grey fog that was clouding my brain. He'd mentioned a name. Kim Weaver.

'What?' I said.

He frowned. 'Stay with me, Harry. Try to keep up.'

'What's this got to do with Kim?'

The frown deepened. 'Nothing at all,' he said. 'But you involved her when you took your friends over to Watt's

Cay. It's up to you now whether she lives or she dies, and the same goes for the rest of your friends. You have their lives in your hands.'

'How did you know about Watt's Cay?' I said, my head spinning.

'I know a lot of things, Harry. You'd be surprised.' He glanced at his watch. 'By now our Cuban friends will have paid Kim a visit. I've told them not to hurt her, but I can't guarantee something of what I said didn't get lost in translation. My Spanish is appalling and their English is almost as bad. Anyway, I'll trust that my message got through and your friends are all right. But whether they stay that way is up to you.'

It dawned on me then that Reynolds wasn't coming. There would be no cavalry riding to the rescue; and for Serena and Jerry Carr it was already too late.

'What do you want?' I said thickly.

'I've already told you what I want. Do try to keep up. Repeating myself just wastes time, and, as far as you're concerned, time is in short supply. In fact you have twenty-four hours to bring Alan to me. If you don't then I'll instruct the Cubans to kill your friends…and I'll tell them to make it slow and painful.'

'What happened to you, Jack?' I said. 'How did you end up like this?'

His eyes narrowed. 'Not sure I'm following you, Harry.'

'The Jack Dylan I know would not kill in cold blood, nor would he hold one of his oldest friends to ransom. This isn't you, Jack.'

'You know, Harry, Alan always said you had a rose-tinted picture of the world. He said that often you couldn't see what was sitting there right in front of you. I guess he was right.'

'But children, Jack. Innocent children!'

'Are nothing more than another commodity. Do you

think they'd be better off if we left them in the slums of Cuba or Haiti? There's every chance they'd end up on the streets selling their bodies.'

'You're not trying to justify what you do, are you? Because if you are you can save your breath. It won't wash, not with me.'

'Harry,' he said. 'I don't give a flying fuck whether you approve or disapprove of what I'm doing. It makes me money. That's all I care about. That's all Alan cared about...at first. Before his conscience kicked in. Bloody fool!'

'I'll bring you down, Jack. I have evidence.'

'You have a few names on a list and a photo album. Hardly what I'd call concrete.'

How does he know all this?

'Then why did Alan leave me the memory stick if the evidence was...' A light flashed on in my mind. 'It was you, wasn't it? The message at the bungalow, the memory stick. You planned this.'

'If I wasn't holding you at gunpoint, Harry, I'd applaud. It's taken you long enough, but you got there in the end. Yes, I left you the note. I've been able to copy Alan's handwriting for years. It came in handy when he wasn't around to sign documents. And yes, I planted the memory stick. A bit John le Carré I know—remember those games we played as kids—but it piqued your interest. No, Alan has all the hard evidence. The bastard raided my computer and copied everything. There's another memory stick floating around out there. At first I thought he may have given it to you for safe keeping—sorry about your bungalow by the way, but I had to be sure. Now I'm convinced he still has it. He was doing a deal with the FBI. He was going to turn everything over to them in return for immunity from prosecution. He'd set up a meeting with one of their agents and I had to stop that happening. Unfortunately Anna chose that morning to leave him and take the car. I wasn't to know it would pan out that way, and I genuinely regret Sally.'

'Add her to the list of children you've destroyed,' I said bitterly.

'Oh, spare me the righteous indignation, Harry. We all follow our own paths. You're not exactly pure as the driven snow yourself. Or doesn't liquor smuggling count as a crime these days. Listen, all you have to worry about now is finding Alan and turning him over to me.'

'And you'll kill him.'

'Of course.'

I shook my head. 'I can't do that.'

Jack Dylan shrugged his huge shoulders. 'It's your choice, Harry boy. Alan or your friends. What's it to be?'

'How do I know you won't kill them anyway?' I said.

'You'll just have to trust me on that one,' he said, without irony. 'Remember what that teacher predicted for us at school? You as the worker, and you've been happy fulfilling that role haven't you. But I was never content to act as the middle manager for high and mighty Alan Lancaster. He owned all his stuff and let me have a few scraps. I'm taking some ownership for me.'

'When this is over, Jack, I'm coming after you,' I said.

'When this is over, Harry, I'll be long gone. I've made my money and the Bahamas has lost its appeal.'

'Then why don't you leave now?' I said. 'Let this go and get out before anyone else is killed.'

He smiled. 'A nice idea, but it doesn't fly. This is *my* mess — I trusted Alan and brought him in — and now the people I work for want me to clean it up. Believe me, Harry, if I don't…well let's just say they have a long reach. I won't be safe wherever I go, and I don't want to spend the rest of my life looking over my shoulder. It's better this way.' He reached into his pocket and produced a mobile phone. 'Here, catch.' He tossed it over to me. I caught it.

'You can reach me on that. Just hit 1 on speed dial and

you'll get through. Twenty-four hours, Harry.'

'Why go to the trouble of encrypting the files on the memory stick if you wanted me to read them?'

He laughed. 'I've never underestimated you, Harry. You're bright. If I'd made it too easy you would never have fallen for it. It added a bit of spice, a bit of a challenge. And you came through. I guessed you would.'

He was still laughing as he backed away into the shadows. There was a small click and the spotlight was extinguished plunging the warehouse into total darkness. I stood there a few seconds more, trying to stop my head from reeling, and then I retraced my steps to the entrance.

Along the way I retrieved the Smith and Wesson and the Beretta. It was a little arrogant of Jack to leave them, but that was a trait he developed very early in life. He thought he had me under control.

I intended to use his arrogance against him.

48

It was raining heavily when I left the warehouse and the wind was starting to whip it into squalls. I pulled up the collar of my shirt and ran back to the car. I started the engine and pulled away, tyres squealing, heading back to town. I had no plan of action, but I needed to put some miles between myself and that slaughterhouse.

When I climbed back on board *The Lady*, my heart rate began to slow and I started to think clearly again. By the time I was out at sea a few thoughts had crystallised in my head. I switched on the autopilot and rang Jim Henderson at home on the mobile phone Jack had given me.

He answered on the third ring. 'Harry, where are you?'

'That doesn't matter, Jim,' I said. 'I want you to listen very carefully.'

For the next five minutes I told him about Serena and Jerry, the warehouse, and Jack Dylan's involvement in their deaths. I was telling him where to find the bodies, no more, no less. I didn't mention the paedophile ring and Alan's involvement, nor did I tell him about Reynolds and how badly he'd let me down. It wasn't safe for him to know any of that. Jim was a friend and I didn't want his blood on my hands as well.

'You realise you're in big trouble,' he said. 'I can't sit on this information, Harry, and I can't keep your name out of it. I'll have to pass it up the line.'

'To Reynolds?'

'No. This has to be reported directly to Assistant Commissioner Brooks. Reynolds is out of the loop on your case. He's disappeared. Brooks is handling everything now.'

I'd miscalculated badly. I'd thought Reynolds was one of the few people I could trust, which was why I had asked for his help. Now he was off the case and Brooks had taken over the investigation. I wondered if he was investigating Hector Reynolds' part in all this as well.

'You've got to come in, Harry, before Brooks issues a warrant for your arrest,' Jim said.

'I can't do that, Jim. I have things to do.'

'We've been friends a long time, Harry, but I can't shield you on this one.'

'And I don't expect you to. Just try to persuade Brooks to hold off issuing the warrant for twenty-four hours.'

'You really think he's going to listen to me? I'm only a sergeant.'

'He'll listen to you if you tell him I've given you my word that in twenty-four hours time I will hand myself over to you personally.'

'And is *that* what you're doing, Harry? Giving me your word?'

One way or another I had a day to resolve this. After that time, my friends would be dead. I had to come through for them, or I'd die trying.

'Yes, Jim. I give you my word.'

'I'll do what I can, Harry.'

Once Grand Bahama disappeared over the horizon I switched off the engines and dropped anchor. We were heading for a storm. The wind was strengthening, pushing the sea into choppy, white-capped waves that buffeted the steel hull of *The Lady* making it difficult for me to keep my feet and, as I walked out onto the deck, the wind drove stinging rain into my face. I lifted the hatch and climbed down into the engine compartment and started my search there.

It had troubled me at the time that while my bungalow had been trashed, my boat had been left untouched. If the Cubans were searching for the memory stick then it would have been an obvious move to rip the guts out of *The Lady's* interior in order to find it; but that hadn't been their objective. Jack Dylan knew I had made the trip to Watt's Cay and, apart from Kim Weaver calling him up and telling him — unlikely- then there was only one way he could have found out.

I searched the boat from bottom to top and then again from top to bottom. I finally found what I was looking for in the wheelhouse, stuck with an adhesive pad to the underside of the drawer in the chart table. It was no bigger than a small MP3 player, but it looked sophisticated enough. The tracking device had been beaming my whereabouts directly to Jack. There was a small grille covering a microphone set in the front of the device, so I guessed he'd been eavesdropping on our conversations as well. It explained why he was so well informed.

I found a piece of polystyrene and a plastic bag in one of the lockers. I slipped the tracking device and polystyrene inside the bag, secured the top with an elastic band and lobbed the whole thing over the side into the sea. I watched it bob along for a second or so, and then another wave took it out of sight. *Track that, you bastard,* I thought, then went back to the wheelhouse and started the engines.

I checked the compass and turned *The Lady* into the wind. I was heading towards Barracuda Cay, in the dark, in an incipient storm. I would negotiate the treacherous, coral-barbed channel, relying mainly on my own navigational skills to get me through without ripping the bottom out of my boat. It was foolhardy to the point of stupidity, but Jack had left me no choice. I couldn't afford the luxury of waiting until daybreak.

49

Thirty minutes later I was questioning my sanity. The storm was increasing in ferocity. The wind was fast becoming gale force, driving the rain horizontally against the windows of the wheelhouse, compromising visibility. The side window, shattered by the Cubans' bullets was a gaping hole through which the rain sprayed, soaking me as I stood at the wheel. I was wet, cold and wondering how much longer it would be before I heard the metallic crunch of the hull grinding against the razor-sharp coral.

I was steering by instinct and little more, and trusting very much to luck to get me through this. The waves crashed over the prow and water ran in a torrent over *The Lady's* deck, carrying anything that wasn't tied down into the sea. A wave lifted us up, bringing the propellers clear of the water and the twin Penta engines screamed at the sudden lack of resistance. As I eased back on the throttle the wave dropped us like a stone and we hit the sea with a tooth-jarring crash. The wheel was wrenched from my grasp and I lost my footing on the sopping wet floor. As another wave lifted us again I found myself sliding towards the door. I spread my legs and jammed my feet against the frame, stopping myself from slipping out onto the deck. When we dropped again I rolled over onto my stomach and hauled myself back to my feet, grabbing the wheel and checking the compass and GPS. By some kind of miracle we were still on course. It was if *The Lady of Pain* had a mind of her own and she'd taken it upon herself to look after me.

I managed to keep on my feet for the rest of the crossing. I could tell from the GPS that we were almost at the Cay, but I could see no lights. In fact I could see very little except rain and white caps. I didn't know how I was going to find the jetty in this weather, and I was debating whether or not to drop anchor and to wait out the storm. I would lose valuable time, but at least I wouldn't run *The Lady* aground on one of Barracuda Cay's beaches.

As I made my way aft I saw a glimmer of moonlight winking through one of the heavy black thunderheads, and it may have been my imagination, but I could swear the wind was dropping and the rain easing off. I looked up at the moon. It was growing in size as the split in the cloud grew wider. The rocking of the boat was calming and the sea was less violent. A half a mile farther on and the rain had practically stopped, and the wind speed had dropped to a moderate breeze. I looked ahead and saw the hump of land that was Barracuda Cay, bathed in moonlight and more welcome than an oasis in a desert.

I eased forward on the throttle and headed towards the jetty.

50

The look on Julius Flood's face after he opened the door to my insistent knocking was priceless.

'Harry, man! Holy Mary! I did *not* expect to see you again so soon.' He looked back over his shoulder. 'Nona,' he called. 'It's Harry. Light the stove.'

'At this time of night?' She stuck her head around the door of the kitchen. 'Cold cuts, Harry. Okay?'

'I don't come here just so you can feed me, Nona,' I said.

Julius held the door wide. 'Come in, man.' As I walked past him he said, 'You're soaked.'

'Blowing up a bit out there,' I said.

'Tropical storm coming. It's been all over the news for the last two days.'

'It's here. I just sailed through it.'

The people of the Bahamas are used to the extreme tricks the weather can play, but over the last few years the Islands have been struck by two hurricanes, and the resulting damage has hit the economy badly. Many businesses have closed and tourism has nosedived leading to unemployment problems and a general rise in the crime rate. The Floods were insulated to a certain degree; living on Barracuda has always been a hard existence so they were the least likely to feel the effects. Julius was still being cautious though — storm warnings make you paranoid. As I approached the house I noticed he had storm shutters covering the windows.

He left me on my own for a moment, returning a few minutes later with a voluminous dressing gown. 'Get out of those wet things. I'll get Nona to dry them by the stove.'

As I stripped off and enveloped myself in the dressing gown he said, 'What're you doing here, Harry?'

'I need to talk to the old man again.'

'Oh?'

'He knows something,' I said. 'About Alan's whereabouts.'

'What makes you so sure?' Nona said as she walked into the room carrying a tray laden with cold meats of every description and colourful mixes of rice and vegetables.

'It was in his eyes, the last time I saw him. I think he only told me he was Alan's father to throw me off the track and stop me asking questions. He always was an evasive old bugger. I've known him long enough to notice the signs. Last time there was too much going on for me to catch on immediately. I've had time to think since then; and the more I've thought about it, the more I'm convinced he knows more than he's telling.'

Julius and Nona exchanged glances; and a whole unspoken dialogue took place in their eyes. I caught it immediately.

'You know something, don't you?'

Julius sighed, forked some meat and rice onto a plate and flopped down into an armchair, resting the plate on his knees.

'Alan was here, Harry,' Nona said.

'When?'

'The same time you were. There's a cove on the other side of Barracuda. It's sheltered from prying eyes by overhanging rocks, pirates used to use it in the seventeen hundreds as a hideout from the authorities. Alan moored his boat there for a couple of days.'

'And you didn't think to tell me that when I was last here?'

'We gave him our word, man,' Julius said. 'He begged us not to tell anyone.'

'Not even me?'

'Especially not you.'

'Is he still there?' I asked hopefully, but knowing the answer would be in the negative.

Nona shook her head. 'He took off a while ago. We're sorry, Harry. We didn't mean to keep you in the dark.'

I stared across at the tray of cold cuts. My appetite had deserted me. 'Nona,' I said. 'People have died because I couldn't find Alan. Good people; innocent people.'

Tears sprang to her eyes. She choked back a sob and ran from the room.

51

'Did he talk to you, Julius? Did he tell you what's going on?'

Julius lowered his eyes; he was finding it difficult to look at me directly. 'He was in a mess, Harry. He'd seen the explosion that took Anna and Sally. He'd been walking back to the house when the car went up. He blames himself.'

'So he should.'

'Hey, man, show a little compassion. You two have been friends for years.'

'So people are fond of reminding me. And yet he's been my brother as well, all along. I know all that, but I also know that Alan got himself mixed up in something so horrible, tragedy was the only outcome. If I blame him for anything it's his greed and stupidity. He must have known that nothing good was ever going to come out of it.'

'He knows that and he's sorry. More sorry than you can imagine.'

'Fine, but that's not enough, not anymore. He came to see me the morning Anna and Sally died…at least he came to the boat. Why?'

'He came to ask for your help. You were the only person on Grand Bahama he trusted.'

'Then why didn't he make more of an effort to track me down? Was he scared?'

'He was,' Julius said. 'But scared *for* you, not *of* you. Once he'd witnessed his car exploding he realised that the stakes were much higher than he'd first thought and he knew he couldn't involve you. He was worried for your safety, man. So he set out to sea and ended up here asking us to shelter him…well, actually he asked your father.'

'And I'll bet the old bastard couldn't wait to help him. Alan is his son after all.'

'Lose the bitterness, Harry. It doesn't suit you.'

'Fuck it, Julius, how do you expect me to feel?'

'I expect you to understand, I suppose. These things happen. Sometimes we don't choose the path life sets out for us. Sometimes it chooses us.'

'And what about free will, Julius? Are you saying we can't decide whether to take the right path or the wrong one?'

'Sometimes.'

'Bullshit! I don't accept that,' I said. 'I accept that the old man fell in love with Robert Lancaster's wife. I even accept that she gave him a son. But to keep that information from me for all these years…that was his choice and, as far as I'm concerned, an unforgivable one.'

'I dare say he was trying to protect you,' Nona said as she came back into the room. She was dabbing at her eyes with a tissue. 'Your father's not a bad man, Harry. He's only human. He made judgement calls—maybe not the right ones when you look back on it, but hindsight makes us wise. He did what he thought was right.'

I wasn't convinced. I lit a cigarette and sank back into my seat, feeling morose and more than a little angry.

'If he did wrong, Harry, he'll be judged by a much higher authority than us.'

Which, if you believe in God, is a comforting thought. I don't, so it gave me no comfort whatsoever.

'We're getting off the track here,' I said. 'The rights and wrongs of my father's actions can wait. Right now I'm racing the clock. I have to find Alan, and I have less than a day to do so.'

Julius narrowed his eyes. 'And why would that be?'

I told him.

When I'd finished he looked visibly shocked and Nona was crying again.

'Let me get this straight,' he said. 'You have to find Alan and hand him over to Jack Dylan, who's going to kill him, and once you've done that your friends on Watt's Cay will be safe. Do I have that right?'

'That's about it,' I said.

'Christ! You have a nerve to sit there in judgement of your father.' Julius was suddenly angry. He was on his feet and towering over me. 'You're a hypocrite, Harry, a bloody hypocrite, with all your fancy talk of the right path and the wrong path. You're handing out a death sentence to Alan. Is *that* the right path to take? And do you honestly think you'll be able to live with yourself after you've taken it?' His eyes narrowed. 'Or maybe that's your plan. Once Alan's dead you'll have your father all to yourself. Is that it? Is that what's driving you on to do this?'

'That's ridiculous. My priority has to be saving the lives of Kim, Stevie and the others. My relationship with my father is a whole separate issue, and one that I'll deal with once all this is over.'

'When this is over Alan will be dead. Very convenient for you.'

I looked up at him. 'It's not like that. Please, Julius.'

He gave me a look that was half contempt and half pity, and then he turned and walked from the room. I heard a door slam.

'Nona,' I said. 'Can't you make him understand?'

Nona sniffed back the tears. 'I'm not sure I can, Harry, because I'm not sure I understand it myself.'

I lit another cigarette, but it tasted sour in my mouth. I ground it to death in the ashtray and went outside.

Julius was sitting on the steps of the porch. He glanced round at me. There were tears in his eyes.

'Is there any point in continuing this conversation?' I said.

'You know where I stand, Harry. I'm not going to shift my position. What you're doing is wrong. Plain wrong.'

'So what would you do, if you were me?'

'I'd sail out to Watt's Cay and rescue my friends, and then I'd see about dealing with Jack Dylan.'

'And Alan?'

'I'd let Alan find me.'

'So I'm meant to sail across to Watt's Cay and take out three heavily armed and very dangerous Cubans single handed. I see the flaw in your plan right there. I'm not Rambo.'

'You wouldn't be single-handed,' Julius said. 'I'm a good man in a fight, Harry.'

I looked at him steadily. 'You're serious, aren't you?'

He nodded his head slowly. 'I don't see what you'd have to lose.'

'Well you for a start. Nona would never forgive me if anything happened to you. Hell, I'd never forgive myself.'

'It would be my choice. Nona would understand.'

'I would understand what?' Nona was standing in the doorway holding two glasses of pineapple rum.

'He thinks we should go to Watt's Cay and rescue Stevie and the others,' I said.

She handed us the glasses. 'Does he now?' she said. She leaned forward and wrapped her arms around her husband's shoulders. 'Julius Flood, what am I going to do with you?' she said softly.

'Harry needs me, Nona. He can't do this on his own.'

She kissed his cheek. 'No, I don't suppose he can.' She turned and looked up at me. 'And when do you plan on going?'

'As soon as possible.'

She shook her head. 'You'll never make it through the channel, not in the dark,' she said.

'I *made* it here in the dark,' I said.

'More by luck than judgement, I'd guess, and you can push your luck too far, you know? Besides, you look ready to drop. Leave it 'til daybreak.' She once again focused her attention on Julius. 'And you, big man, if you get yourself killed I'll never forgive you.'

'That wasn't part of the plan,' Julius said. He turned to me. 'Harry, why do you think Reynolds left you high and dry?'

'I've been wondering the same thing myself. Maybe he didn't believe my story. He said he had to consult with Assistant Commissioner Brooks. Maybe Brooks didn't believe it and pulled the plug on the rescue mission.'

'There is another, more sinister explanation,' Julius said.

'Yes, I know. But if you knew Hector Reynolds as well as I do you'd discount the possibility that he could be involved in all this. The man's as straight ahead as they come.'

'In your opinion.'

'Not just mine, Ray Burgess thinks so too, and he's a much better judge of character than I am.'

At that moment light spilled out onto the yard as my father opened the door of his house.

52

'You got a conference going on, Julius?' he called.

'Sorry. Didn't mean to disturb you,' Julius called back. 'I've got Harry here.'

My father didn't reply. I heard a door close and the light was extinguished. Seconds later he was there on Julius' porch. He noticed the glasses of rum immediately and a tremor went through his emaciated body. He closed his eyes and tried to gather himself. He had his teeth in this time, and he'd shaved away the stubble. He didn't look great; his eyes had sunk into their sockets and he was breathing heavily through his mouth, as if the effort of walking the few yards from his house to the Floods' had drained him, but he didn't look one breath away from a coffin as he had the last time I'd seen him, so that was an improvement.

'I owe you an apology,' he said. 'I shouldn't have told you about Alan, not like that.'

'What, you mean you should have dressed it up? Maybe you should have hung flags and banners to announce it.'

'Harry,' Nona said soothingly. 'Give him a chance.'

I stared into her eyes, saw the compassion there and something went out of me. A few hours before I'd seen two people shot dead before my eyes; their only crime was that of being in the wrong place at the wrong time. Somehow the knowledge that my father had sired an illegitimate son, and that son was my best friend, just didn't seem that important in comparison.

'Do you know where Alan is?' I said.

The old man took a breath, and then he nodded his head, slowly.

'Well?'

'Do I have your forgiveness?'

'Just tell me where he is.'

'Please, son.'

I could feel three pairs of eyes watching me, willing me to make the right decision. 'Yes,' I said after what seemed like an eternity. 'I forgive you.'

It was a lie.

The old man's shoulders sagged and tears welled up in his eyes. Nona put her arm around his shoulder and hugged him. 'I told you, Lucas,' she said softly. 'Harry's a good man.'

'Not like his father, eh,' the old man said with a rueful smile.

'So where is he?' I said. 'Where's Alan?'

'Can I sit down?'

Nona pulled him up a chair. The old man sat down heavily. 'The FBI let him down badly,' he said. 'He'd set up a meeting, the morning the car bomb went off. An agent was coming to interview him and Alan was going to give them everything, all the information they needed to bring down the cartel in the States. But someone at the Bureau ratted him out. The bomb was meant for him, not Anna and Sally. It's why he ran. He knew, once they'd figured out it wasn't him driving the car, they'd come for him again and that they'd catch up with him sooner rather than later. He came here. We hid him.' He licked his lips and glanced at the rum glasses again. 'A small one. Julius?' he said.

'You know better than to ask, Lucas.'

I was getting impatient. 'So where is Alan now?'

The old man licked his lips again. 'All this talking. Makes me dry.'

'Give him a drink, Julius,' I said.

'Harry!' Nona said.

Julius glared at me. 'Harry, you're no better than the Cubans who got him drunk.'

'I'm not telling you to get him drunk,' I said. 'One drink. A small one.'

'Thanks, Harry,' my father said.

Nona looked at Julius, a question in her eyes. Julius gave a small nod of his head. She went inside and came back with a glass containing a finger of rum, handing it to my father who took the glass in both hands and brought it up to his nose. He sniffed the sticky-sweet aroma, put the glass to his lips and took a sip, and then he set the glass down on the table.

'Watt's Cay,' he said.

'What?'

'Alan. He's gone to Watt's Cay.'

'Why?' I looked at him incredulously.

'He wouldn't say.'

I couldn't see why he'd go there of all places. I wasn't aware Alan knew Kim that well.

'This is bad, Harry. He's walking straight into their arms,' Julius said.

'Yes, I know. Can you get in touch with him?'

Julius shook his head. 'He's not using the radio on the boat and his mobile phone's switched off.'

'When did he leave here?'

'A few hours ago.'

'Then there's no way we're going to head him off,' I

said. 'We'll do as you suggested, Nona, and leave at day-break.'

'You're going after him?' my father said.

I nodded and went to pour myself another rum. My hands were shaking.

53

'So do you think Lucas was telling the truth about Alan meeting with the FBI?' Julius said once we'd cast off and *The Lady* was ploughing through the waves.

'Jack Dylan said the same. Besides I think I know who Alan's contact is. I've met him. Sam Goldberg. He spun me a line about meeting up with Alan for research on a book he was writing. And I swallowed it, damn it!' I slapped the wheel with the flat of my hand. 'Writer, my ass! He damn near told me he worked for the Feds.'

'And he's on Watt's Cay too?'

'Oh yes, he's there too.'

'What are the chances he'll still be able to contact the Bureau?'

'Not a hope in hell. Remember my father also said that Alan had been ratted out by someone at the FBI. So I would hazard that Jack and the Cubans are well aware of Goldberg's status. Besides, the FBI have no jurisdiction over here. If they got involved in an internal Bahamian affair it could open a political can of worms, and I don't think they'd be willing to do that.'

'So we can count out any help from that quarter.'

'I think it's safe to say we're on our own.'

'A comforting thought,' Julius said with heavy irony.

We made good time to Watt's Cay. Julius was an experienced sailor and didn't suffer from seasickness, so I was able to open out the twin Pentas and build up some considerable speed. Yesterday's storm had moved on and the morning was fine with a sky of deep azure streaked with a few high bands of cirrus. There was a darker cloud-line on the horizon that suggested the storm may be back later in the day, but the forecast was non-committal.

At a little after midday we saw the faint outline of Watt's Cay in the distance. I throttled back and let *The Lady* drift.

'We can't take the chance they'll be watching the jetty. It can be seen from Kim's house,' I said.

'What do you suggest?'

'We circumnavigate the cay at a distance and come up on the opposite side to the house. We can anchor some way out and use the dinghy to get ashore. If my memory serves me correctly there's a long stretch of beach on the north shore with a fair bit of cover. Unless we're seriously unlucky we should be able to get up to the house without being spotted.'

'It's your call,' Julius said.

It was a plan of sorts. What happened when we reached the house though was still a vague shadow-play in my head, but nothing would be any clearer until we got there and assessed the situation.

The noise of the dinghy's outboard motor blared through the morning silence and I was very aware that this wasn't a subtle method of approach. Half a mile out from land I cut the motor and we used the oars.

'No sight of Alan's boat.'

'He would have tied up at the jetty,' I said. 'He wouldn't be expecting a reception committee.'

We landed on the beach and dragged the dinghy across the sand, hiding it in a patch of dense foliage at the base of a stand of palm trees. When I was satisfied that it wouldn't be noticed by any casual observer we struck out towards Kim's house.

We were both armed. I had the Beretta and the Smith & Wesson, both tucked into the waistband of my chinos; Julius had surprised me back at his house by producing an old Colt .45 revolver. 'It scares away the sharks,' he said.

'Are you any good with it?'

'Pretty fair. I get a lot of target practice. You?'

'I could hit a barn door if you painted it bright red and stood me two yards in front of it,' I said.

'*That* good, eh?' Julius said with a chuckle. 'Let's hope the threat of the guns is enough.'

We could hope, but I wasn't feeling terribly optimistic.

54

By the time we reached the rear of Kim's house that lack of optimism had developed into a deep pessimism. I was out of my depth here and had been right from the start. I was no hero, and certainly no action hero. The thought of confronting the Cubans with their guns and utter ruthlessness filled me with nothing short of total dread. As we crouched behind the small rise overlooking Kim's house my palms were sweating, and that had nothing to do with the trek across the island.

Julius produced a pair of binoculars from the small rucksack he had slung over his shoulder. He handed them to me. They were strong enough to give a clear view through the windows.

The first person I saw was the Cuban woman. She was dressed in combat fatigues, her thick, black hair tied back from a plain face. Her eyes were heavy lidded, nose prominent and there was a determined set to her heavy jaw. She was standing at the window of the lounge, glancing out occasionally as she smoked a cigarette. She turned to speak to someone and I caught a glimpse of the machine pistol she was holding at her hip.

I looked beyond her and saw Stevie, Billie and Sam Goldberg sitting together on Kim's cream leather couch. From the awkwardness of their postures it was obvious they were tied up, their hands secured behind their backs.

The smaller of the Cuban men came into view. He too was holding a machine pistol. He crouched down in front of the three on the couch. He was saying something to them, to Billie in particular, and then he reached out with his free hand and grabbed Billie's breast, his fingers digging into the soft flesh. She squirmed but could do nothing. I saw the Cuban woman laughing and making gestures to urge her colleague on. Sam said something to the man. The Cuban released Billie's breast and swung his hand, catching Sam across the mouth. Sam rocked backwards, his split lip dribbling blood. Stevie was struggling against her bonds and mouthing a stream of invective I had no problem lip reading. The Cuban woman raised her weapon threateningly and then took her cigarette and blew on the lighted end, making it glow red. The implication was obvious and Stevie's mouth snapped shut like a clam shell.

There was no sign of Alan and so far I had seen nothing of Kim, her young lover Philippe or the larger of the Cuban men. I was guessing they were in another part of the house, but even as I thought it another, much darker possibility entered my mind.

I swung the binoculars from window to window and was about to give up when a door at the side of the house opened and the big Cuban stepped into view. He had something slung over his shoulder. With a feeling of dread I refocused the binoculars. He was carrying something rolled up in one of Kim's Persian rugs and it didn't take too much to imagine what the rug contained. I felt a knot of nausea settle in the pit of my stomach. We had left it too late. I should have followed my instincts and set sail last night instead of being convinced by Nona to wait until morning.

I felt Julius nudge me in the ribs. He too was staring at the Cuban; watching as the big man dumped his burden unceremoniously into a bed of Kim's flower garden.

We waited until he had disappeared back inside and then crept forward, finding cover where we could; behind trees and a couple of small wooden structures where Kim kept her gardening tools.

We reached the house, ducking down to avoid being seen from the windows, and crept along in the lee of the house wall. Julius reached the rolled up rug first. I could see him hesitate as he reached down to unroll it. By the time I joined him he'd exposed the body and was staring down at it, a confused expression on his face. He looked up at me, an unspoken question in his eyes. I stared down at the chiselled Gallic features, almost serene in death. There was a small bullet hole in the forehead, but that was the only imperfection in Philippe's handsome face.

'Kim's lover, Philippe,' I whispered.

'I thought I was going to find Alan.'

'Yes. So did I.'

'Poor Philippe. He loved me so much he had to play the hero. Such a waste.'

55

I spun around at the sound of the voice.

Kim was standing there, not two yards away from us. In her hands she held the shotgun, cocked and aimed at us. 'This old thing may not shoot straight, but from this range it will take you both out, so don't make any sudden movements or try anything stupid.'

'Kim?' I said, not really understanding what was happening. The world had lurched under my feet again, leaving me disoriented.

'I take it this is Kim Weaver?' Julius said.

'Yes,' I said, glaring furiously at her.

'A famous man once said, *choose your friends wisely.* You should have listened, Harry.'

'Tell me something I *don't* know,' I said. 'Kim, what's going on?'

'We can talk when we're inside. I don't trust you not to do anything rash, Harry. You always were a little hotheaded. A great fuck, but a hot-head. Take out your guns very carefully and throw them into the flower bed.'

I pulled the Beretta from my waistband and tossed it into the flowers. Julius did the same with the Colt.

'Both of them, Harry. I saw you had two when you were bending over Philippe. You don't want to play the hero as well and end up like him, do you?'

I took out the Smith and Wesson, wondering if I'd have time to raise it and fire before Kim pulled the trigger of the shotgun. The back door opened and the large Cuban stepped out into the late morning sun. He said something to Kim in Spanish. She replied and, with an alacrity that belied his size, he was behind me and yanking the gun from the waistband and in doing so tore an inch-long gash in my buttock.

I think I swore, or said something insulting. He didn't miss a beat. Without even looking he threw the gun into the flower bed and swiped me with the back of his hand. I don't know whether he wore a signet ring or whether it was just his knuckle, but something very hard cracked into my temple and something exploded in front of my eyes. I sank to my knees, clutching my head with my hand.

Kim twitched the shotgun. 'Right,' she said. 'Inside.'

Julius hauled me to my feet. 'Are you all right?' he whispered in my ear.

I felt groggy. My vision was blurred and my head felt as if someone was trying to penetrate my brain with a pneumatic drill. I stumbled a couple of times as Julius helped me towards the door, but his strength kept me on my feet.

'Harry!' Stevie gasped as Julius hauled me into the room where they were being held. As Kim walked in behind us with the shotgun aimed at our backs, the flame of hope that had flared briefly in Stevie's eyes guttered and died. 'So she fooled you too,' she said bitterly.

'For a long time,' I said, the bitterness in my voice matching Stevie's.

'Not *that* long,' Kim said. 'I really cared about you, Harry, truly I did. But as I told you yesterday, I've changed more than you know.'

'So how long have you been working for these clowns?' I said nodding towards the Cubans.

'No, Harry. You've got things about face. They work for me. Or to be more precise, they work for Jack and me. And believe me, Harry, they're not clowns. They'd kill you as soon as look at you.'

I tried to digest what she'd just said, but my thoughts were woolly from the blow on the head and nothing was making much sense. I thought she'd said "me and Jack", but that couldn't be right, could it? 'You and Jack?' I said.

She shook her head, a sad little smile playing on her lips. 'Oh, Harry, Jack always said you never knew what was going on right under your nose. Now I believe him. Jack and I have been lovers for years. Since his last wife left him.' Her smile turned coquettish. 'Well actually, for a few years before she left him.'

Julius lowered me onto the other couch. Kim aimed the shotgun at him. 'You sit too.' She said something in Spanish to the big Cuban and moments later our hands were being tied behind our backs.

At the window the Cuban woman was lighting yet another cigarette. She didn't offer me one which was a shame because I hadn't smoked since we left the boat and I was starting to feel slight nicotine withdrawal and that wasn't helping my thought process, but at least my head was starting to clear and the pain was easing. 'So,' I said to Kim. 'You and Jack are making a handsome profit trading in human misery.'

The smile didn't drop from her face. If anything it intensified. 'A very handsome profit. Yes, Harry, we are.'

'But why? Ted left you a fortune and you're a successful writer. You don't exactly need the money.'

'Don't be so bloody naïve, Harry. You can never have enough money. And besides, the books aren't selling anywhere near as well as they used to. I'm no longer flavour of the month. I'm looking at this little venture as my...our, pension.'

'I don't know how you, or Jack for that matter, can live with yourselves.'

'I don't have any trouble looking myself in the mirror, Harry,' she said coldly. 'We're not the ones fucking children. Each other, yes, and Jack allows me to have my lovers, just as I turn a blind eye to his, but we're not perverts.'

'Maybe not, but you're *supplying* the perverts. Is that any better?'

She shrugged. It was obvious she didn't care.

Her mobile phone rang.

She pulled it from the pocket of her jeans and answered it, turning her back on us. The Cuban woman trained her semi-automatic on us, just in case we got any ideas.

'Hi, darling. Where are you?'

She listened for a while. 'No, he hasn't got here yet... Oh yes, he'll come. And some other guests have arrived... Yes, Harry, and he's brought a friend with him. I think it's Julius Flood...Yes, that's what I was thinking. No loose ends...Love you. Bye.'

She turned to us

'Jack will be here soon,' she said brightly. 'Although he's a little disappointed in you, Harry. He thought you were out hunting down Alan.' She went to the bar in the corner and poured herself a brandy. 'Though I must say you would have wasted your efforts. Alan telephoned me earlier. He's on his way here.' She sat down on a cream leather armchair and tucked her legs underneath her.

On the couch Stevie, Billie and Sam were sitting in silence, watching the exchange. 'They're going to kill us, Harry,' Stevie said in her usual direct way.

'That's right, isn't it, Kim?' I said.

'I expect so,' she said. 'Though, ultimately that will be Jack's decision.'

Julius made a sound of disgust. 'How can you sit there, woman, and contemplate cold blooded murder?'

229

'Because, Mr Flood, I'm a survivor. And neither Jack, nor I, want to spend the rest of our lives behind bars.' She sipped at her brandy. 'We didn't bring about this situation. If you want somebody to blame for your current predicament then blame Alan Lancaster. Jack made a mistake. He trusted Alan and brought him into this venture. He thought capital investment would be useful, and he thought Alan would be the man to provide it. He miscalculated badly. He didn't realise that Alan actually had scruples.' She laughed. 'Well, he'd never consciously displayed them before; screwing that nightclub singer while he had a wife and child at home were not the actions of a man with high moral values.' She glanced at her watch, swallowed the last of her brandy and got to her feet. She walked to the window and looked out. 'Here he is,' she said.

She could have been talking about Alan or Jack, but I guessed from the look of infatuation on her face it was the latter. She turned to the Cuban woman. 'Watch them carefully, Maritza,' she said, 'Shoot if they give you any reason.' She then walked quickly from the room.

56

The five of us sat there under the watchful eye of Maritza, who stood with her back to the window, smoking and holding the machine pistol steady. I noticed her trigger finger twitch occasionally. She was trying to convey nonchalance, but her body language gave her away. She was strung out. She may have got her kicks from torturing young girls and old ladies, but guard duty was out of her comfort zone.

'How are we going to get out of this, Harry?' Stevie whispered to me.

'*Silencio!*' Maritza snapped and jerked the gun threateningly.

'She told you to watch us,' Sam Goldberg said. 'She didn't say we couldn't speak.'

Maritza glared at him, but there was uncertainty there in her eyes as well.

'Are you three okay?' I asked, testing Maritza's resolve. This time she said nothing, just continued to glare.

'As fine as can be expected,' Billie said. 'But Luis has wandering hands and seems to have formed a deep attachment to my breasts.'

'Where is he?' I hadn't seen the smaller of the Cuban men since arriving at the house.

'Oh, he's around,' Sam said. 'The bastard shot Philippe. He seems to be the leader of the Terrible Trio. Miguel, the big one, doesn't say a lot, and the ugly bitch,' he nodded in Maritza's direction, 'seems to be on something. She pops the odd pill every now and then, and seems pretty strung out. But it's your friend Kim who's calling the shots here. Didn't you suspect she was involved?'

'I had no reason to. I didn't know she and Jack were a couple. I take it the FBI didn't know of the involvement.'

'How should I know?'

'It's okay; you can drop the pretence now. Alan was meeting with an FBI agent here for a trade off. All the information about the cartel in exchange for immunity from prosecution. But the meeting never took place. Someone in the Bureau sold him out to the cartel and Jack Dylan had the bomb planted in his car.'

'And you think I'm an FBI agent?' He shook his head. 'I'm flattered, but sorry; I'm a journalist, nothing more, nothing less.'

'Well if it isn't him,' Julius said. 'Who is it?'

I scratched my head. 'I don't know,' I said. 'I was convinced it was Sam.'

'I think the more important question is who sold Alan out?' Billie said.

'Well, that would be me,' Kim said as she walked back into the room.'

'*You*?' I said

Kim smiled. 'I just keep rocking your safe little world, don't I, Harry? You never knew this, but Ted was very involved with the Bureau. He had a huge network of contacts on Wall Street and the FBI recruited him years ago to make use of his knowledge. It was during the insider trading scandal of the '80s. Ted was able to provide names and dates. The information he supplied led to many arrests and prosecutions; and he continued working for them right up to his death.

'At his funeral the head of the Baltimore office approached me and asked if I would carry on his work.'

'But you weren't part of his network,' I said. 'What use were you to them?'

'I had a network of my own, Harry. The wives. You'd be amazed how many indiscretions were revealed during our coffee mornings and fund raisers. I was just as valuable to them as Ted, sometimes more so. So they put me on the payroll; undercover of course.'

'And now she's my mole.' Jack Dylan strolled into the room. 'You'd be amazed how useful it is to have someone who has inside access to an organization like the FBI. It keeps me one step ahead of the game.' He went across to the bar and poured himself a whisky and another brandy for Kim.

'You two are a piece of work,' I said in disgust.

'Yes, we are, aren't we?' Kim said with something like glee in her voice. 'Alan was aware of my relationship with the FBI—I'd used my contacts to help him out in the past—but he knew nothing of my relationship with Jack. So when he decided he wanted to wreck the cartel I was the first person he contacted. Of course, I had to set up a meeting or he would had suspected something was wrong, and if he'd contacted the Bureau direct and voiced his suspicions about me...well, let's just say it could have made my life a little awkward.'

'Once Kim told me what had happened I had no option but to take him out before the meeting could take place,' Jack said, and took a gulp of whisky. 'But you know the outcome of that attempt.'

'And Alan still trusts you?' I said to Kim.

'Apparently so, which I'm sure is why he's on his way here now.'

'Anyway,' Jack said. 'Enough of the history lesson.

Harry, come with me. There's something I want to show you.' He turned to Kim. 'Call me when Alan finally arrives.' He checked his watch. 'I don't know what's keeping him.'

He came across to where we were sitting and hauled me to my feet. 'We're going for a little walk. Just you and me.' He pushed me towards the door.

'Harry!' Stevie cried out. I could see the panic in her eyes. To Jack she said, 'Don't kill him. Please don't kill him.'

I saw something shift in Jack's eyes. 'Actually, you come too,' he said to her. 'You should find it interesting.

'Leave her out of this,' I said.

'No, I don't think I shall. It will be an education for her.'

'Stevie, stay here.'

'They're going to kill us anyway, Harry. This way neither of us die alone.' Hesitantly Stevie got to her feet. There were tears in her eyes, but she was willing them to stay there.

57

Moments later we were outside and walking back across Watt's Cay the way Julius and I had come.

'Where are you taking us?' I said.

'You'll see soon enough.' He was walking two paces behind us. There was no gun in his hand, but the pocket of his jacket bulged heavily. If we tried to run we'd end up with bullet in our backs. Of that I had no doubt.

We breasted the rise from where Julius and I had observed the house, and from there it was a clear run down to the beach. When we reached the stand of palms where I had hidden the dinghy I saw immediately that it was gone. I turned and looked at Jack.

'Almost there,' he said.

As we stepped onto the beach I saw the dinghy. It was out at sea, midway between *The Lady of Pain* and the beach, being steered back to land by Luis, the smaller of the Cubans.

'What the hell is this, Jack?' I said, but alarm bells were ringing so loudly in my head I wouldn't have heard his answer had he given one.

The dinghy finally glided to a halt on the silver sand. Luis killed the motor and jumped out, running up the beach to where we stood. He stopped a yard away.

'You haven't been properly introduced,' Jack said. 'This is Luis Aldama. Luis has worked for me for many years now. He's a killer by profession. He likes killing people. Even more he likes getting paid to kill people. I pay him so he kills for me when necessary. He's very good at it.'

Luis Aldama gave a small bow, proud of the accolade.

Beside me Stevie shuddered.

'Why don't you just get this over with,' I said. 'We don't need the theatrics.'

'Impatient to meet your maker, Harry? I would never have guessed you had a death wish.' Shielding his eyes from the sun he looked out to sea. 'That wasn't why I brought you down here. Remember what I said about loose ends?'

I nodded.

'Well I'm looking at one now.'

I followed his line of sight.

In the distance *The Lady* was rising and falling on the gentle swell of the sea, the sunlight glinting on her white superstructure and on the waves surrounding her.

Jack tapped Luis on the shoulder and from his pocket the Cuban produced a small device with an aerial and a red switch.

'Luis is also an explosives expert,' Jack said.

Luis flipped the switch and *The Lady* was engulfed in an orange ball of fire.

Stevie's eyes widened. I think she screamed as the only real love of her life was blown apart.

A second later the sound of the explosion reached land; a terrifying, deep throated roar of destruction that I felt throughout my entire body. Stevie had sunk to her knees and was sobbing, hot tears of grief and anger coursing down her face. 'You bastard! You bastard!' she said over and over again, repeating it like a mantra as she rocked backwards and forwards.

Maynard Sims

As I watched the column of black smoke rise up from *The Lady's* scorched hull something inside me snapped. I hurled myself at Jack, head butting him in the chest. Taken by surprise he went down landing flat on his back and laid there laughing. I was straining against the ties that secured my hands behind my back. I needed my hands free so I could wrap them around Jack Dylan's throat, but the more I strained the tighter the restraints became until the blood supply was virtually cut off. I kicked out, aiming for Jack's head but missed by a mile and, while I was off balance, Luis moved in and kicked my other leg from underneath me making me tumble to the sand. I landed on my bound wrists, but the pain was insignificant compared to the pain of losing *The Lady*. I rolled over onto my side and watched as my precious boat, my life for the last seven years, listed to port and then slipped beneath the waves. I have never hated anyone more than I hated Jack Dylan at that moment.

For him this had nothing to do with loose ends. This was sadism of the first order; he'd proved that by bringing Stevie along to witness this destruction. She was still sobbing, bereft and alone. There was nothing I could do or say to comfort her. I felt impotent, but from that feeling of utter helplessness a new, deep-rooted resolve was forming. Jack Dylan wasn't going to triumph. I was going to bring him down, and I was going to bring him down hard. I would make him suffer the way he was making Stevie and I suffer now; and like him, I would show no mercy.

58

'There's something else I want to show you before we head back,' Jack said.

We were on our feet and stumbling through the sand. Stevie's tears had dried and her face looked like stone. No emotion showed there at all. It had been wiped.

Jack and the Cuban walked behind us, both carried guns and they were watching us carefully. 'Turn right at the next palm and make your way up the rise,' Jack said.

Neither Stevie nor I said a word, but as we came to the next palm tree we turned and started to climb up the sand bank. At the top we stopped and waited.

'Keep walking,' Jack said. 'We're not there yet.'

There was a small house in the distance, small and decaying. Storm shutters covered the windows, but were starting to fall apart. Paint peeled from the clapboard and the roof was missing great patches of shingles. The house reminded me of a rotten tooth sticking out from the ground, badly in need of extraction.

A low picket fence ran around the perimeter of the property, but it too had been neglected and the wood was starting to decay, crumbling to dust. Jack moved forward and stepped over it. 'This way,' he said.

We followed with Luis Aldama bringing up the rear, the gun in his hand ready and cocked.

There were three steps leading up to a narrow porch, and a door that had once been painted a pastel blue, but was now so streaked with bird lime that the original colour only showed through in sparse patches, like the sky peaking through storm clouds.

From his pocket, Jack produced a key and slotted it into the lock. He turned and pushed the door open. 'Follow me.'

There was little illumination, although a few stray beams of sunlight managed to slip in through the broken shutters, catching the dust motes in the air and making then glisten.

There was a narrow staircase with a few broken risers. Jack stood at the bottom and called out. 'Elena! We're back.'

The door at the top of the stairs opened and a pretty, teenage girl stepped out. Her hair was a mass of black curls that tumbled to her shoulders. She wore a white tank top and tight denim cut-offs.

She stared down at us, saw Luis as he stepped into the house and the pretty face split into a wide grin, showing a row of perfect white teeth. 'Luis!' she cried and ran down the stairs, throwing her arms around Luis Aldama's neck and covering his face with kisses.

'Elena is Luis' sister. She keeps house for me here.'

In all my time on Watt's Cay I had never seen the house before. 'What is this place?' I said, my own curiosity overriding my desire not to waste any more of my breath on Jack Dylan.

'It's all that's left of the original settlement. There were five houses like this. Back in the thirties a few Hollywood stars hung out here on Watt's Cay. From what I can gather all sorts of debauchery was indulged. Drink, drugs...sex, lots of sex. I rather like the ambience.'

'You're sick,' Stevie said. It was the first words she'd uttered since the sinking of *The Lady*, and the words were spoken with such venom even Jack winced a little.

The torrent of kisses finally abated and Elena pulled away a little breathlessly. Close up she looked slightly older than I'd first thought—maybe early twenties—and the resemblance to her brother was marked. Siblings. The word drifted through my head. Luis and Elena, Serena and Jerry, Alan and I…I blocked the thought. I needed to keep a clear head.

'How are they?' Jack said to Elena.

'They're well, Jack. I've told them a boat was coming from America tomorrow to take them off on an amazing adventure. They're very excited.' Unlike her brother Elena's English was flawless, and I wondered about her background. She sounded like a typical American college kid.

'Let's go and take a look, shall we?'

We followed Jack up the stairs, along a short passageway and into a bedroom.

The room was decked out like a dormitory with six single divan beds, three on each side of the room, and on each bed was a child. It was lighter in here; the storm shutters at the two windows had long since rotted away, and I could see the children clearly. Not one of them was more than seven years old. There were three boys and three girls, and they were all smiling. Big beaming smiles that reached their eyes and made them sparkle. They didn't know the nature of the *amazing adventure* they'd been promised, but I did, and that knowledge broke my heart.

'Well, Harry, what do you think?'

'What do you mean, what do I think?' I said. 'I think Stevie was right. You are one sick fuck.'

'Harsh, Harry, harsh. I'm giving these children the opportunity of a better life.'

'What, as sex slaves to other sick fucks? Don't insult

240

my intelligence by trying to pretend your motives are altruistic. These are the golden eggs. Your passport to wealth. A testament to your greed.'

'Very poetic, Harry. Funny, I never had you pegged as a poet.'

'It just shows how little we know those we consider to be our friends. Funny, I never had you pegged as a thoroughgoing bastard. Seems we were both wrong.'

'You're still pissed at me for blowing up your boat,' he said. 'Guess it's going to take me a long time to get back into your good books after that one.'

He was mocking me. Did he really hate me that much; and for how long had he been harbouring those feelings? 'What happened to us, Jack? We were friends.'

'Friendships wither and die, Harry. And let's face it, I'm not Alan, and Alan's your true friend—always was. I was always the one on the outside. Remember when we were kids, it was always Harry and Alan, Alan and Harry. I was the tall, freaky one who you'd indulge sometimes. Maybe you'd let me into your games if it suited you, and if it didn't you'd drop me like a stone. Outside looking in, Harry, that was me. Outside looking in.'

'So this is about our *childhood*? You have to be kidding me.'

He grabbed me then and pushed me up against the wall, his fingers burying themselves in the flesh of my throat. 'There have been times over the years when I've wanted to smash you, to beat you to a pulp, both of you, both you and Alan. To wipe the supercilious smiles off your faces. I've had nothing but bad luck in my life. Three marriages down the tubes; the bastards closing down my restaurant...'

You can't blame us for that,' I managed to get out, but the grip on my throat tightened.

'Shut your mouth! How do you think I felt having to ask Alan for help? And knowing that he wouldn't even consider helping me before he'd run it by his best buddy Harry. It stuck in my craw, and even now, all these years on, it sits there, like bile, threatening to choke me.

'Well this is my time; this is my venture; my *passport to wealth*. These *are* the golden eggs. Look about the room, Harry, and you're looking at two hundred thousand dollars. We bring in two shipments a week, fifty-two weeks a year. I'll leave you to do the math. And even this, *even this* both you and Alan want to take away from me. Well, it's not going to happen this time, Harry. Not this time.'

He released me; his anger spent, and let me crumple to the floor.

Stevie was on her knees at my side. 'He's mad, Harry. Totally fucking insane!'

I looked up at Jack who had his arm around Elena and was whispering into her ear. Luis Aldama looked on approvingly.

'No, Stevie, it's the world that's insane. Jack's bitter and twisted and playing out his game of vengeance against that madness. But he's not insane. Evil, yes, but he's no more mad than we are.'

Jack's mobile phone rang. He pulled it from his pocket and put it to his ear. 'What do you mean he hasn't arrived? You spoke to him hours ago and he said he was on his way.' He listened for a moment. It was quite satisfying to see that the smile had slipped from his face. 'Okay, okay. Tell Miguel and Maritza to take them down to the jetty and get them on the boat. I'll meet them down there shortly.' He snapped the phone shut and dropped it back into his pocket. 'Fuck!'

'So Alan hasn't walked into the trap you set for him,' I said. 'That must be very disappointing.'

'Shut up!' He was rattled. That too was satisfying. He turned to Luis. 'Get them out of here.'

Luis Aldama raised his gun. 'Move,' he said.

59

Jack's boat was a 57-foot Marko Sambrailo, with a fibreglass hull and powered by a V12 MTU engine capable of up to 22 knots. It was a spacious vessel with a large aft deck and accommodations below. Designed originally as a fishing boat it had been converted to better suit Jack's purposes. There was plenty of room, both above and below deck for contraband.

The boat rocked gently at its moorings as we climbed aboard. Julius, Sam and Billie were sitting on the starboard side of the deck, wrists and ankles bound. In the wheelhouse Miguel was smoking a cigarette, while Maritza was consigned to guard duty once more and was pacing the deck irritably, clutching the ever-present machine pistol.

The first thing I noticed as I stepped down onto the deck were the coils of anchor chain stowed at the rear of the deck. They were an ominous sign as I had a pretty good idea what the chains were going to be used for, and it had nothing at all to do with the anchor.

Jack went straight to the wheelhouse and had a few words with Miguel. The big Cuban was smiling. Luis, in the mean time, forced Stevie and I down with the others and set about binding our ankles with nylon cable ties.

243

Finally Miguel started the engine and Jack came out from the wheelhouse. He looked down at the five of us who were trussed up like Christmas turkeys and just as helpless. 'This is where you take your leave,' he said. 'I'm afraid your roles in this little adventure are over.' He moved to the rail and prepared to climb ashore.

'Not coming with us, Jack, to wish us *bon voyage* as you toss us over the side?'

He looked at me for a long moment. Finally he said, 'No. I'm lousy at goodbyes.' He jumped ashore, untied the ropes and the boat started to move back from the jetty.

'Is that what they're going to do?' Billie said. 'Throw us over the side?'

'It's what the anchor chain's for.' I nodded towards the metal coils lying in the corner. 'They'll wait until we reach a blue hole. There's one a few miles out from here. Three hundred feet deep.'

'That's not very comforting, Harry,' she said.

'You asked.'

'I wish now I hadn't been so fucking curious.'

I glanced across at the others. Julius was staring stoically ahead, his face impassive; Sam Goldberg looked green, though whether it was the motion of the boat or just plain terror I couldn't say. I suspected it was a combination of the two. Stevie looked back at me and tried for a smile, a reassuring smile. It tugged at my heart. I'd got her into this mess and now I didn't have a clue how to get her out of it. I sat there praying for a miracle that seemed very unlikely to manifest itself.

A while later the three Cubans had gathered in the wheelhouse and were talking amongst themselves. They had a chart open and seemed to be arguing about the direction they were taking. As sailors they didn't seem that experienced. Maritza came out of the wheelhouse and went across to the side rail, peering down into the water.

'It's the coral beds you have to watch out for,' I said.

'They rip through fibreglass like a knife through butter. And this hull is fibreglass.' I was exaggerating the risk. Compared to the run to Barracuda Cay this stretch of water was easy to navigate; but the Cubans didn't know that and I thought a little anxiety on their behalf might be helpful

I don't know if Maritza understood me, but she gave me a poisonous look and went back to join her colleagues. Moments later another argument ensued and Miguel cut the power to the engine.

'I think they're lost,' Julius said.

'It's easy to lose your bearings here,' I said loudly for the Cubans' benefit. 'Maps, compasses and even GPS devices are great, but you need to really know this stretch of water to safely navigate it.'

Julius looked at me as if I were mad. He opened his mouth to say something, but I gave a small shake of my head and he clamped his lips shut.

Luis emerged from the wheelhouse. He walked up to me and kicked my ankle. 'You,' he said. 'On your feet.'

'Why?'

'On your feet!' He grabbed my shirt and tried to haul me up.

'You'd find it easier if his legs were untied, dumbass,' Stevie said.

He glared at her, but produced a lock knife from his pocket and cut the cable tie that bound my legs together. When he hauled again I was able to assist him.

Pressing the knife against my spine he propelled me towards the wheelhouse. He jabbed at the chart that was lying on the table, his finger landing in the centre of the blue hole. 'You take us there,' he said.

I shook my head. 'No, I don't think so.'

He pressed harder with the knife. I felt my skin pop and the blood start to trickle down. 'Kill me and you're stuck here,' I said.

The pressure eased. He said something to Miguel in Spanish then went back out onto the deck. I heard Billie cry out. Luis was standing over her and had sliced her shirt open with his knife, now he was working on her bra. He severed the straps and her bra came off. Blood rushed to her cheeks in a hot blush.

'Leave her alone!' I shouted.

'You steer the boat.'

He had one hand planted in her hair and the other was holding the knife which was pressed against her left breast. Another ounce of pressure and he'd cut her.

'Deal,' I called.

Miguel understood that much English at least. He started the engine, standing aside to let me take the wheel. I glanced back at the deck. Luis had released Billie and was now talking to Maritza. Billie was sitting, visibly shaking, tears streaking her cheeks. I caught her eye, but she turned her face away. 'At least let her cover herself up,' I called to Luis.

He turned to look at her. 'I like the view,' he said.

'Take the wheel,' I said to Miguel. 'Keep steering straight ahead.'

Incomprehension spread over his face.

'I said, take the fucking wheel!' I jabbed my finger at the windscreen. 'Straight ahead. *Comprender?*'

I stormed out of the wheelhouse and back along the deck. Luis swore and Maritza raised the machine pistol, but Luis grabbed the barrel and pushed it down until it was aimed at the deck. I crouched down in front to Billie and pulled the severed halves of her shirt together, tying them in a knot just under her breasts. It was hardly a fashion statement, but at least it covered her. 'Are you ok?'

She was biting her bottom lip, trying to stem the flow of tears. She nodded. 'I'm okay,' she said. 'Scared shitless, but okay.'

'We'll get through this,' I said. 'All of us. I promise.'

She stared into my eyes, searching for the lie. Finally a wan smile curled her lips. She sniffed back the tears. 'Yeah,' she said. 'Course we will.'

I went back to the wheel house and pushed Miguel out of the way, taking the wheel again and checking the bearings. We had about an hour before we reached the blue hole and the fate Jack Dylan had dreamed up for us. Which meant I had about sixty minutes to come up with some kind of plan so I could make good my promise to Billie.

I stared out at the ocean. On the horizon thunderheads were gathering. The storm was still out there and we were heading directly for it. The first few spots of rain spattered against the windscreen and I noticed Maritza's frizzy hair was being blown across her face by the rising wind.

I eased back slightly on the throttle. Miguel looked at me sharply as the sound of the engine changed. 'Coral bed,' I said, pointing vaguely through the window.

He frowned.

Luis came into the wheelhouse, grabbed my shoulder and spun me around. 'Why we slow down? I not say slow down!'

'We're over a coral bed. The water here is shallow, so unless you want me to tear the bottom out of the boat leave me alone to do my job.'

He hesitated, indecision flickering in his eyes. Finally he made a noise of frustration in the back of his throat, turned and went back on deck. I eased the throttle back more. With any luck the storm would hit us before we reached the blue hole and, if it was as ferocious as the one I'd encountered on the run to Barracuda Cay, the situation could change drastically. At the very least it would even out the playing field slightly. I slowed the boat to about three knots, making a great play of looking out of all the windows to check the depth of the water and the closeness of the coral. Next to me Miguel was looking anxious.

'How deep?' he said, a tremor in his voice.

'Three feet. Maybe less.'

He shook his head, not understanding what I'd said. I held my hand roughly a yard above the floor of the cabin. 'Three feet.'

If he'd bothered to go outside and look over the side he would have seen that the water we were passing through was at least ten times deeper than that. Instead he crossed himself and started to pray.

I ignored him. I was staring at the storm clouds ahead, willing them to come closer. Beside me Miguel gave a small grunt and sank to his knees, his eyes rolled back in their sockets and he collapsed unconscious onto the floor of the wheelhouse, blood seeping from a gash in the back of his head.

For a moment I couldn't understand what had happened; and then a very familiar voice said quietly, 'Hello, Harry.'

I turned and stared at the smiling face of Alan Lancaster who was standing in the corner of the wheelhouse holding a metal bar streaked with Miguel's blood.

60

The hatch to the below deck storage area had been pushed back. How he had sneaked into the wheelhouse without being seen was beyond me, but he had managed it and he'd cracked Miguel over the back of the head. I glanced back at the deck, but Luis and Maritza were both now staring over the rail trying to catch a glimpse of the imaginary coral beds. Any moment they could turn and look up at the wheelhouse. We had to act fast. I gestured for Alan to stay where he was and went to the door.

'Hey! Give me some help up here. Your friend's collapsed.'

Luis reacted immediately. He snapped something at Maritza, pulled out his gun and ran towards the wheelhouse. At the door he pushed me out of the way and looked down at Miguel. He saw the gash on the back of Miguel's head and turned to me angrily and as he did so Alan brought the metal bar crashing down on his arm, shattering his wrist. Luis screamed in pain and the gun clattered to the floor. As he clutched at his wrist I swung a punch and connected with the point of his jaw. His head snapped back and he crumpled.

On deck Maritza watched all this happen with an expression of complete shock on her face and, as Luis fell, she shook herself and raised the machine pistol. 'Down!' I yelled as she sprayed the wheelhouse. Glass shattered as bullets tore through the windows.

I looked out in time to see Stevie swing her legs and connect with the back of Maritza's ankles, taking the Cuban woman's legs out from under her. Maritza toppled backwards, smashing the back of her head on the unforgiving wood of the deck as she landed. Before she had time to gather herself Stevie raised her legs and brought her heels crashing down into Maritza's face, knocking her out cold.

The whole thing had taken less than a minute and I found it hard to grasp that a situation could change so quickly. I felt in Luis' pocket and found the knife, bolted out onto the deck and severed the others' bonds. Stevie was on her feet quickly and ran to the hatch.

'Where are you going?' I said.

'To find some rope. I want to get these bastards tied up.'

Billie and Sam were getting to their feet. Julius just sat there, a huge smile on his face.

'Nice moves, man,' he said.

'Thank Alan. I couldn't have done it without him.'

Alan was standing in the doorway of the wheelhouse, sunlight glinting on his dirty blonde hair.

'Who are you, bloody Houdini? How did you manage that?' I said.

'I've been hiding below. When I saw the welcome Kim gave Jack as he arrived at Watt's Cay I realised she was the one who'd sold me out.'

'So you've been hiding out on the boat ever since.'

'No. I followed them to the house. Once I saw the situation there I realised they'd be coming back to the boat sooner rather than later so I thought I'd form my own one-man reception committee.'

'That was a long shot.'

'Not really. Jack has a propensity for tying up loose ends...and I'd seen the anchor chain on the deck so I guessed what he was planning. When we were kids playing our games Jack was always the one who'd come up with the ruthless endings to make sure the games had some kind of conclusion. He hasn't changed.'

I'd forgotten that, or at least thought I had; but it was true. As soon as I climbed aboard the boat and saw the coils of chain curled in the corner of the deck I knew what Jack had in mind, so maybe those games had left more of an impression than I thought.

'So what's next?' Alan said.

'You can start by introducing us,' Billie said. She'd recovered from her ordeal and the spark had been reignited in her eyes.

At that moment a fork of lightning split the sky, closely followed by a low growl of thunder. 'I'll leave Stevie to make the introductions,' I said. 'I'm going to race the storm back to Watt's Cay.'

I headed back to the wheelhouse and gunned the engine, spinning the wheel and turning the boat around. From wishing the storm to find us I was now anxious to get back to land before it hit. I was unfamiliar with Jack's boat and didn't know how she'd handle in a storm. *The Lady* had never let me down, but the Marko was a different beast altogether. I soon pushed her up to fifteen knots and, although the rain was beating against the windscreen and reducing visibility, I was confident we'd make landfall before the worst of the storm struck.

A short while later Stevie joined me in the wheelhouse. The Cubans had been tied up and left on deck to suffer the rain. Alan and the others were sheltering in the Marko's small and sparsely furnished kitchenette.

'Do you want me to take the wheel?' she said.

'No. Why?'

'I thought you might want to speak to Alan.'

I shook my head. 'It'll wait.'

'I still can't believe she's gone.'

'*The Lady*?'

She nodded. She was close to tears and was biting her bottom lip to distract herself. 'Why did the bastard do that?'

'I don't know, Stevie. I think he wanted to hurt me, and you too.'

'Well he succeeded. Quite a week so far, eh?'

'It's not over yet,' I said. 'There's Jack and Kim to deal with first. And those children. The boat's coming from Florida for them tomorrow. I want to get them off Watt's Cay and to safety before it arrives. We don't know how heavily it'll be manned.'

'You don't have to play the hero you know? You could call the authorities and let them deal with it.'

'I could do that, but where would that leave Alan? They'd arrest him, and I can't imagine his prison sentence would be lenient.'

'Jesus H Christ, Harry! Alan's not your concern.'

'He's my brother,' I said.

61

'Oh enough with the hippie stuff. Alan's your friend, best friend maybe, but he's not your brother.'

'That's just it, Stevie. He *is* my brother. My father told me when I visited him on Barracuda Cay. He had an affair with Alan's mother. Alan was the result.'

She ran her hand through her already tousled hair. 'Okay,' she said. 'I guess that changes things.'

'Yes, but only a little. I still can't forgive him for getting involved in all this. He went into it with his eyes open, and because of his stupidity people have died. Anna, Sally, Serena Carr and her brother. Even Philippe would still be alive if it wasn't for Alan. But I won't be the one responsible for sending him to jail.'

'Does he know how many people have died because of him?'

'He does now.' Alan was standing in the doorway of the wheelhouse, his face ashen. 'Serena's dead?'

I nodded.

'How?'

'Jack shot her through the head.'

'And Jerry?'

'The same. They didn't know where you were so they were surplus to requirements, and for Jack they were just more loose ends.'

He sagged against the doorframe. 'I had no idea.' Tears started rolling down his cheeks. 'I loved that girl so much.'

'And Anna, Sally? Did you love them too?' Stevie said. She was looking at Alan will ill-concealed contempt.

'Of course I did…well, Sally. Anna and I had our issues.'

'Well it saves you an expensive divorce,' she said.

'Stevie, that's enough!' I said.

She looked at me hotly. 'Harry! Don't take his side. Remember what those bastard Cubans did to me. It wouldn't have happened if it wasn't for him. He's caused so much damage, so much harm, and I don't care if he *is* your brother, you can't let him get away with it.' She stormed out of the wheelhouse, barging past Alan.

He looked at me bleakly. 'Lucas told you? About him and my mother?'

'Yes, he dropped that bombshell the other day. I think he enjoyed it although he's claiming remorse now.'

'You must hate me. Stevie's right. I have to pay for what I've done.'

'First things first,' I said. I took a couple of steps towards him and punched him hard in the face.

He staggered back, holding out an arm to steady himself. 'I guess I deserve that.'

'Is what Jack said true? Do you have the information needed to bring down the paedophile ring, the cartel?'

He nodded. 'Names, dates, what child went where. Everything.'

I had to ask him. I didn't want to, but there was no avoiding it.

'When Jack asked me to invest in a business venture I thought it would be another restaurant. You know the

Oyster Bar and the *Tar* are mine? I'm not a hands-on owner, not with someone I've known such a long time, not with Jack. It took me a while to realize what was going on.'

'Where's the hard evidence?'

He fished in his pocket and produced a memory stick identical in size to the one Jack had sent me, but this one was red. I held out my hand and he dropped it into my palm. I closed my fingers around it. So many people had died because of Jack's search for this small plastic device I was expecting it to resonate, but it didn't. It just sat there in my fist, inert and unspectacularly ordinary. I made to hand it back to him, but he shook his head.

'No,' he said. 'You hold on to it, as a mark of good faith.'

'Okay. But...'

I was interrupted by Jack's voice blaring from the radio. 'Luis? Luis! Come in. Is the job done?'

'Fetch Luis up here. I don't want Jack getting suspicious and running. I want to nail that bastard.'

As Alan went to get Luis and bring him to the wheelhouse I listened to Jack repeating the message over and over, each time getting a little more irate and a little more impatient.

Finally Alan returned holding on to Luis by the collar of his shirt. In his other hand was Maritza's machine pistol and he'd rammed the barrel under Luis' chin.

Jack sounded again, swearing this time.

'Right, listen to me and listen carefully,' I said. 'Tell him the job's done. We're all over the side and you're heading back to Watt's Cay. Got that?'

Luis spat in my face.

As I wiped the saliva from my cheek I said, 'You'll tell him, or you and your friends will find yourselves swimming home. But just so you know, there's blue sharks in these waters and I'll make sure all three of you will be bleeding when you enter the water. They'll sense you from a mile away, maybe more. So I think it'll be a short swim.'

Fear flashed in his eyes. He said something in Spanish that sounded crude, but held out his hand for the handset.

'It's Luis.'

'About fucking time!' Jack came back. 'What's the score?'

'It's done. All of them. We're coming back.'

'Good. I'll see you when you get here.'

I took the handset back from him. 'Get him and the other two below,' I said to Alan. 'And lock them in.'

I was finally alone in the wheelhouse. I could see Watt's Cay, a speck in the distance. Although it was raining heavily now and the sea was getting choppy, we would make it back before the storm. Although in my head another storm was raging.

62

Julius joined me in the wheelhouse.

'Did you get the Cubans below?' I said.

'They're secure.'

'Are you planning to tie up at the jetty?'

We were half a mile out and my plans were still a woolly tangle in my head. 'I don't know what's for the best. If Jack's watching from the house he'll see there's something wrong.'

'Alan moored his boat in a cove on the west of the island that can't be seen from the house. We could tie up alongside and make land that way.'

'Yes, but Jack's expecting the Cubans. He'll get suspicious if I don't take the boat back soon.'

'Then go round to the west to where Alan's moored, and then you and the others change boats and leave me to take this one back to the jetty. He won't question a black face at the wheel. He'll think it's Miguel. We're about the same size and I'll keep my face averted. He won't suspect anything.'

It sounded like a plan. 'Okay. We'll leave Stevie, Billie and Sam on the boat, then Alan and I will get to shore and make our way to the house. We'll signal you when we get there. Take the wheel. I'll go and tell the others what's happening.'

When I told them Sam and Billie looked relieved.

'I think I've had enough excitement for one day,' Billie said.

'Yeah, I'll second that. Though this is going to make one helluva story. The *Post* will be tearing my arm off to get hold of it.'

'How are we going to signal Julius when we get to the house?' Alan said.

'There's a flare gun in a locker below,' Stevie said. 'I saw it when I was looking for the rope to tie those bastards up. Oh, and I'm coming with you and Alan.'

'No!' Billie said. As we turned to look at her the blood rushed to her cheeks and she blushed. 'I mean, there's no point risking your life like that. You've been through so much already.'

'I'll be fine, hun.' Stevie said. 'I want to witness the fall of Jack Dylan. I want it more than anything else in the world.'

'When she's in this kind of mood,' I said to Billie. 'You won't get anywhere trying to change her mind.' To Stevie I said, 'Go and fetch the flare gun.'

Alan and I went back to the wheelhouse. 'So are those two an item?' Alan said.

'Stevie and Billie?' I shrugged. 'I don't know. But then I don't know a thing about any of my friends, do I?'

* * *

Julius brought us up alongside Alan's Princess V85 V-Class Sports Yacht. Eighty-five feet of sheer class and the type of boat I could only own in my dreams. We climbed aboard and Julius moved away.

'There is a slight problem with this plan,' Alan said. 'I went across to the Cay in the dinghy. It's still there. I have a small inflatable, but we'll have to row.'

'That's not a problem,' Stevie said. 'Though calluses might not sit well with your manicure.' She was baiting him.

'I'll live with it,' he said.

Calluses were the last thing on my mind as I took up the oars. The wind had increased dramatically as the storm approached the shore and it was raining heavily. The sea was starting to get rough and it took all my strength to keep us on course. The waves were lifting the lightweight inflatable and carrying it along for a while before dropping us into a trough. The constant impacts were jarring my teeth.

Both Alan and Stevie were grim faced and I guess all of us were wondering if we were going to make it to shore alive. Stevie glanced behind her and said, 'Harry!' The warning was in her voice, but I'd already seen the wave. It was at least twenty feet high and it was barrelling down on us. It picked us up like flotsam and we rode it for what seemed like an eternity. The oars were ripped from my grasp and went spinning off into the storm. The inflatable flipped and the three of us were flying through the air.

I landed flat on my back on the white sand shore, air rushing out of me like an express train. I lay there winded for an age, with the rain lashing my face, before turning my head to see if I could see the others. The first thing I saw was the inflatable. It had been carried several hundred yards inland and was upside down on the sand. The oars too had made it to the cay. I thought vaguely that I should gather them up and stow them somewhere safe in case we needed them later, but then I caught a movement out of the corner of my eye and turned my head more to get a clearer view.

It was Stevie. She was sitting up, rubbing the back of her head and drawing in long, deep breaths, letting the rain pummel her and wash the salt water away. Beyond her Alan lay face down in the surf and I couldn't tell if he were alive or dead. Stevie crawled over to him, rolled him over and checked for a pulse in his neck. 'He's alive,' she called.

Alan coughed once and sat up, looking about him with wild and frightened eyes. 'What the fu…'

'It's okay. We made it,' I shouted.

'Jesus!' he said.

'Are you both all right?'

'I cracked my head, but I'll live,' Stevie called above the howl of the storm.

Alan just nodded and pushed himself to his feet, leaning into the wind to maintain his balance.

'Do you still have the flare gun?' I shouted to Stevie.

Panic flared momentarily in her eyes. She checked the waistband of her shorts and produced the gun, raising it high. 'Got it. Seem to have lost the extra flares though.'

'Don't worry. We should only need the one. Come on. Let's get out of this weather.'

63

The storm wasn't as fierce as *Noel*, the tropical storm that had swept through this part of the world in 2007 and claimed over a hundred lives, but it was wild enough.

We made our way inland, fighting the storm all the way. We were soaked to the skin and the wind was chilling us as well as making it very difficult to walk.

'This is useless,' I shouted. 'We can't fight it.'

Alan brought his face to within inches of mine. 'What do you suggest?'

'There,' I said. We were five hundred yards away from the ramshackle house that held the children. 'We'll sit out the worst of it there.'

'What about Julius?' Stevie said. She'd joined the huddle.

'He's no fool. He won't be expecting us to signal him any time soon. He'll wait on the boat until we do.'

By the time we reached the broken-down porch of the house, Stevie was shivering. I hammered on the door. A storm shutter was swinging backwards and forwards in the wind, banging against the side of the house. With that and the howling wind it was hardly surprising that Elena did not respond. I tried again, and called out this time, but the words were whipped away by the wind as soon as they left my lips. 'It's no use,' I said to the others. 'We'll try round the back. There may be a door open.'

'To hell with that,' Alan said and kicked out at the door; it shook a little in its frame but stayed shut. 'Both of us, together,' Alan said.

We kicked and the door crashed inwards.

Elena stood there, just inside the doorway. She was holding a shotgun, but I could see from her eyes she wasn't going to use it. She was too young and this was beyond her sphere of experience. Added to which she was frightened, badly frightened.

Stevie took a step inside the house, swung a left hook and caught Elena just under the eye. The girl dropped the shotgun and threw her hands to her face. Stevie drew her fist back to hit her again.

'That's enough,' I said.

Alan and I stepped inside and pushed the door closed. Elena had sunk to her knees and was sobbing. We pulled her upright. 'Is anyone else here?'

'Only the children,' she gasped between sobs.

We took her into one of the downstairs rooms and sat her down on a threadbare couch. 'It's all right, we're not going to hurt you,' I said to her.

She looked up at me with frightened rabbit eyes. 'She hit me,' she said, switching her attention to Stevie.

'Well, to be fair, you were pointing a shotgun at us,' Alan said.

'It's not loaded.'

'Well, she didn't know that when she hit you,' I said. 'Stevie, go up and check on the children. They're probably scared out of their wits.'

'I'm not a fucking nursemaid.'

'Please.'

Stevie made a grand shrug and left the room. I turned back to Elena. 'Is there any way to contact anybody? A phone, radio?'

'In the next room. A radio.'

'Keep an eye on her. I'll check it out,' I said to Alan.

A table stood in the middle of the adjoining room and on the table a short wave radio transmitter. Jack or Kim probably used it to communicate with the boats that came in to pick up the children.

I switched it on and turned the dial. I'd have to broadcast on an open channel as I had no idea of the frequency of Jack's radio on the boat. It was hit and miss. Getting through to Julius without alerting anyone else would be a matter of luck. I hit the button. 'Julius, this is Harry. Come in.'

I was hoping Julius had the radio switched on, but there was no response. I tried again. The third time round the speaker crackled and Julius' voice rang out. 'Harry, man, where are you?'

'Sheltering from the storm. It's too fierce to get to the house. Visibility is poor. How are you doing?'

'Tossing about like a pea in a pot. But I'm hanging in there. I wouldn't like to be the Cubans at the moment; they're probably being thrown about in the hold.'

'My heart bleeds. It'll do them good to suffer. Listen, we're going to give the storm a few hours to die down. I'll call you again when we're ready to move on Jack.'

'Got it. I'll wait to hear from you.'

Alan was sitting next to Elena on the couch when I returned to the other room. 'I got through to Julius,' I said.

'Good. Elena and I have been having a little chat. The boat from Florida's due here at eleven tomorrow. It's only a small craft with a three man crew. I think we can take them if the worst comes to the worst.'

'You mean if we're stuck here until the boat arrives.'

'We don't know how long this storm's going to take to blow itself out. It could well be that we're here tomorrow. You really need to rethink your plan.'

That wasn't going to be easy as I didn't have a plan. I'd been winging it ever since we overpowered the Cubans. If anything was driving me onwards it was the overwhelming desire to bring Jack and Kim to justice and to stop any more children being sold into slavery, but the finer points that make up a plan of action remained elusive.

Julius' voice sounded from the radio speaker in the other room.

'Julius, I hear you.'

'Just listened to the weather report. The storm's going to turn in a couple of hours, so we might be able to...'

His next words were drowned out by what sounded like a gun shot.

A few seconds later another voice came over the speaker.

'Is that you, Harry?' Jack Dylan said.

I hesitated for a moment before I said, 'Yes, Jack, it's me.'

'Damn it. I thought you were dead.' There was a mocking tone to his voice.

'Put Julius on.'

'Difficult. He's too busy bleeding.'

'You bastard!'

'Harsh words, Harry. Harsh words. Now you have a choice. Either you get your ass back here or I let your friend bleed himself to death. What's it to be?'

I didn't need to think about it. 'Okay, Jack, you win. Keep Julius from bleeding. Keep him alive. I'll be with you as soon as I can.'

'I'm looking forward to it already.'

The radio went dead.

As I walked back into the other room Alan said, 'You look ill. What's happened?'

I told him.

'Shit! Does he know I'm with you?'

'He'll know that as soon as he releases the Cubans and

speaks to them.'

'No, they'll tell him I helped you, but he won't know I'm still with you. You can tell him I took off on my boat. He's not to know I didn't.'

It was an idea, but I didn't think Jack would swallow it. 'We have Elena. We could trade her for Julius.'

'Believe me, Harry, I know Jack better than anyone. He'd put a bullet between her eyes rather than let you use her as a bargaining chip. Let's go and give Jack what he wants. We'll work out how to handle this on the way.'

I sighed. It had been a long day; and it had just gone from bad to worse. 'Okay,' I said. 'Let's do it.'

64

Jack was waiting at the door of Kim's house, an automatic in his hand, watching me as I struggled against the buffeting wind along the winding path.

'I should kill you now,' he said.

'Why don't you then? You're the one holding the gun.'

'All in good time.'

'Where's Julius?'

He pressed the barrel of the automatic into my side and patted me down, looking for a weapon. Finding none he said, 'Get inside.'

Julius was lying on one of Kim's leather couches. There was a blood-soaked cotton pad taped to his chest. His eyes were closed and he was breathing deeply.

'I think I missed his lung when I shot him, but never mind,' Jack said.

Kim sat on the other couch, her legs crossed, glass of brandy in her hand. 'Well,' she said. 'Here we are again, just the four of us. How cosy. Where's Alan?'

That question had been following me around for days and I was getting sick of it.

At the sound of our voices Julius' eyes flickered open. He stared up at me from the couch.

'How do you feel?' I said.

'It could have been worse. I'll live,' he said. 'I let you down. Sorry, man.'

'You did no such thing. Don't talk. Save your strength.'

'Very touching,' Jack said. 'But you haven't answered Kim's question. I know he was with you, so where is he now?'

'He took off once we reached his boat,' I said.

Jack pressed the gun harder into my ribcage. 'Now why do I find that hard to believe?'

'It's true,' I said. 'He knew if he stayed with me I'd turn him over to the authorities.'

Jack exchanged looks with Kim. She raised her eyebrows. 'Why would you turn him in? He's your best friend. Oh no, of course, he's your brother. Sorry, Harry, you're going to have to do better than that.'

'He's telling the truth,' Julius said. 'Alan Lancaster's scum.'

'He stopped being my friend the day he threw in his lot with you and your filthy business. He killed any loyalty I might have for him when he let his wife and daughter get blown to bits.'

Kim put her glass down on the coffee table and got up from the couch. 'Jack, a word.'

With the gun Jack urged me to sit on the couch next to Julius. 'One wrong move and I'll blow your head off.'

Kim had crossed to the far side of the room. Jack joined her and they started to talk quietly, occasionally glancing back where we sat.

'Are you really okay?' I whispered to Julius.

'Sure,' he said. 'I'm letting them think it's worse than it is. Biding my time.'

'Where are the Cubans?'

'He dragged them up from the hold, got the information he wanted then cut their throats and threw them over the side,' Julius said. 'Shark bait.'

'More loose ends tidied away.'

'He's a psychopath, Harry.'

I glanced across at Jack who was still talking to Kim. 'Yes, I think he is.'

Suddenly he wheeled away from her and pulled his gun, aiming at the door on the far side of the lounge. 'You can come in now, Alan. We've been expecting you.'

There was a moment of absolute stillness. Nothing moved. Julius and I were holding our breath.

The door opened a crack.

Jack fired twice at the door, splintering the wood.

There was another beat and the door flew open. I caught a brief glimpse of Stevie as she raised the flare gun and fired at Jack.

Kim screamed and threw herself in front of her lover and the flare took her in the face. She hit the floor, her head a ball of fire. Jack emptied his gun into the doorway, but Stevie was nowhere to be seen. He glanced down at Kim then ran from the house.

The whole encounter had taken less than thirty seconds. I sat on the couch, frozen into immobility by the suddenness of it all.

'Get after him,' Julius said. He shook my arm. 'Harry, get after Jack. He's getting away.'

But I had other things on my mind. 'Stevie? Stevie!'

I ran across to the doorway. Stevie was leaning against the wall on the other side of it. A bullet had winged her shoulder, but it didn't look serious. 'You silly little fool,' I said. 'What the hell did you think you were doing?'

'Covering your ass, Harry,' she said, a wan smile playing on her lips. 'As usual.' Then she slid down the wall in a dead faint.

I carried her into the lounge and laid her on the couch, trying hard not to look at Kim. Julius had hauled himself up and extinguished the flames, but it was too late for her. Much too late. 'Cover her up before Stevie comes round and sees what she's done.'

Julius pulled a cloth from the dining table and draped it over Kim's body. I ripped my shirt and made a small pad with the material, dabbing away the blood from Stevie's shoulder. It was as I'd thought, a flesh wound, nothing more, but it would sting like hell when she woke up.

As if on cue Stevie groaned and her eyes fluttered open. She jerked her head round and stared at the covered body lying on the floor. 'Is he dead?'

I shook my head. 'Kim threw herself in front of him.'

'I liked her.' Stevie flopped back onto the couch. 'If she hadn't been a child trafficking piece of shit we might have been friends.'

'Yeah. She had me fooled, that's for sure.'

'So that bastard is still free?'

'After you shot Kim with the flare he ran. I thought he'd killed you.'

'I wouldn't give him the satisfaction.'

'This wasn't how it was meant to go,' I said.

'You mean you were banking on Alan rushing in to save the day.' She shook her head, genuine sadness in her eyes. 'Oh, Harry, you never learn, do you? Alan had no intention of putting himself in danger. When you left the house I tied Elena up and followed you, right up until the point where you split up. I guessed what your plan would be. You'd offer yourself up to Jack while Alan moved around to the back of the house and came up behind him. But Alan had other ideas. As soon as you were out of sight he doubled back and headed off to his boat.'

'Then he'll be miles away by now.'

She smiled. 'I don't think so.' She fished inside the pocket of her shorts, wincing from the pain in her shoulder, and produced a set of keys. 'I never trusted him so I relieved him of these. He's going nowhere fast.'

'You never cease to amaze me,' I said. 'Stay here with Julius. Give them to me. I'm going after Alan.'

'What about Jack?' Julius said.

'His boat hasn't the speed to match Alan's. I'll catch up with him.'

'And then?' Stevie said.

I didn't reply.

'Let me come with you,' Julius said.

'With that hole in your chest? I don't think so. Stay here with Stevie.'

'The walking wounded,' Stevie said. 'He's right, Julius, we'll just slow him down.' She clasped her hand to her shoulder and hissed through her teeth. 'Christ! It stings.'

'I thought it would,' I said with a smile. 'See? You're not as tough as you think you are.'

'Bastard!' she said, matching my smile with one of her own. 'Get out of here.'

'Take care, man,' Julius said.

'Don't worry, I will,' I said.

65

At least the storm was dying away. The wind direction had changed, taking it out to sea once more. It made running easier.

I reached the shore where the Cubans had left *The Lady's* dinghy. I pushed it into the water, climbed aboard and started the outboard motor.

I stuck to the shoreline and minutes later I was coming up on Alan's Princess. I eased back on the throttle. I could see Alan on deck. He seemed to be searching for something.

'Looking for these,' I called, holding the keys to his boat aloft.

He looked up from his search, saw me and ambled over to the rail. 'I might have known,' he said, a smile spreading over his face.

Sam and Billie appeared behind him.

'What's going on?' Sam Goldberg said. 'He told us you'd been shot and that he'd managed to escape.'

'We were going to head back to Freeport and contact the police,' Billie added. 'But Alan seems to have lost the keys.'

I held them aloft again, giving them a shake for good measure.

'Drop the ladder. I'm coming aboard.'

Moments later the rope ladder rolled down the side of Alan's boat. I tethered the dinghy and climbed aboard. 'Jack's made a run for it,' I said to Alan. 'We can catch him if we move quickly.' I turned to Billie and Sam. 'You two take the dinghy and head back to Watt's Cay. When you get there call Sergeant Jim Henderson. You'll find his number on here.' I tossed them my mobile phone. 'Tell him what's happened and say we need medical assistance urgently.'

'Who's been hurt?' she said, alarm flashing in her eyes.

'Stevie and Julius. Both shot.'

She groaned. 'Oh Christ!'

'Stevie's fine. Just a flesh wound. Julius is a bit more serious. He took one in the chest, but he's tough is Julius. He'll be fine, but stress the urgency of the medical assistance. It doesn't pay to take chances, especially with bullet wounds.'

'And Kim? Is she with Jack?' Alan said.

'Kim's dead. She took a flare in the face. She was dead before she hit the floor.'

Billie gasped. 'Stevie had the flare gun. Did she…'

I nodded.

'Poor kid. She's going to feel so bad.'

'Not a word to the police about Stevie and the flare gun, and, when you see her, tell her to keep her mouth shut about it. If they press her she's to say she was outside the door and saw nothing. Okay?'

Billie nodded. 'Not a word. Do you want me to get rid of it?'

'Throw it into the sea as far as you can.'

'Yeah,' she said. 'I can do that.'

Sam was peering nervously over the side at the dinghy as it kicked and bucked on the waves. 'And you want us to get back to the island in that?'

'You'll be fine,' I said. 'The storm's dying out.' I tried to hurry them along. Every moment we spent in conversation Jack put more distance between himself and us. Billie squeezed his arm. 'Come on. It's down to us now.' She hopped over the rail and onto the rope ladder, descending to the dinghy. Sam was slower, but he made it aboard. Billie started the motor, released the tether and they were away.

'Well,' Alan said. 'Just you and me. Like old times.'

I shook my head. 'No, this is nothing like old times, Alan. We used to be friends. And apparently we're supposed to be brothers.'

'Ouch,' he said. 'Harry, I'm sorry I ran out on you, okay, but I couldn't take the chance you'd have a change of heart and turn me over to the police. I can't go to jail, Harry, it would finish me. And remember, I know you very well. You *would* have had that change of heart.'

'Do you think about anyone but yourself?' I said as I climbed up to the flying bridge. I slotted the key in the ignition and the engine started smoothly.

'That's unfair,' Alan said.

'I don't think so. We could have all been killed back at the house. You knew that and still you ran out on us.' I eased the throttle forward, the propellers spun, churning up a white spume and the boat began to move. 'This has all happened because of you.'

'It's all happened because I've been trying to stop it.'

'You wouldn't have got involved in the first place if you cared more about people than you do for making more money. I've known you all my life and any respect, any love I had for you has just about been drained out of me.'

Alan moved to the long, leather seat at the back of the flying bridge and sat down, crossing his legs. 'How do you know where Jack's headed?' he said.

'I don't know for certain, but my guess is he's going to make for Florida. His luck's run out on the Islands and he knows it. He'll head for Florida because he's obviously got contacts there and, once he's in the US, he'll find it easy enough to disappear. So that's the course I'm taking. What's the top speed of this thing?'

'35 knots,' he said.

'Then we'll catch him. Jack has a maximum speed of 22.'

'I admire your optimism,' Alan said.

'Good,' I said. 'You just sit there on your ass and admire it, because I promised Jack Dylan I was going to bring him down and, unlike some, I don't go back on my word.'

66

The storm had blown back out to sea and the sun was breaking through the clouds, glinting off the wave caps. The exhilaration of feeling the wind blowing through my hair was making me feel light-headed. It was almost possible to put all thoughts of Jack Dylan out of my mind and just settle into enjoying the ride.

Alan's boat handled like a dream and I felt the adrenaline rush of being in charge of a vessel that was responsive to my every whim. *The Lady* used to handle like that, though not at this kind of speed. Already I was thinking about her in the past tense, and it was a sickening thought. She was insured, but I knew I'd never be able to replace her. I could buy another boat with the insurance money, sure, but whatever craft I bought next I knew I'd never be able to recapture the sheer buzz of almost elemental excitement I felt whenever I started *The Lady's* engines. I had loved that boat with a passion bordering on the obsessive. She may have cost me my relationship with Katy, but she had more than compensated for that loss over the years.

'There he is,' Alan said.

I turned. He was still sitting casually on the long seat, but he was holding a pair of binoculars to his eyes and was pointing off to starboard. I followed his line of sight and saw a small speck on the horizon.

'Are you sure it's him?'

'It's him.'

I turned the wheel and the boat responded. The small speck grew larger as we closed in on it and ten minutes later I had Jack Dylan in my sights. 'Right, you bastard,' I said under my breath. 'Payback time.'

We were half a mile away from him when he began firing at us. I could see the flare from a machine pistol's barrel, but could not yet hear it over the roar of the boat's engines. A bullet whistled past my ear and took a bite out of the superstructure of the flying bridge.

'Get down to the cockpit and take over the controls,' I shouted at Alan. 'I want you to bring us alongside him. Close.'

'How close?'

'Close enough for me to board him.'

'You are out of you mind,' he said, but was already moving down the stairs to the cockpit and the duplicate set of controls.

Once I felt him take over I let go of the wheel and moved down to the sun deck. Alan was sitting in the cockpit steering the Princess like the expert he obviously was. He glanced back at me and made an OK sign with his finger and thumb.

I looked across and saw Jack Dylan. He was standing on the bridge of the Marko, steering one-handed and trying to aim the machine pistol in my direction. He was smiling. The bastard was actually smiling! Alan tweaked the controls and brought us up alongside. Realising what we were doing Jack swung the pistol round and sprayed the cockpit. Windows shattered and I felt the Princess lurch. I only had one chance at this. I ran for the side and jumped.

For a brief few seconds I was airborne and then with

a bone-crunching jolt I landed in a heap on the aft deck of the Marko.

I rolled and hauled myself to my feet, glancing back at the Princess, but she had veered away and was slowing down. We were leaving her and Alan behind. Jack killed the engine and was moving down from the bridge advancing on me, machine pistol cocked.

'Jesus, Harry, you just couldn't let it go, could you?' He raised the pistol. I looked back again at the Princess, but she had slowed to a halt and was dead in the water.

With almost a fatalistic fascination I watched Jack's finger tighten on the trigger and I held my breath, waiting for the hail of bullets to cut me in two.

Nothing happened.

A frown crossed Jack's forehead and he shook the weapon, willing it to work; but the magazine was empty. The gun was useless. With a frustrated roar he threw the machine pistol into the sea and launched himself at me.

Jack was six inches taller and forty pounds heavier and he came at me like a bear, catching me around the waist and taking me down to the deck. We had fought as children and even then he'd had the advantage of size. The results of those fights were inevitable. Jack would win, usually by pinning me down and trapping one part or another of my anatomy in a crippling submission hold; but that was when we were children. I'd learnt a few things since then, and one of them was how to fight dirty. As we tumbled to the deck I rammed my knee up between his legs and listened with satisfaction as the air rushed out of him and he groaned.

He rolled off me and lay there for a moment, clutching himself. I struggled up to my feet again, but he shot out a hand and grabbed my ankle, tugging hard and taking me off balance. I fell back to the deck, landing badly on my elbow. A numbing pain shot up my arm and turned to fire in my shoulder. I lay there for a moment fighting down a wave of nausea, but Jack was back on his feet, reaching down and hauling me upright by my hair. He smashed a fist into the side of my head that sent me reeling across the deck like a drunken puppet. I crashed into the side rail, but had the presence of mind to grab the cold metal and stop myself tumbling overboard.

The bear was coming for me again. The civilized mask Jack Dylan usually wore had slipped away completely and in its place was a face filled with a killing rage; eyes wild, lips pulled back in a savage snarl. The *real* Jack Dylan.

I leaned back against the rail and stuck out my foot, catching him in the stomach, and then wheeled away and staggered across the deck looking for something to use as a weapon. Jack could keep this up for hours. He was stronger than me and hyped up with adrenaline from the fight. As he came at me again I grabbed at one of the coils of anchor chain still stowed at the rear of the deck. It was only about six feet in length, but as heavy as hell. Using what was left of my strength I swung at him. The chain caught him a glancing blow on the head, opening a deep gash on his brow. Blood poured down his face and he reeled backwards, but he didn't go down.

I dropped the chain. I didn't have enough strength for another swing. Jack glared at me. His hand went to his head and came away covered in blood. He stared down at his hand and then growled deep in his throat and bar-relled towards me, hands outstretched, ready to separate me from my limbs.

When he was a yard away I dropped flat onto the deck, but his momentum kept him coming. He tripped over me and crashed into the aft rail. For a moment he hung there, doubled over, flapping his arms, trying desperately to re-gain his balance, but then his canvas shoes slipped on the deck, his centre of gravity shifted and he tumbled over the rail and into the sea.

67

A current must have taken him, because by the time I pulled myself upright and looked over the stern, he was over a hundred yards away, treading water. The mask was back and he was smiling.

'Come on, Harry. Throw me a line. You know you want to,' he called.

'But that's just it, Jack. I don't want to. I want to let you drown.'

He laughed. 'You haven't got it in you. You're not like me.'

I shook my head. 'No, Jack. I'm not.'

There was a lifebelt stowed under a locker at the front of the deck. I went across and hauled it out, unravelling the nylon line. 'Swim closer,' I called when I reached the aft rail. 'The line's not long enough.'

He started to swim towards me. When he'd halved the distance I tossed the lifebelt into the water. It landed just in front of him. 'Cheers, Harry,' he said and struck out towards it. He had it half over his head when he suddenly vanished beneath the water.

It took me a moment to realise what was happening, and then I saw four triangular dorsal fins cutting through the waves towards the lifebelt.

Sharks. Four of them blocking off his route back to the boat. A fifth had taken him under.

He surfaced a second later, farther away.

'Oh, Jesus Christ! Help me, Harry! Hel...' and he disappeared again.

I looked on helplessly as the four fins switched direction towards the point where Jack had vanished. He reappeared briefly once more, but the water around him was already turning red with his blood. He was flailing with his arms and looking about him frantically. Our eyes met. There was terror in his, and something else. Resignation.

He went under again and this time he didn't resurface. I watched the water boil as the sharks began their feeding frenzy. Finally, sickened, I turned away and went back to the wheel, started the engine and steered off in the direction of Alan's boat.

I pulled up alongside it, cut the engine and tied the two boats together. I climbed over the rail onto Alan's Princess. I could see no movement in the cockpit, but I could see the back of Alan's head. As I drew closer I saw the cockpit was a mess. Bullets from Jack's machine pistol had shattered most of the windows and pock-marked the superstructure. As I entered Alan turned his head.

'Well?' he said.

'Jack's gone.'

'Gone as in got away?'

'Gone as in dead.'

'Good riddance.'

He was curiously still; not moving in his seat.

'Are you okay?'

'A ricochet got me.'

'Let me see.' I crouched down next to him. His hands were clamped over his stomach. As I tried to look, to assess the damage, he turned away. 'I'm fine. It's just a scratch. Get back on Jack's boat and we'll take them back to Watt's Cay.'

'Alan, don't be ridiculous. You're in no condition to pilot this boat anywhere. You need medical attention.'

'In the middle of the ocean?'

'Just let me see how bad it is.'

'Sometimes, Harry, you're bloody hard work. I heard you tell Billie and Sam to call for medical assistance for Julius. They'll send a helicopter to Watt's Cay. They can take a look at me when we get there. Now, will you do me a favour and climb back on board Jack's boat and follow me back there.'

'Okay, if you're sure there's nothing I can do.'

'I'm fine. As I said, it's just a scratch, but it stings like hell, so if you could move your ass quickly it would be much appreciated.'

Our eyes met. I smiled at him and he smiled back.

Something happened in that moment; something unspoken and very profound.

There was a fundamental shift in my perception of Alan Lancaster.

I wanted him as a friend.

I needed him as a brother.

I climbed back on board Jack's boat, untied the lines and started the engine. I heard the roar of the Princess' twin MTU engines as Alan started her, and then we were heading back to Watt's Cay.

I followed Alan at a steady ten knots. If he'd had a mind to he could have opened out the throttle of the Princess and left me cold, but I knew he wouldn't do it. Not this time. The look we had exchanged told me everything I needed to know about Alan Lancaster, and I knew, at last, I could trust him.

68

Three helicopters had landed on Watt's Cay. One, an air ambulance in its usual red and white livery, the other two belonged to the police.

We pulled in on either side of the jetty. I climbed from Jack's boat and tied her up, half expecting Alan to emerge from the cockpit of the Princess. When, after five minutes, he still hadn't shown I boarded the Princess and made my way to the cockpit.

Alan was in his seat, but slumped over the controls. There was a puddle of blood beneath his seat. I rushed up to him and pushed him back. He was barely breathing and for the first time I got a look at his wound. The bullet from Jack's machine pistol had ricocheted and entered Alan's stomach just above the waistband of his chinos tearing a ragged hole. The chinos were crimson as was his shirt. God knows how much blood he had lost, but I felt for his pulse and it was hardly there.

I could do nothing for him. The wound was still leaking blood, and if it was allowed to go on much longer Alan would be dead.

I rushed ashore and up towards the house. Halfway along the path I met two medics carrying Julius on a stretcher. He had an oxygen mask over his mouth and nose, but his eyes were open wide. He pulled the mask off as I reached him. 'Jack?' he said.

'Shark bait.'

He smiled. 'Good, Harry, the world's a better place without him.'

'But Alan's hurt. Badly hurt.'

A third medic was following behind the stretcher carrying a large medical kit, Stevie beside him, her arm in a sling.

'What's happened?' she said.

'Alan's been shot.'

'Another one?' the medic said incredulously. He looked about twelve years old.

I grabbed his sleeve. 'You need to come with me. Bring your kit.'

'I don't know. I'm only authorised...'

'A man's dying. Do you want his death on your conscience, just because you don't have the necessary paperwork?'

He hesitated for a moment, indecision fluttering in his eyes, and then he said. 'Okay. Show me.'

As soon as we reached the Princess the medic went to work, taking Alan's blood pressure, sticking a cannula into a vein in his wrist and connecting up saline drip. He handed me the polythene drip bag. 'Hold this. I need to call this in. We've only just made it in time. Another five minutes and we'd have needed a body bag.'

Despite his ridiculously youthful appearance he certainly knew his job. He pressed a sterile swab against Alan's wound. 'Hold this here. Keep applying pressure. There's too much bleeding.'

I did as I was told, holding the saline bag with one hand and pressing down on the swab with the other. While I did this he got on his radio.

'They're holding the helicopter until we can get him

aboard. We need to get him to the hospital as soon as we can,' he said as he came off the radio. 'Joey and Dave are coming down to give us a hand getting him there.'

Minutes later Joey and Dave, the stretcher carriers, arrived and together we got Alan off the Princess and onto the stretcher.

Stevie met us at the door of the helicopter. 'Is he going to be all right?' she said, though there was an unusual coldness in her eyes. Stevie wasn't the forgiving type and Alan would have to do a lot to convince her he was worth saving.

'I don't know. He's lost a lot of blood, and God knows what damage the bullet's done to his insides.' I rubbed the back of my hand across my lips. They were dry, parched. 'Jesus Christ, Stevie, he told me he was okay; said it was just a scratch. I let him bring the boat back to the Cay. I just don't know how he had the strength to do it; he's lost so much blood. I never should have left him alone like that.'

'You can't blame yourself, Harry. This was always going to end up badly. I just thank God it's not you on the stretcher. At least then any tears might have been justified.'

I made to get into the helicopter. The depth of my emotions was surprising me, and although some of it would be through shock and pumped up adrenaline, there was no doubting there was a lot of relief as well, relief that perhaps, no make that probably, Alan was innocent in all this.

'Where do you think you're going, buddy?' one of the medics said.

'The hospital. You've got two of my friends in there.'

'Sorry,' he said. 'No can do. Authorised personnel only. Besides, there's no room.'

'And,' the other stretcher carrier said, 'Assistant Commissioner Brooks is waiting up at the house to talk to you.'

'Don't worry, Harry, I'll keep you posted,' Stevie said.

'*You're* going to the hospital? I didn't think your

wound was *that* bad.'

'Billie insisted. She said I needed to go and get it checked out. Don't sweat it. With me there at least you'll be kept in the loop.'

I watched her climb aboard and then backed away as the rotor began to turn. Moments later the helicopter was airborne and wheeling back across Watt's Cay heading towards Nassau and the Princess Margaret Hospital.

I watched it fly for a few seconds and then wearily made my way up to the house.

69

Chaos had arrived at Watt's Cay.

There were police everywhere. Floodlights had been set up and switched on to combat the dwindling evening light. I could see through the lounge window scenes of crime officers dressed in white coveralls combing every inch of the room, and the grounds around the house were teaming with more officers. It was slightly alarming, but at the same time strangely reassuring to see that so many were armed. I counted at least eight of them and they looked like they were prepared for a small war.

I told one of them who I was.

'The lounge is off-limits,' he said. 'They're conducting interviews in the sun-room at the back. You can go straight through. Before you do though...' He spread his arms.

I got the message and stood there, arms stretched out, legs wide apart while he patted me down, checking for any weapon I might be carrying. Finally he let me through.

Brooks was in the sun-room as well as two detectives who he introduced as Inspector Grant and Sergeant Cooper. They were both black and, in their shorts and T-shirts, were much more informally dressed than Brooks himself.

Assistant Commissioner Brooks, like me, was a white

Bahamian and he was standing in the corner of the sun-room, dressed in an immaculate blue serge uniform. Billie and Sam were sitting on a cane couch, watching him with something like amusement in their eyes. I looked through the French doors that connected the sunroom to the lounge and saw that Kim's body had been removed, but there was a white taped outline and a scorch mark on the wooden floor to show where she had fallen.

I could feel Brooks' eyes boring into my back. He had the demeanour of a European policeman, precise, deliberate in his questioning and relentless when he thought he was on to something.

I tore my gaze away from the outline and turned to face him. He was in his forties, good-looking in a thirties-film-star kind of way. His dark hair was slicked back and a thin neatly-trimmed moustache hugged his top lip. The dark eyes, though, were sharp and incisive.

'Take a seat, Mr Beck,' he said. To Sam and Billie he said, 'That will be all for now. Constable?' he called.

A young police constable entered the room

'Show Ms Martinez and Mr Goldberg the way out. We won't be needing them again tonight.'

As I sat down on the couch he said, 'Carnage seems to follow you around like a stray dog, doesn't it, Mr Beck? I take it Mr Dylan won't be joining us?'

I shook my head.

'Because?'

'He's dead. He fell off his boat. Sharks.'

'Sharks.' He digested this piece of information. 'That's a shame. I have a warrant for his arrest. A waste of paper.' He produced the warrant from his pocket and ceremoniously tore it in half. 'Tell me, Mr Beck, are there any other criminals we might be after who you would like to feed to the sharks? You could probably halve my workload.' His sarcasm was heavy and unwelcome.

'We were fighting. He fell. It was an accident.'

'And Mrs Weaver? Was that too an *accident?*'

'Jack shot her with the flare gun,' I said.

He raised his eyebrows at that. 'Really? I was under the impression that they were lovers.'

'They were.'

'So why would Mr Dylan shoot his lover in the face with a flare gun?'

'He was trying to shoot me. Kim got in the way.'

The eyebrows climbed higher. 'How?' he said.

'Deliberately. She was trying to protect me.'

'Are you trying to tell me that Mrs Weaver deliberately put herself between yourself and a crazed lunatic with a flare gun to protect you? Why would she do that?'

'We were lovers too. Albeit a long time ago.'

The eyebrows slid back down. 'I see,' he said. 'So when we locate the flare gun and test it for fingerprints, we're going to find Jack Dylan's. Is that what you're telling me?'

'I would expect so.'

'Yes,' he said, thoughtfully nodding his head. 'I'm sure you would.' He suddenly clapped his hands together. 'But I'm doing Inspector Grant and Sergeant Cooper here a disservice. They've been assigned to this case and it should be them asking the questions not me. But if they don't mind I should like to sit in. Inspector?'

'No problem, sir,' he said gruffly.

The young police constable returned, pulled up a chair and took out his notebook.

It was Cooper's turn to speak. 'Ms Martinez told us about the other house on the island where Dylan and Weaver were keeping trafficked children. We sent a team over to it and indeed that was the case. They found the children, all safe and sound, along with a young woman, Ms Elena Aldama, who is wanted in several states on mainland America on charges ranging from credit card fraud to murder.'

'Murder?'

'Indeed.' Brooks butted in. I got the impression he was a man in love with his own voice and had a well developed sense of his own importance. 'It seems she dispatched her boyfriend with a carving knife when she found he'd been sleeping with her best friend. And then Ms Aldama hurled a flask of sulphuric acid at her best friend's face but let her live...not that I imagine the poor girl wanted to after that. I saw the photographs they took after the attack. The girl is blind and horribly scarred for life.' He gave a theatrical shudder.

I remembered vividly Elena holding the shotgun on me and thinking she would never use it. *Another great judgement call, Harry.* I thanked God now it wasn't loaded.

'Sorry, Sergeant. I interrupted you,' Brooks said. 'Please continue.'

Cooper managed a tight smile and was about to continue when Grant said, 'So, Mr Beck. Would you mind telling me now just what has been going on here?'

Cooper made a noise of frustration and wheeled away, walking across to the window and staring out, his foot tapping an impatient tattoo on the wooden floor.

I glanced at my wristwatch. It was a little after eight. I had a feeling I was in for a long night.

70

Two hours later I'd more or less finished the story. It would have been quicker if Grant and Cooper hadn't kept interrupting me with searching questions trying to make me explain parts of the story I wanted to gloss over. They were a good team and effective inquisitors and I could see why they had been assigned the case, but I held my nerve and only gave them the answers I wanted them to have.

Finally I said, 'I have a question for you.'

'Go ahead.'

'What happened yesterday? Why weren't Reynolds and his squad at the warehouse when Jerry Carr and I went to rescue his sister?'

Brooks stepped in again fielding the question effortlessly; almost as if he'd been waiting for me to ask it and had prepared the answer in advance.

'I'm afraid you'll have to ask Reynolds that yourself. But you might find it difficult as nothing has been seen or heard from the Inspector since yesterday afternoon when he left the station.'

'So you knew nothing of his idea to provide an armed squad to back us up. He told me you had approved the plan.'

'I assure you, Mr Beck, I knew nothing of Reynolds' plan, if indeed he ever had one. We are conducting an internal investigation into Hector Reynolds' role in this matter, the results of which will be made public in due course. In the meantime I've issued a warrant for his arrest.'

'So what you're saying is that Reynolds set us up.'

He spread his hands in a conciliatory gesture. 'That would seem the most likely scenario.'

'Can we move on?' Grant said, obviously irritated by Brooks' presence and his constant interruptions. 'Where is the memory stick now?'

I fished it from my pocket and handed it across to him.

'May I?' Brooks held out his hand.

Grant scowled, but passed it to him.

Brooks looked pleased. He held the black plastic device between his finger and thumb and stared at it for a moment. 'So this is the McGuffin,' he said.

'Sorry?' Grant and Cooper said, almost in unison.

'You see, they don't know their Hitchcock, Mr Beck.'

'I'm not big into films myself,' I said.

Grant and Cooper just looked bemused.

'Well, the late, great Alfred Hitchcock would have called this memory stick a McGuffin, a random object of desire, the quest for which drives people to murder and treachery in the plots of so many of his films, and those, I might add, of many other directors.'

I really couldn't care less. It was getting late and I was tired. I needed to be horizontal and asleep. Eight hours, no less. I'd sleep on the Princess tonight. There was a double bed in the Princess' main bedroom, and at that moment it was calling me.

I watched as Brooks slipped the memory stick into the top pocket of his uniform jacket.

'Excuse me, sir,' Cooper said. 'Shouldn't we be turning that over to forensics?'

Brooks looked at him sharply. 'And that's exactly

what I intend to do, Sergeant. I appreciate the urgency of this case, even if you don't.'

'I think what Cooper means, sir, is that the chain of evidence...'

Brooks held his hand up to stop him. 'I do not need a lecture about evidence chains, Inspector, or anything else for that matter. I shall drop this into the forensic department myself and I will stress the need for urgency in processing it. I'm in a position to expedite the matter. You're not. Is that clear?'

Grant shifted uncomfortably from foot to foot. Cooper just looked furious.

'Yes, sir,' Grant said.

'So have we finished here?' I said hopefully. 'Because I'm bloody tired and I need to sleep.'

Cooper and Grant exchanged looks. 'Yes,' Grant said. 'That will be all for tonight. But when you're back in Freeport you'll have to come in to the station and make a formal statement. When is that likely to be?'

'I'll be heading back there tomorrow,' I said.

'Tomorrow will be fine,' Grant said.

'Right, I think that will be all for tonight,' Brooks said. 'Thank you for your co-operation, Mr Beck.' He smiled. It wasn't pretty. It looked like he had indigestion. 'It's going to be interesting reading through the transcripts of the interviews we've already conducted with Ms Martinez, Mr Goldberg, Mr Flood and Ms Bailey. I may even look in on Mr Lancaster at the hospital in Nassau if he's well enough. It will be interesting to see how all your stories compare.' He walked to the door.

'What about the boat coming in from Florida to pick up the children?' I said.

'You need not concern yourself with that, Mr Beck. That will be dealt with. They won't reach Watt's Cay.'

He walked out into the night.

Grant and Cooper followed him. Grant paused at the

door. 'Goodnight, Mr Beck,' he said. 'I'll be expecting you at the station tomorrow.'

'Is Brooks always like that?'

'What, an asshole you mean? Yeah, pretty much.'

'You have my sympathy.'

He smiled. 'I appreciate it.'

A few minutes later, as I was walking back to Alan's boat I heard one of the helicopters start up and take off.

71

'I didn't know they made them like Brooks anymore,' Billie said as I walked into the Princess' lounge. She went across to Alan's drinks cabinet and poured herself a stiff whisky. 'Can I get anyone else a drink?'

'Chivas Regal,' I said. 'Brooks is one of a kind. Jim Henderson said he was a stickler for the rules. He wasn't far off the truth.'

'Do you think he believed your story about Kim's death?'

'Not for one moment, and I don't think Grant and Cooper were convinced either, but they're going to have a difficult job proving otherwise, as long as Stevie keeps her mouth shut. I take it you got rid of the flare gun?'

'That's long gone,' Billie said. 'And Stevie won't say anything. She's got no desire to spend the next twenty years in prison.'

'Good.'

'Do you mind if I ask a question?' Sam Goldberg said.

'Oh, not tonight, Sammy,' Billie said. 'Harry looks all in.'

'No, I'm okay. Ask away.'

'It's just that something doesn't hang together. Dylan planted the bomb in the car to stop Alan making the meeting with an FBI agent. After the car exploded Alan ran. The meeting never took place. So where is the FBI man now? Is he still on the Islands? And what part is the Bureau playing in all this?'

I nodded. 'I'm asking myself the same question, and it will probably occur to Brooks too, once he's gone through all the statements. He'll be furious.'

'Good,' Billie said. 'He deserves a sleepless night.'

'Yes, but I don't,' I said. 'I'm turning in. There's another bedroom if you and Sam don't mind sharing. Single beds.'

'Suits me.'

'Yeah, me too.' Sam said.

'As long as you don't snore,' Billie said.

'As if I'd dare with you in the same room.'

They disappeared below decks and I had every intention of doing the same; but then I saw the laptop computer sitting on the desk in the corner of the lounge. I went across, sat down at the desk and switched it on. It took a moment to boot up. I took the memory stick that Alan had given me out of my pocket, the red one, the *real* one, and slipped it into the USB socket. A menu appeared on the screen and I clicked on Open Files.

Unlike the Jack Dylan mock-up I'd handed over to Brooks, this one was not encrypted and I spent the next few hours searching through files, making notes, studying photographs and trying to digest the implications of everything Alan had downloaded onto the memory stick. I'd thought the information on Jack's mock-up was dynamite. This was, in comparison, a nuclear warhead.

When I finally removed the stick and closed down the computer my head was reeling, and I was starting to feel totally out of my depth.

I hadn't mentioned this memory stick to the police,

and I'd had no intention of handing it over to them, at least not until I'd checked it out and removed any evidence that might have incriminated Alan. Now I doubted my wisdom.

I went to bed and lay there tossing and turning for another hour before finally falling into a fitful sleep, filled with dreams of friendship, betrayal and murder.

72

The weather had cleared by the next morning. The sun was set in a clear blue sky and sharing its warmth with everyone. So why did I wake up feeling incredibly gloomy? The prospect of going to Freeport to give my statement and another run-in with Brooks certainly didn't lighten my mood, and thoughts of Alan in his hospital bed depressed me still further. As if she was reading my mind, Stevie rang me on my mobile phone.

'How's Julius?' I said.

'They've patched him up. Now he's sitting up in bed and flirting with all the nurses.'

I laughed. 'That's Julius; never can resist a pretty face.'

There was a pause. I could sense Stevie standing there, waiting for me to ask the question.

'Well?' she said finally.

'How's Alan?' I said.

'Not good. He's conscious and he's pulled his lawyers in for a meeting. They're in there now.'

Lawyers? I thought. *Perhaps he's preparing his defence.*

Stevie continued. 'But I spoke to one of the doctors when we arrived last night and he didn't sound optimistic. There's a lot of *internal trauma*, as he put it.'

I took that in. 'Okay,' I said. 'And how are you?'

'I'm fine. They stuck a Band-Aid on my arm and kept me in overnight for observation, but they're letting me go this morning. I'll have to find a way to get back to Freeport.'

'What are you doing for money?'

'Credit card.'

'Right, find a hotel close to the hospital and book in. I'll be over as soon as I can.'

'Harry, you have to be kidding. Do you know the rates of the hotels around here? I can't afford it.'

'Don't worry about the money. I'll cover the bill. But I want you close by. If Alan takes a turn for the worse I want you to call me.'

'Okay,' she said lightly. For once she didn't argue with me. 'I'll hang around the hospital and call you if I have any updates on his condition.'

'Thanks,' I said. 'It's important. I know how you feel about him, what he's done. This is for me, okay?'

'Yeah,' she said. 'I know it is.' She rang off.

Alan's boat was well appointed. I showered quickly. Alan had some clothes in one of the wardrobes. We were close to the same size. I found a cream T-shirt and a pair of grey slacks that more or less fitted, slipped them on and went down to the kitchen.

Billie was already there and she'd made coffee.

'Want a cup?'

'Sure. Is Sam still in bed?'

'Sleeping like a baby. And guess what? He doesn't snore. Relief. I actually managed to get some sleep.'

'I'm taking the boat over to Nassau this morning. Alan's in a pretty bad way.'

'Sorry to hear that. Don't the police want you in Freeport to give your statement? They want us there to give ours.'

'Yeah,' I said. 'But they can wait. I have things to do

first. Stevie's at the hospital and she said she'll call me if there's any news, but it should be me there, not her.'

'She's a good kid,' Billie said.

'One of the best. She's been through a lot lately and I'd hate to see her hurt again,' I said pointedly.

Billie looked at me steadily. 'She's a big girl, Harry, and more than capable of looking after herself. But no. I won't hurt her,' she said.

'No. No, of course you won't,' I said. 'If I get you and Sam to Nassau you can get a charter back to Freeport. Would that suit?'

'That's fine. Don't worry about Sam and me. Regular rolling stones, both of us.'

'I don't think Sam's going to get his interview with Alan.'

'That's a shame.' Sam Goldberg appeared in the doorway of the kitchen looking dishevelled and half asleep. He yawned. 'A shame, but I think I can carry on with the book without his input. It'll just be a slightly different book, that's all.'

73

We were halfway to Nassau when Billie said, 'You're very quiet.'

'I've a lot on my mind,' I said. We were on the flying bridge and I was pushing the Princess' engines hard. Goldberg seemed to be getting over his seasickness problem and was sitting on the sundeck looking for all the world as if he was enjoying the trip.

'You're worried about Alan?'

'That…and other things.'

'Want to share?'

'Not just at the moment.'

'Fair enough. You're a dark horse, Harry Beck,' she said. 'Sometimes I think you're one of the most open people I've ever met, other times you're about as deep as a blue hole. It's unusual. I'm normally pretty good at reading people, but a lot of the time you have me baffled.'

I was concentrating on piloting the Princess. 'How do you want me to respond to that?' I said without looking round at her.

'I don't, I guess. I just wanted you to know that if you need to talk things through, you could do worse than bend my ear, that's all.'

Maynard Sims

'I appreciate that, Billie,' I said.

'But keep my nose out of your business, right? It's okay. I understand.' She made her way down to the sun deck and sat herself down next to Sam.

My stomach lurched as my mobile phone rang. It was Stevie.

'You need to get here fast, Harry. Alan's asking for you.'

'I'm on my way there. How is he?'

'Bad, Harry. Really bad. They've called in a priest.'

'Alan's not Catholic. He's not religious at all. Why call a priest?'

'I think they're working on the assumption that he needs as much help as he can get.'

I felt sick. 'We're an hour away from Nassau,' I said glancing at the read-out on the GPS. 'It will take another thirty minutes to get from the harbour to the hospital. Can you get in there and sit with him? Tell him I'll be there shortly.'

'I'll do what I can, Harry.'

'Thanks, Stevie.'

I eased the throttle forward, nudging the Princess towards her maximum speed. As the boat bounced over the waves my mind replayed events of the past few days. I hadn't really had time to digest them.

Since the explosion of Alan's Mercedes I'd been carried along on a raft of action and reaction, but now, standing on the flying bridge of the Princess, with the wind blowing in my face and the waves disappearing under the boat's hull I had time to review what had happened and to consider what my next move would be. Despite the police involvement this affair was a long way from being over; at least as far as I was concerned.

It didn't look as if Alan was going to make it through the day. Another death, another victim of a group of evil men and women who had chosen a path in life alien to

301

my own and to the rest of decent humanity. I couldn't in all conscience sit back and let the police take over the case from here on in.

My time spent reviewing the information on Alan's memory stick had been well spent. I was in possession of a lot of information now; I was no longer shooting in the dark. I now had names and faces to hang this evil on, and I was damned if those who had been sacrificed to feed the perverted lust of a few sick bastards would have died in vain.

74

Stevie was there to meet me as I pulled up in a taxi outside the hospital. I had moored at the harbour and said my farewells to Billie and Sam Goldberg, promising to look them up once I got back to Freeport. I owed it to them to let them know the conclusion to this affair.

Stevie had been crying. There were damp streaks down her cheeks.

'Am I too late?'

She shook her head. 'I'm not crying for him, though I was so horrible the last time I spoke to him.'

'We've all said things and done things over the past few days we'll probably live to regret,' I said. 'Alan included.'

She sniffed back the tears. 'Come on,' she said. 'I'll take you to his room. I should warn you though, Nona Flood's here. She's brought your father.'

I swore under my breath. He was the last person I wanted to see right now.

Stevie led me through the antiseptic corridors to the elevator. We reached the second floor and stepped out into another corridor. Nona Flood was the first person I saw. She approached me, her face inscrutable.

'What can I say, Nona? I'm sorry.'

She ignored my apology. 'I've spoken to Julius. It was his own damned fault. Getting shot, at *his* age. The man ought to know better. Still, he's going to be all right, so no harm done. But if he keeps on flirting with the nurses, he'll realise that a bullet in the chest is the least of his worries.' She threw her arms around me and held on tight. 'Thank you, Harry, for bringing my man back to me.' I realised she was crying. I stroked her hair.

'Stevie said my father is here.'

I felt her nod her head against my chest. 'He's in with Alan now. He's not handling it very well.'

I wondered if he'd handle it any better had I been the one on the hospital bed. 'I should go in,' I said. 'Stevie, keep Nona company.'

I left them in the corridor and walked into Alan's room. My father was at the bedside, holding on to Alan's hand, mumbling to him, tears coursing down his face. He looked round as I entered. 'Come and sit with your brother.'

He pushed himself up from the chair, leaned over Alan and kissed him lightly on the forehead. 'Goodbye, son,' he said and left the room, pausing at the door to look at Alan one last time, then he gave a sob in his throat and stepped out into the corridor, closing the door behind him.

I felt a lump form in my throat. I swallowed and went to sit next to the hospital bed,

Alan was unresponsive. He was wired up to a vital signs machine. There were tubes in his arms drip-feeding him drugs, electrodes on his chest, and an oxygen mask over his nose and mouth.

I rested a hand on his arm. 'I'm here, Alan.'

For a second or two he didn't respond, but then his eyes flickered open. 'I fucked up,' he said in a voice that sounded like two pieces of sandpaper rubbing together. He gestured to the carafe of water on the nightstand.

I poured some into a glass, moved the oxygen mask to one side and put it to his lips. He took a sip.

'Sally…Anna…look after her,' he said, his eyes rolling in his head. Wherever his mind was it was a place where his wife and daughter were still alive. I had no desire to shatter the illusion.

'Sure,' I said. 'I'll look after them.'

'Knew you would. You're a good friend, Harry. My brother. How about that, eh?'

'Don't talk. Save your strength.'

His eyes cleared. 'Save it for what? I'm dying.' He gripped my hand fiercely and hauled himself up so that his face was just inches from mine. 'Bring them down. Harry. Bring the bastards down.'

'I will, Alan. I promise.'

He flopped back on the bed. 'Yeah,' he said weakly. 'I know you will.' He closed his eyes.

An alarm went off in the room and seconds later two medics rushed in pushing a crash cart. They defibrillated him, but it was too late.

Somewhere Alan Lancaster was touching the sun.

I hoped he was satisfied at last.

Stevie wrapped her arm around me as I walked from the room. 'I'm sorry, Harry. I'm so, so sorry.'

'I need some air,' I said.

'Sure.'

As I walked out into the hospital car park my mobile phone rang. It was Jim Henderson.

'They found Reynolds,' he said.

'Oh?'

'Dead. They found him in a warehouse downtown. He was shot up pretty bad.'

'Jim, I need you to do me a favour.'

'I don't know, Harry. They're waiting for you to come in to the station. You should be here.'

'Alan died five minutes ago. I'm in Nassau at the Princess Margaret hospital.'

'Oh, Harry, man, I'm sorry.'

'Yeah. So will you do something for me?'

'Go on,' he said, and then listened as I told him what I wanted him to do.

75

I hung up the phone and headed back to the hospital. Nona and my father were approaching the door, Stevie trailing along behind them.

'I'm taking Lucas back to Barracuda,' Nona said. 'There's nothing for him here now.'

My father didn't look up at me. He was lost in a very private world of grief, and it was a world that had no place in it for me. I wondered briefly if I'd ever see the old man again. I doubted that I would, and the thought didn't trouble me too much.

'What about Julius?' I said.

'They're keeping him in for few days. I'll be back in Nassau the day they release him. In the meantime he's got lots to occupy him. So many pretty girls. The best tonic a man like Julius can have.' Nona played the role of the long-suffering wife well, but there was never any doubt in my mind that their marriage, if not made in Heaven, was formed in one of its anterooms.

'I'm going to check out of the hotel, Harry,' Stevie said. 'I take it you're going back to Freeport?'

'I'm taking a detour first. Billie and Sam are booking a charter flight to take them back. Come with me in the taxi and I'll get the driver to drop you off at the airport. You can travel back with them.' I turned to Nona. 'What about you and Lucas?'

'Don't you worry yourself about us, Harry. We'll make our own arrangements.'

I kissed her on the cheek and waited until their taxi had pulled away.

'You're not going to do anything stupid, Harry, are you?' Stevie said.

'I don't know what you mean,' I said.

'You can't kid me, Harry. I know you too well.'

We climbed into a taxi. 'The airport,' I said to the driver.

* * *

'Stevie tells me you're about to do something really stupid,' Billie said to me shortly after we hooked up with her and Goldberg at the airport.

'Stevie exaggerates,' I said. 'She always exaggerates.'

We were in the main concourse, but Billie pulled me to one side, away from the others. 'Don't bullshit me, Harry. Are you following a lead? It's important I know.'

'Why? Do you want to come along and take pictures?'

She glared at me. 'You really are the most stubborn son of a…' She reached into the pocket of her jacket and took out a small laminated card, handing it to me.

With everything else that had happened lately I really should have been expecting to see an FBI identity card, but I wasn't and it shook me. 'You?' I said.

'Yes, me. Special Agent Martinez. Just like it says on the card.'

'Does Sam know?'

She raised her eyebrows. 'No, of course not. As far as he's concerned I'm just Billie Martinez the photographer who gate-crashed his party in the Bahamas. But who do you think it was who facilitated his meeting with Alan Lancaster in the first place?'

Wheels within wheels. I was getting sick of the machinations. I just wanted someone, anyone, to be straight with me and not be working from some kind of hidden agenda.

'So what do you want?' I said.

'*I* want to know what *you* know. And if you're planning to go out there and bring down the bad guys, I want to come with you.'

'Not going to happen,' I said, shaking my head.

'So I ring Assistant Commissioner Brooks and tell him you're withholding vital evidence and planning to do the whole Charles Bronson vigilante bit?'

I stared at her and she stared back; a challenge.

'You'd do that.' It wasn't a question. I could see in her eyes that she didn't make threats lightly.

'I'd do that.'

'Right. But get used to the idea that this is *my* show. For me this is personal. Don't expect me to be looking out for you.'

'That's fair. We'd better tell Sam and Stevie to go back to Freeport without us.'

*   *   *

After a token protest from Stevie and a look of confused resignation from Sam Goldberg, Billie and I took a cab back to the harbour.

As we boarded Alan's Princess, Billie said, 'This really is a beautiful boat. I'm not big into boats, but this one has the *wow* factor. Does it have a name?'

'It's written on the side.'

She read it aloud. I knew she would.

'*Sallyanna*,' she said and saw the expression of pain on my face. 'Sorry, Harry. I wasn't thinking.'

'It doesn't matter. Not any more,' I said.

'No, Harry, it does. What we're about to do now, well, it's for them, isn't it?'

'Yes,' I said. 'I suppose it is.'

As I steered the Princess out of the harbour Billie said, 'So, are you going to tell me now?'

I handed her the red memory stick. 'There's a laptop down in the lounge. Run this and then you'll know what I know.'

She took it and disappeared below.

76

I flicked on the radio and called Max Donahoe on *The Minotaur*.

'Harry, good to hear from you,' the ebullient voice came over the speaker.

'I'll be passing by your way soon. Mind if I come aboard for a chat?'

'I'd be delighted, old boy. What time should I expect you?'

'Give me an hour.'

'An hour. Splendid. I'll look forward to it.'

After he disconnected I rang Jim Henderson again. 'What's your ETA?'

'We're just coming in to land at Linden Pindling Airport. There's a police launch waiting for us. I reckon we can rendezvous in just over the hour,' he said.

'Is Brooks with you?'

Jim lowered his voice. 'Yes, he's here, but he's not happy, Harry. Not happy at all.'

'I can live with that. See you soon.' I rang off.

Fifty minutes later Billie came up to the flight deck.

'You read fast.'

'I've skimmed it, but I know all I need to know. I've sent all the salient details to my computer at the Miami field office, so it will be waiting for me when I get back.' She sat down in the seat next to mine on the flight deck, pushing her hair away from her face. 'This is big, Harry. Much bigger than I thought. Once this story breaks and the guilty parties are exposed the media is going to have a field day. Some of the names mentioned in the files took my breath away. I know a few of them personally. *That* made me feel a bit queasy.'

'I know,' said. 'I had a similar reaction last night when I went through the files. Did you look at the photos?'

'Yes, I did. Did you?'

'Some of them,' I said. 'But they turned my stomach as much as reading the names and the details of the transactions did. I couldn't carry on with them.'

'That's a shame, because the photos answer a lot more questions; but I can understand your reticence. They're revolting. The fact that these people want to indulge in such perverted acts is one thing, but wanting to be photographed whilst doing them, that's something else again. The photos made me feel sick, but they also made me sad, very sad, that there are people like that out there. For them there can never be enough victims to satisfy their sick lust. I think the worst thing, Harry, is that we can expose this cartel and its clients, but across the world there are others just like it, indulging in the same trade; trafficking innocents to satisfy their needs. And once we've shut this one down here, another just like it will pop up in its place. We're only scratching the surface.'

'It's a start,' I said. 'I'm just hoping that the media will turn the spotlight on what's happening here. Perhaps if people worldwide start reading about it in their newspapers and magazines, and see features and documentaries on their TVs, the outcry will be so great their respective governments will be forced into action. At the moment they just treat the whole human trafficking issue as an unsavoury fact of life and sweep it under the carpet.'

'You're an optimist, Harry. I like that about you,' she said.

'You don't think it will happen?'

'I'm a realist. At the last count there are twenty-seven million people worldwide in one form of slavery or another. It's an indigestible statistic and one that most governments shy away from. But you're right about one thing. Once people see their favourite film stars, politicians, or whoever on the cover of their gossip mags and tabloids charged with paedophilia and other sex crimes, they may just stand up and demand something's done about it. We live in hope.'

I could see *The Minotaur* in the distance. I slowed the engines. I searched the ocean in the hope that I might see the police launch, but so far there wasn't a sign of it.

I had a choice. I could either wait for it to arrive or I could go and confront Max Donahoe with just Billie to provide backup if events turned nasty. I ran both scenarios past her.

'I don't like waiting around,' she said. 'Let's move in.'

'Fair enough,' I said and eased the throttle forward.

77

As we pulled up alongside *The Minotaur*, Max was there to greet me. He took one look at Billie and the smile froze on his face.

'I didn't realise you were bringing a guest,' he said frostily.

'Billie Martinez, Max Donahoe,' I said.

'Pleased to meet you,' Billie said, beaming mischievously.

'Likewise, I'm sure,' Max said not thawing at all. 'You'd better come aboard.'

I scanned the surrounding ocean again, but there was no sign of the police launch. I was starting to fear they were going to let me down again, but then I saw a boat in the distance, growing gradually larger. It had to be them.

We boarded *The Minotaur* and Max led us down to the stateroom, settled us into chairs as far away from each other as he could manage and went to pour drinks.

'So, Harry, how have you been?'

'Since I last saw you, Max, positively lousy.'

'Oh, come on, Harry, you do Ms Martinez a disservice. How can life be that *lousy* as you put it, when you have such an attractive consort?'

Maynard Sims

'I agree, Max, Billie is very attractive, but as for being my consort is concerned, I'm afraid you've jumped to all the wrong conclusions. We're not a couple. Ms Martinez is here because she wanted to witness me blowing a hole in your self-absorbed, perverted lifestyle.' I said it with a smile and for a moment I don't really think Max Donahoe actually heard me; but then the words registered and his face creased into a confused frown.

'I'm sorry, Harry, I don't think I'm following you.' He stopped pouring.

'The children, Max. I'm talking about the children you, and others like you, are using for your own sick purposes.'

The confusion cleared a little. 'Ah,' he said. 'Katy warned me you had me in your sights. I didn't really believe her. I thought you knew me too well to consider, even for a moment, that I'd be capable of such a thing. It seems I was wrong.'

'If someone had told me that about you a week ago I wouldn't have believed it. But now I have no choice. The evidence is damning.'

He handed me a Chivas Regal. 'Drink that and I'll explain. And believe me, I will tell you *everything*.' He sat down on the chesterfield, crossing his stubby legs with difficulty.

'Perhaps you'd better wait until the police get here.' I heard another vessel draw alongside *The Minotaur* and cut its engines. 'In fact that sounds like them now.'

This was confirmed a few seconds later when a crewman burst into the stateroom. 'It's the police, sir. They're asking to come aboard.'

'Then let them,' Max said. 'I have nothing to hide.'

A few minutes later Assistant Commissioner Brooks strode into the stateroom followed by Jim Henderson. Brooks seemed furious. 'Mr Beck, I was expecting you at the station this morning to make your statement. I was not expecting you to summon me to New Providence.'

'I'm sorry, Brooks, but this really couldn't wait. I asked you to come out'here so you can make your first arrest in the child sex slavery case.'

'Really?' he said. 'And who is it I should be arresting?'

I took out the memory stick. 'I'm afraid I wasn't entirely straight with you last night. The stick I gave you was one that Jack Dylan had mocked up to get me interested in the case, hoping that I would lead him to Alan Lancaster. *This* is the stick Alan gave me, the one on which he downloaded pages of evidence against the cartel and its clients. On this one you'll not only find a list of names of all those involved, but also details of transactions each of them had with the company Tarradon Exports, the name the cartel hides behind. One of their more prominent and prolific customers is Max Donahoe, who has purchased six children, in the last year alone.'

A heavy silence settled over the stateroom, broken finally by Max himself. 'Harry, I said I could explain everything, and I will.' He went across and poured himself another drink.

78

I looked across at Billie, but she was looking troubled, her eyes darting around the room, settling on faces and moving on. When her eyes finally met mine I really didn't like the look of uncertainty I saw there.

Max sat back down and took a sip of his drink. 'I admire you, Harry, always have. The way you've pursued this case says a lot for your moral character and your sheer, bloody doggedness. I realise that the evidence against me looks to be overwhelming. It's true; I did purchase children from Tarradon Exports. But not for any perverted sexual need. I bought them to protect them from exactly the kind of person you think I am.'

'Bullshit!' I said. I turned to Brooks. 'Aren't you going to do anything?'

'I think we need to hear Mr Donahoe out first,' he said.

Max Donahoe took another mouthful of his drink and swallowed. 'I first became aware of Tarradon Exports when it was brought to my attention by A.C. Brooks here. He was involved in a joint US and Bahamian investigation into sex slavery and paedophilia, and they needed someone on the inside of the cartel; someone with money who would be seen as a very useful customer for the organization. I was approached and asked to act as that customer.'

Brooks picked up the story. 'Through Mr Donahoe here we gained a much broader insight into how the cartel was run. Their shipping patterns, where they sourced the children they were selling, and all manner of peripheral information we could only guess at before we had someone on the inside. Mr Donahoe presented himself as a client with an insatiable lust for the product they were offering. As you said, Mr Beck, six children in the last year alone. That's six children Mr Donahoe has personally settled in safe and secure foster homes, with trust funds established to see them comfortably into adulthood.'

'Why go to all that trouble?' Billie said. 'Why not just reunite them with their families?'

'What, so they can be sold again when the next bastard comes along with a wad of cash?' Max said angrily. 'No, I assure you, my way's better.'

'I misjudged you, Max,' I said. 'Badly misjudged you.'

'Yes, you did, Harry,' Katy said.

I spun around in my seat as Katy walked into the stateroom and sat down next to her father.

'And I think you owe him an apology.'

I sighed. I'd just made a complete and utter fool of myself. Again. 'I apologise, Max. I got it so wrong.'

He waved it away. 'To be honest, Harry, presented with the same evidence I would have reached the same conclusion. So don't feel bad about it.'

'So I'm afraid, Mr Beck, I won't be arresting anyone.'

'I wouldn't be so sure, Assistant Commissioner,' Billie said.

All eyes turned to Billie who was sitting forward in her seat. 'Mr Donahoe, do you have a computer we can use?'

Max looked surprised. 'I have a laptop. Katy uses it when she's staying over to search the Net and keep up with her friends on the social networking sites. Would that be any use to you?'

'Sounds perfect,' Billie said.

Katy got to her feet. 'I'll go and fetch it. It's in my bedroom.'

'What are you playing at?' I said to Billie.

'You'll see soon enough.'

Katy returned and set the computer down on the coffee table in the centre of the room. 'It won't take long to boot up,' she said.

The screen quickly flickered into life and went speedily through its start up programs. Even though it must have taken just a few seconds I tapped my foot impatiently while I waited. This day was not turning out how I had envisaged it, and it was making me nervous.

Then the computer was ready.

'Harry, can I have the memory stick?'

I passed it across to her and she inserted it into the USB socket at the side of the laptop. It brought back memories of the hotel in downtown Freeport and the day I had first met this remarkable woman. So much had happened since then, and so many people had died.

'Okay,' she said as her fingers flew over the keys.

She entered an images file and was searching through it. Finally she hit the touch pad and a young girl's face appeared on the screen. It was one of the children whose picture we had called up before. A young black girl, her hair neatly plaited into cornrows. *Michelle, 8yrs, Cuban, Experienced, $15,000.* I remembered the picture instantly and felt the same wave of sadness I had felt then.

'This is a small part of a bigger picture,' Billie said. She clicked the touch pad again and another image filled the screen.

The girl, Michelle was there, but this time she was flanked by two larger figures. It took me a while to absorb what I was seeing. Each of the two men was holding one of Michelle's hands. They were both smiling, both black, both smartly dressed in the uniforms of the Bahamian police. One of them was Hector Reynolds, the other…the other…I turned in my seat. 'Jim?'

79

Jim Henderson stood there staring at the screen, clutching his cap, turning it over and over in his hands. 'Sorry, Harry,' he said. 'He got me into this. It was easy money and Reynolds said it was totally safe. He was getting a huge retainer from the cartel in return for doctoring evidence, tipping them off when there was any threat to their security. He offered me a cut if I'd help him. It was too good an opportunity to turn down.'

'So when did it all go sour between you?' I said.

'The other day, when you called Reynolds and asked him to back you up at the warehouse. He tipped Jack Dylan off to what you were planning and he was going to go along there to make sure you wouldn't present a problem to Jack or the cartel.'

'You mean he was going along there to kill me.'

Jim nodded. 'I'm sorry, Harry,' he said again. 'I'm not a bad man, really I'm not. I couldn't let him kill you. I love you too much, man.'

'I'm touched. So, if I've got this right you killed Hector Reynolds before he could kill me. Is that it?'

Jim Henderson nodded and tortured his cap. 'We were in the car on the way to the warehouse. He was on his mobile to Dylan, and I could hear Dylan giving him his instructions. I was driving so I took a wrong turn deliberately and ended up on another part of the estate. Reynolds was furious. He started accusing me of sabotage, of putting my concern for you before the needs of Dylan and the cartel. I thought he was going to kill me.'

'So you shot him.'

'It was the only way to stop him, Harry. The only way.'

I stared at my old friend for what seemed like an eternity. I didn't know what to say. I could have wept.

'Well,' Billie said. 'You have your man, Assistant Commissioner.'

Brooks looked sick. His face was bleached white. 'All this going on, right under my nose, in my own *fucking* station!' He wheeled away from the computer screen. 'Sergeant James Henderson, you are under arrest for the murder of…'

He didn't get any further. Jim Henderson dropped his cap and in its place was a sleek, silver automatic pistol. In one move he had grabbed Katy and wrapped his arm around her throat. He pressed the muzzle of the automatic to the side of her head. 'Right,' he said, his voice quavering. 'If anyone moves, I'll shoot her.'

Max was struggling to his feet, but when Jim cocked the gun he collapsed back onto the chesterfield.

'Daddy!' Katy said.

'Do as he says!' Max barked. 'All of you!'

I met Katy's eyes. They were silently pleading.

Jim moved backwards towards the door of the stateroom, dragging Katy with him. 'I'm not a bad man, Harry,' he said again. 'But I can't go to prison, really I can't. Can you imagine what it would be like for me?'

'You made your bed when you threw in your lot with Reynolds. Don't expect me to have any sympathy for you.'

Something flickered in Jim's eyes. 'You sanctimonious bastard,' he said venomously. 'I knew you'd never understand. Throw me the keys to your boat.'

I took them from my pocket and tossed them across to him. If there was ever a moment when we could have taken him it was then. But he was fast. Too fast. He released Katy for a millisecond, caught the keys and then his arm was around her throat again. He was through the door and onto the deck.

The pilot of the police launch had come out of his wheelhouse and was reaching for his gun. 'Stop right there!' Jim shouted at him. 'One more move and I blow her head off.'

Katy was whimpering now, fat tears rolling down her cheeks. 'Harry, please.'

I couldn't move. I could see the panic in Jim Henderson's eyes. Rational thought was a thing of the past. He was nothing more now than a cornered animal, and that animal would do anything to protect itself.

'Stay calm,' I said. 'And do exactly as he says.'

Several of Max's crew had noticed the commotion and were gathering at the rail of the upper deck.

'And you can tell them not to do anything as well,' Jim called. 'I *will* kill her if I have to.'

'Yes, Jim. We believe you. No one's going to do anything.'

He reached the rail of *The Minotaur*. I wondered briefly if there was any way I could take him as he transferred to the Princess, but he'd worked it out. He took his arm from Katy's throat and planted his hand in her hair, grabbing it so tightly her face screwed up in pain. He forced her to climb onto *The Minotaur's* rail and then climbed up next to her.

'Jump!' he said to her.

Katy hesitated. 'I said jump, you bitch!'

80

He leapt into space still holding tightly to Katy's hair. She had no option but to follow. They disappeared from sight. I ran to the rail, but he was already on his feet and grabbing Katy again. He looked up at me and fired the automatic. I ducked back as the bullet zinged off the rail. When I looked over again, he'd dragged her up the steps to the flight deck and was starting the engine. He pushed Katy down onto the floor, but kept the automatic pointed at her head as he spun the wheel and started to move away from *The Minotaur*; but Jim was no sailor and he'd forgotten about the ropes tethering the two craft together.

The Princess lurched as the ropes strained. For a moment he looked bemused, wondering why his getaway was being compromised, and then he saw the ropes.

'Untie me, Harry. Now!'

I hesitated and Jim shot Katy in the arm. She looked down at the wound, gave a small groan and fainted.

'The next one goes through her head. Now untie me.'

'Do it,' Max urged. 'Do it quickly. He'll kill her.'

I tried, but the Princess had pulled too far away, stretching the ropes to their limits and making the knots impossible to unravel. 'Give me a knife. Somebody give me a knife!'

A knife was placed in my hand and I sawed first through one rope and then the other. Once he was free, Jim Henderson gunned the engines. The propellers spun, found their grip and the Princess took off, out into open sea. I looked around to see Max climbing into the seat behind the wheel of *The Minotaur.* 'What do you think you're doing?' I said.

'Following him. We can't let him get away. He has Katy for Christ's sake.'

I pulled him out of the seat. 'How many times have you piloted this boat, Max? Once? Twice?'

He shook his head. 'Never.'

'Then let me.' I took the seat, started the engine. 'Somebody weigh the anchor!' I shouted.

A few moments later someone shouted back, 'Clear!'

I pushed the throttle forward and we were riding Jim's wake. The Princess was a powerful boat and Jim had put a few hundred yards between us. *The Minotaur* was built for luxury and endurance but not for speed, and even with the engines flat out there was no way we were ever going to catch them. But Jim didn't know that. He wasn't pushing the Princess to anywhere near her limit, and he was panicking.

He looked back at us, aimed the gun at Katy again and screamed at us. 'Stop following me! I'll kill her! I swear!'

Then his head exploded and he fell forward over the wheel of the Princess.

It took me a moment to realise what had just happened, but then I looked back along the deck and saw Max Donahoe, skeet gun still tucked solidly into his shoulder, both barrels smoking.

'Right, Harry,' he said calmly. 'Let's go and get my daughter.'

81

Six months later.

Stevie took an age to answer the door. I checked my watch. It had gone ten and she was usually an early riser. When she finally pulled it open I walked past her into the apartment. She had pulled on a thin cotton robe but had forgotten to tie it, and her make up had streaked, giving her panda eyes. I could see straight through to her bedroom. The covers on the bed were messed up but still covering a figure lying there, and I could just make out a tangle of chestnut brown hair spread over the pillow.

'I see you're still banging the tourists,' I said with a smile.

She yawned and glared at me at the same time and reached past me to close the door. The figure on the bed stirred and rolled over. 'Not so much of the tourist, Beck,' Billie Martinez said.

'Does the Bureau give its agents the time off to indulge in such debauchery?'

She yawned sleepily and raised her middle finger before flopping back onto the pillow and closing her eyes.

Stevie padded out to the kitchen and switched on the coffee maker. 'What do you want, Harry?' Stevie said, running her fingers through her tousled crop. 'Shouldn't you be at the casino or something? You're certainly dressed for it.' She looked me up and down. 'You in Armani. I never thought I'd see the day.'

'We all have our crosses to bear, Stevie. This is mine,' I said.

'Only you would describe a five thousand dollar suit as a cross to bear.'

I heard the shower start and then Billie's voice floated out from the en suite singing a Fleetwood Mac song.

'Jesus!' Stevie said as she poured coffee into a mug. 'Why is everyone so…so *awake* this morning?'

She picked up the mug and padded back to the couch, sitting down and curling her legs underneath her. 'So what have I done to deserve the pleasure of your company at this godforsaken hour?'

'It's ten-twenty. Hardly the middle of the night.'

She groaned. 'Is that all it is? We were still clubbing at five. Billie only hit Freeport last night. We're trying to make up for lost time. The FBI work her so hard, poor lamb.'

Poor lamb was not an epithet I would use to describe Billie Jean Martinez.

The singing stopped and the shower was switched off. Moments later Billie opened the door of the bedroom and walked into the lounge wrapped only in a towel, her hair dripping and her bare feet leaving a damp trail across the wooden floor. 'Thought I could smell coffee,' she said.

Stevie waved her hand airily in the direction of the coffee maker. 'Help yourself, hun. You too, Harry, if you want one. Why *aren't* you at the casino?'

'I had a chat with Max,' I said. 'I told him that my initial thoughts about running a casino had been right. I'm a fish out of water there, Stevie. A square peg in a round hole.'

'A cliché in an otherwise perfect paragraph,' Billie said

with a smile. She curled up on the couch next to Stevie and threaded her arm through hers, their hands locking, fingers intertwined. 'You don't mind me joining you?' she said.

'Not at all. How's the case going?'

'Just tying up a few loose ends. Jack Dylan would be proud of me. You've probably read most of it in the press.'

'A lot of famous people totally discredited; a number of politicians both here and in the US falling on their swords; a political scandal in the UK that's rocked the stability of the British government; and a lot of arrests and court cases. An awful lot. Yes, I've read some of it.'

'You see,' she said. 'You made good your promise. You brought down the cartel.'

I shook my head. 'I played a part. A small part.'

'Harry, give yourself some credit,' Stevie said. 'You, more than anyone else, lost an awful lot bringing these sick bastards to justice. Friends, family...*The Lady.*'

I winced slightly. I didn't need reminding.

Stevie picked up on it immediately. She was always good at reading me. 'Anyway, let's change the subject. What did Max say?'

'He agreed with me. He said he's never seen me as miserable as has over the past few months. He thinks I need to get out of the gambling business.'

'So will you?'

'I already have. I'm just going in this morning to clear my desk. Hence the suit.'

'So what will you do now?' Billie said.

'That's what I came here to talk to Stevie about.'

'Shoot,' Stevie said.

'How do you fancy resurrecting the old firm?'

'Beck Charters?'

'I can't think of any other old firm I've been involved in.'

She took a swig of coffee. 'Not one of your best ideas,

Harry.'

She saw my face drop.

'No, no, don't get me wrong. I'd come back and work for you in a heartbeat. They were great times, probably the happiest times of my life…at least until I met Billie. But I would draw your attention to the major flaw in your plan. You haven't got a boat.'

'Big flaw,' Billie said, nodding her head sagely.

I smiled 'Well, you see, you're both wrong.'

Stevie's expression changed to one of intense curiosity. 'Come then,' she said. 'Explain how we're wrong.'

'Remember when you called me from the hospital in Nassau and told me that Alan had called his lawyers in. I thought at the time he was preparing his defence. But I was wrong. Alan knew he was going to die and he was just setting things straight.' I took a breath. 'In those few hours of his life he changed his will to benefit his remaining next of kin. His fortune has been divided between my father and me. And,' I said, reaching into my pocket and producing a set of keys. 'He left me his boat.'

Stevie's eyes widened in shock. 'You're kidding me.'

'I'm not. He actually told me in those last few minutes I spent with him before he died. I thought he was rambling when he said look after Sally and Anna, but what he actually said was, "Look after Sallyanna". *Sallyanna*, the name of his boat.'

'Looks like you're back in business, babes,' Billie said, squeezing Stevie's hand.

Tears sprung to Stevie's eyes. She got up from the couch and came over to me, wrapping her arms around my neck. 'I love you. Harry Beck,' she said and kissed my cheek, and then whispered, 'Beck and Bailey Charters. How about does that sound?'

I laughed and pushed her away. 'You're a rogue, Stevie Bailey,' I said. 'But yes, I like the sound of it.'

They walked me to the door. 'So when do we start?'

Stevie said.

'Tomorrow morning. Nine sharp at the harbour. *The Sallyanna* was badly shot up. She needs some work.'

'And I'll bet the engines need an overhaul.'

'Reckon they will.'

'And what does The Lady of Pain think of the new career?' Stevie said, looking beyond me to Katy who was sitting in her Porsche waiting patiently for me.

'*The Lady of Pain* doesn't exist anymore…in any way, shape, or form.'

I looked across at Katy. She turned in her seat smiling and waving at the girls.

Stevie waved back and grinned. 'No,' she said. 'I don't suppose she does.'

ABOUT THE AUTHORS

(www.maynard-sims.com)

Five supernatural novels, *Shelter, Demon Eyes, Nightmare City* and the two *Department 18* books (www.dept18.com) *Black Cathedral* and *Night Souls*, have been published paperback and ebook in the USA. *The Eighth Witch, Department 18* book three, is out 2012 and a standalone supernatural novel, *Stronghold,* is out in 2013. They have delivered the fourth *Department 18* book, *A Plague Of Echoes,* and are working on another standalone, *Stillwater.*

They have begun to write thrillers, and their first one is *Dark Of The Sun.* There are more thrillers in progress.

Collections include, *Shadows At Midnight* (1979 and 1999), *Echoes Of Darkness* (2000), *Incantations* (2002), *The Secret Geography Of Nightmare, Selling Dark Miracles* (both 2002), *Falling Into Heaven* (2004), *The Odd Ghosts* (2011) *Flame and Other Enigmatic Tales* (2012), and *A Haunting Of Ghosts* (2012).

Novellas, *Moths, The Hidden Language Of Demons, The Seminar,* and *Double Act,* have been published in 2001, 2002, 2003 and 2007 respectively.

They have worked as editors, publishers, essayists and reviewers.

CPSIA information can be obtained at www.ICGtesting.com
Printed in the USA
BVOW09s0919220714

360047BV00001B/2/P